TO CAMBRIDGESHIRE
(CREATION PHARMACEUTICALS AND ELY)

HORNSEY
POLICE
STATION

HORNSEY
SCHOOL
FOR GIRLS

CROUCH END
CLOCK TOWER   POST OFFICE

PARK RD

TOTTENHAM LANE

INDERWICK RD

WOLSELEY RD

CROUCH END

SHELTER

WESTON PARK

GLADWELL RD

CROUCH END HILL

CECILE PARK

EDIE'S HOUSE

LANE

Parkland Walk (South)

CROUCH HILL

STROUD GREEN RD

FINSBURY PARK

TO CENTRAL LONDON

FINSBURY PARK STATION
AND BUS TERMINAL

ANTHONY KESSEL

DON'T DOUBT THE RAINBOW

THE FIVE CLUES

Crown House Publishing Limited
www.crownhouse.co.uk

First published by
Crown House Publishing Limited
Crown Buildings, Bancyfelin, Carmarthen, Wales, SA33 5ND, UK
www.crownhouse.co.uk

and

Crown House Publishing Company LLC
PO Box 2223, Williston, VT 05495, USA
www.crownhousepublishing.com

British Library Cataloguing-in-Publication Data

A catalogue entry for this book is available from the British Library.

Print ISBN 978-178583555-1
Mobi ISBN 978-178583557-5
ePub ISBN 978-178583558-2
ePDF ISBN 978-178583559-9

LCCN 2021932197

Printed in the UK by
Clays Ltd, Bungay, Suffolk

To Mum and Dad
No longer here, but always here

CONTENTS

HOW IT ALL STARTED

'Shall we start in Marie Curie, Cancer Research or just go straight to Shelter?' asked Mum, as we walked down Gladwell Road towards the centre of Crouch End.

'Straight to Shelter!' I exclaimed, grinning. 'They always have the best stuff.'

With Dad and Eli watching football on the telly, Mum and I had developed a weekend habit of sauntering into Crouch End and, best of all, browsing around the charity shops for hidden treasure. I also loved our coffee shop chats after the shopping, when Mum would share with me her latest human rights investigations. She was so passionate about standing up for people and making the world a better place, and some of her stories were incredible: corruption in government, workers being taken advantage of, the dumping of toxic waste. Mum said that Dad and Eli weren't interested, but I couldn't get enough – and I even helped her out sometimes. She once joked that if she wasn't careful I'd take over her job!

I knew the walk by heart: cross over Landrock to Drylands Road, left on Weston Park, right down Elder Avenue and left onto Tottenham Lane. From there, we marched down the busy high street, past the Post Office and made a sharp right through the red door into affordable shopping heaven. Inside, our pattern was well established: we split up, perused what was on offer separately, then shared our findings. According to Dad, I rifled through the clothing racks in a manner identical to Mum. I told him he watched football just like Eli.

I'd gathered a pretty blue cotton blouse and silver earrings by the time Mum beckoned me over. She'd found a book of puzzles – for a daughter who loved problem-solving – plus an old paperback.

'This is one of my all-time favourites,' Mum pronounced. 'I read it when I was …' she sized me up with a smile, 'maybe a year or two older than you.'

I looked down at the cover: '*The Midwich Cuckoos*,' I probed.

Mum took a moment, which she often did, before replying: 'People think that John Wyndham was just a science fiction author because of *Day of the Triffids*, but he was much more than that. He wrote about how people behave when put in unusual circumstances – and what lengths they'll go to in order to survive.'

I thought that through and then asked: 'So what's this one about?'

I could sense Mum's mind ticking over. 'It's been a while but … as I remember … in a quiet English village the minds of children are taken over by an alien force, which then exerts telepathic control over objects and humans.'

'Sounds horrible!' I reacted.

'You should read the book,' Mum continued. 'They made it into a creepy black-and-white movie in the sixties called *Village of the Damned*.'

'I'm not sure I fancy it right now, Mum. I've only just finished *Lord of the Flies* … which was pretty disturbing.'

But Mum paid no attention and leant in: 'You should read it.'

'Mum, I don't really want to—' I started to explain.

'Read it!' Mum pressed in a louder voice, completely out of character. Other customers looked over in concern.

I started feeling anxious and became aware of a pounding in my chest. Something wasn't right.

'Read it!!' Mum repeated insistently, her eyes now glazed and intense.

No, something really wasn't right. I'd had this dream a few times before and Mum had never behaved like this. In fact, this was the only dream that brought back good memories, at least until I returned to reality.

'Read it!!' Mum urged again, but her words were entangled, confused, a combination of forcefulness and plea. I looked down, on the verge of tears, and the book seemed to have disappeared, replaced by something else on her palm.

'Read *me*!!' Mum demanded oddly, but I'd had enough. I needed to wake up and get out of the dream. Right now. And I did – eventually.

What I didn't know then, however, was that this dream would be the moment – the very moment, a year after Mum's death – when my world would transform yet again. When, over the next few weeks, I would change from regular schoolgirl to national celebrity and star detective.

Along the way I've become stronger, tougher and more self-aware. But I've seen things that nobody, let alone someone my age, should ever see.

My name is Edie Marble, and this is my story.

CHAPTER 1

FROM BEYOND THE GRAVE

Unable to sleep, Edie lay in bed and tried not to think about the day she'd been dreading for weeks. Staring at the ceiling, she wondered about what determined the different things that happened to different people: whether you had a brother or a sister, whether you were born into a slum in the suburbs of New Delhi or a privileged home in north London, whether you were popular at school or not, whether your mum lived or died.

Eventually, Edie's dad came into the room.

'How are you feeling?' he asked, perching on the edge of Edie's bed.

'Okay,' Edie replied, although 'numb' would have been a truer answer.

'I know this will be a hard day,' Dad continued, gently touching her hand. 'But we'll get through it together and move on.'

The evidence around Edie suggested that nobody had moved on yet. Her brother Eli, who was now ten, had withdrawn into his shell since Mum's death. He refused to talk about her or even join in looking at old photographs. Although he had friends, Eli seemed increasingly to prefer playing alone. And he wetted his bed – not every night, but two or three times a week since the tragedy. Dad had done his

utmost to keep everything together, but he was still suffering badly himself. In the evenings, Edie sometimes heard her dad sobbing quietly in the lounge, turning up the volume on the TV to mask the noise. He'd immersed himself in work and was drinking more whisky than ever.

As for herself, Edie knew that she hadn't moved on yet and still couldn't understand – truly understand – why her world had been turned upside down. Edie woke up every day thinking about Mum and fell asleep comforted by the image of her mother – her beautiful, dark-haired, dark-eyed mother – stroking her hair. Edie's schoolwork had suffered and her friends didn't seem to know what to say to her. Worst, perhaps, were the nightmares that just wouldn't go away.

Edie eventually managed to drag herself out of bed, put on her slippers and a fleece, and made her way downstairs. On the last step, still half asleep, Edie slipped and lost her footing. She gasped and looked down at the Buffy slippers with their poor grip. Mum had bought them the week before she died and seemed to find them cute. It was just like Mum, so busy with her own work that she didn't realise the vampire slayer was old news.

'Crunchy Nut cornflakes?' asked Dad, too perkily for this day.

'I'm not hungry,' Edie replied.

'You've got to eat something, luv,' he continued. 'It's going to be a long day. What about your favourite, one of those Müller yoghurts?'

'I'm not hungry,' Edie repeated more firmly. She glanced over at Eli sitting quietly at the table, munching on some peanut-buttery toast. He seemed oblivious to it all, concentrating on the football pages of the newspaper. Inside, though, she knew he was anxious.

'I'll make you something else then, maybe some eggs on—'

Edie raised her voice further. 'I told you, I'm not hungry!' After a short-lived but fierce glare, Edie grabbed something from the fridge then turned defiantly and left the kitchen for the playroom.

It was here that Edie found solace, not just on this day but often since her mum had died. In truth, it wasn't the playroom that provided the comfort but what lay right outside on the outdoor decking. Edie opened the back door, took a couple of steps into the garden, crouched down and looked inside the cage.

'Where are you Günther, my little fella?' she called.

A shuffle of claws on wood, the shifting of straw and her treasured guinea pig's face popped out from the bedding. Edie released the cage door, felt around and pulled out her cuddly brown and white friend. Back inside the playroom, she held him up to her chest and peered into his eyes. Günther squeaked at her lovingly, twitching his little whiskers. 'What's it like to be a guinea pig?' Edie wondered momentarily, then instinctively knew the answer: a lot less complicated than being a human.

Edie sat on the sofa and stroked her warm companion's furry back as he gazed around the room. Günther nibbled on the carrot Edie had brought from the fridge, then decided he preferred her fleece zipper. His little claws held on to her thumb. Fifteen minutes of quiet affection, including changing his water and food and freshening up his hay, was all Edie needed in the mornings. By then, she normally felt emotionally refreshed. Today, however, Edie lingered, until interrupted by a shout from the next room.

'Come on, luv – we're leaving at nine o'clock.'

Taking her time, Edie placed Günther carefully back in his cage, locked the door and went back upstairs to get dressed.

'What does a thirteen-year-old girl wear for a stone-setting?' Edie pondered as she rummaged through her wardrobe. The sombre occasion marked a year after a person's death in the Jewish religion, probably meaning similar clothes to a funeral, so Edie picked out black tights, a grey sleeveless dress with thick shoulder-straps and a white long-sleeved T-shirt to go underneath. Another reminder: her mum had bought her this dress for an eco-award ceremony a month before her death, where she'd been given a prize for exposing a water pollution scandal. Just the two of them went, as Dad had been on call for the surgery, and Edie had been so proud of her mum.

Last, Edie opened the top drawer of her bedside table and reached for the ceramic dish that contained her few items of jewellery. Edie picked out the heart-shaped locket that Mum had given her on her eleventh birthday. The locket had originally belonged to Edie's mum's mother – or Mama, as the kids called her – and had been lovingly handed down. The gold was tarnished and the chain had been replaced, but the locket still opened with a crisp click to reveal a tiny old photo of Mum as a young teenager. Edie had carefully cut out and inserted that photo the day before the funeral, and Edie wore the locket at those times when she really needed her mum's presence. A day like today.

Downstairs they were still getting ready. Eli was wearing an olive coloured shirt and brown corduroy trousers which made him look too grown-up and silly. Her dad wore a dark-blue suit, white shirt and plain tie. Always appropriate, never wanting to stick out. The doorbell rang.

'Are we ready, then?' Dad asked. Nobody answered.

'Come on, kids,' Dad continued. 'Let's not make this harder than it needs to be.'

Eli put on his black school shoes and Edie was about to do likewise, but then noticed her brown calf-length suede boots which would be more comfortable for trudging around the cemetery.

As Edie reached for her warm school coat something stirred within her, but she couldn't work it out for a moment. Then Edie remembered. It was one of her dreams, a recent one in which she was at the cemetery but she wasn't wearing her school coat. Instead, Edie had on the sheepskin coat her mum had bought for her – the coat Edie had been wearing when the teacher had approached her in the school playground with the forlorn expression of someone bearing dreadful news. The coat Edie associated with that moment and had never worn since.

Edie bolted upstairs, grabbed the sheepskin from her cupboard and slung it on. She ran back down to join the others in the minicab and off they set.

'Can we watch the game later?' Eli asked, as they snaked through the traffic towards Edgwarebury Cemetery in north London.

Dad didn't answer at first and stared blankly through the window.

'I don't know,' he responded eventually, without averting his look to face the children. 'Let's see how things go and what time we get back.'

'Will Aubameyang be playing?' her brother continued, seemingly oblivious to the gravity of the day.

'Can't you ever stop talking about football?' Edie interrupted angrily. 'We're on the way to Mum's stone-setting and all you can think about is stupid footballers.'

Eli winced for a moment when Edie raised her voice, then just continued to gaze out at the road. He still seemed to be keeping his sadness deep inside.

'I know how hard today is,' Dad said quietly. 'But it's hard for us all, luv. Please try not to take it out on your brother.'

Edie knew her dad was right, but she found it hard and got upset easily. As silence descended, Edie went to that familiar place inside her mind. If her dad had only driven Mum to the appointment that fateful day a year ago, Edie's world wouldn't have changed forever. Edie remembered almost by heart the conversation she'd overheard. Dad had said he was too busy with work to take Mum to the meeting, though, in truth, they'd argued about her latest human rights investigation. Despite being supportive of Mum's work, Dad felt the latest case was taking a toll. After bickering briefly, they'd eventually settled on a drop-off at Finsbury Park Tube station. Within ten minutes, the Victoria line was closed with a dead person on the tracks.

Edie knew the accident wasn't her dad's fault but she found it hard not to blame him, a little. Right now, though, she needed comforting herself. Tears were welling up as Edie turned to her dad.

'This is the worst day of my life,' she said gently, in a way that invited an embrace.

Edie burst out crying and held on tight, eyes closed. For a few minutes, Dad stroked her back and slowly the tears receded. When the car turned a sharp corner, Edie instinctively reopened her eyes to catch a glimpse of the cemetery gates as they passed by.

'Actually,' she said to her dad. 'It's the second worst day.'

Half an hour later, and with all the preparations done, the crunch of tyres on gravel heralded the arrival of the others. Edie recognised the silver Honda Jazz before Eli blurted out: 'That's Mama and Papa.' Eli ran over to their grandparents and Papa lifted him up. Mama came over and wrapped her arms around Edie. Back came the tears.

Edie's mum's parents, Anya and Maurice (Mama and Papa, according to the kids), had tried to be helpful since the death of their daughter. Although desperate themselves from the tragic occurrence, they'd tried to help Dad, their son-in-law, but he'd been largely resistant. Offers of meals were spurned, conversations rebutted and answerphone messages ignored. The only exception was assistance with the kids: Mama and Papa had been a real support to Edie and Eli, whenever they were given the chance.

Edie was particularly close to her grandmother. Mama was never fazed by Edie's driven nature and was always open to patiently talking things through. Undoubtedly, Edie reminded Mama of her own daughter: strong-willed, passionate and inquisitive. Mama had once remarked: 'One day, Edie, all your questions will get you into trouble – just like your mum!'

On the other side of the family, connections were not so strong. Edie had never known her dad's mother, who'd died before she was born, and Edie's dad's father lived in Toronto – a retired doctor who played golf and kept to himself. Although Grandpa David had made it to England for the funeral, he wasn't here for the stone-setting.

'How are you doing?' Mama asked with concern.

'I just want it to be over,' Edie answered honestly.

Mama looked her straight in the eye. 'Me too,' she said.

The moment of kindred spirit was broken by a tap on Edie's arm. She spun around.

'You came!' exclaimed Edie. 'I was worried that—'

'Of course I came, silly,' was the response. 'I wouldn't

miss this for the world!'

Edie wouldn't have let anybody get away with that kind of comment – except for her best mate, Lizzie, who'd befriended Edie through her transition to Highgate Hill from state school over a year ago. Whilst Edie's other classmates hadn't known how to deal with Edie and her loss, Lizzie kept on trying. Some things worked, some things didn't, but Lizzie wasn't deterred, although her natural kindheartedness was beginning to be tested. Edie smiled, turned away from Mama and hugged her best friend hard.

'Stay by me through the whole thing,' Edie whispered into Lizzie's ear.

'Just what I was planning,' came the hushed reply. Edie turned to Mama, who gave her a smile that said it was okay if she headed off.

'Is anybody else from school coming?' asked Lizzie, as they made their way around the side of the car park to the back of the main building.

'I didn't ask anyone else,' replied Edie curtly. 'You're the only one I don't mind seeing me in this state.'

'What do you mean – *in this state*?'

Edie contemplated for a moment and then replied truthfully. 'Helpless,' she proclaimed.

Away from the hubbub, the girls watched quietly as people arrived: friends of her parents, whom Edie hardly ever saw any more, plus some of her mum's work colleagues from the human rights movement. Edie recognised a couple of old friends of her dad's – Richard, from Dad's schooldays, and a friend from university, Miles, with his partner, John. Despite their kindly efforts, Dad had kept them all at a distance as he soldiered on.

Gradually, people stopped arriving and the crowd congregated in the main reception room. Dad called the two girls over. The ordeal was about to begin.

Thinking that today would be a bit like the funeral, Edie had been expecting a repeat of the eulogies of a year ago. Those had been awful: her dad choking his way through heartfelt but restrained words about Mum – what a wonderful wife and mother she'd been, her professional achievements. When he finally got to how much he'd miss her, his voice had cracked and his stare had become locked in the distance. Eventually, Papa had gone over, put an arm around Dad and tenderly led him away. Auntie Ruth, Edie's mum's sister, had been next up but she couldn't get a word out before bursting into uncontrollable tears. Next was a director from Amnesty International, who'd spoken powerfully about Mum's crusading work. Edie had been supposed to follow: she'd insisted, against her dad's advice, on saying some words, but her feet had stayed rooted to the floor, the chance missed.

To Edie's surprise, however, the stone-setting was different. All her dad did was greet people and thank them for coming, then after a short service they all trudged off along the winding cemetery paths. As promised, Lizzie didn't let go of Edie's hand. So many buried people, Edie thought: each so significant but also so insignificant.

Then they were there, at the so-called final resting

place: her mother's grave. Although the sun was out, Edie felt a chill come over her and pulled the sheepskin collar up around her neck. It was surprisingly comforting to have the special coat on again.

Quiet descended and the rabbi began with the prayers. Edie looked over at some of the black lettering beneath the Hebrew on the smooth, light-grey headstone:

ALEXANDRA LEILA FRANKLIN
A WONDERFUL MOTHER AND A CHERISHED WIFE –
WE MISS YOU DEARLY.

They'd argued at home for days about the wording. Edie had wanted something more direct, more honest: 'The best mum ever, we love you more than words can describe. P.S. Life isn't bloody fair.' But her dad had trumped her with something more 'appropriate'.

One by one, close family members then followed a Jewish ritual. A year ago at the funeral, each had taken the spade, spooned some gravel and earth onto its flat surface and deposited the material into the grave, a hollow clang sounding as each spade-load landed on the coffin. To mark the stone-setting, though, a personally chosen small stone was carefully placed onto the flat slab of granite at the base of the headstone. Edie had brought with her an oval, dark-grey piece of pumice that she'd found with her mum when walking on the beach in the Canaries. Edie felt hypnotised by the little rock, resting peacefully beneath the word 'Alexandra'.

'It's over, Edie,' said Mama suddenly.

'Can you stop squeezing my hand so tight,' pleaded Lizzie. Edie looked down to see her friend's hand turning blue. She loosened her grip but didn't let go.

'Let's head back,' said Dad.

Edie nodded, but then asked, 'Can I have a little time here by myself?'

'Of course, luv,' Dad replied. 'Don't be too long, though.'

Something caught the corner of Edie's eye. Initially, she thought it was a spade, left carelessly at a nearby graveside, but then another glint. Edie turned her gaze towards the edge of the cemetery, where the sun was bright and she had to shield her eyes. A cloud briefly gave respite, but when it passed, there it was again: the glimmer of a parked car.

At first, Edie thought little of it, but then noticed that the car was inside the cemetery perimeter, on a track around the edge. Next to the vehicle stood a man. He was about sixty metres away but, undoubtedly, was staring directly at Edie. One thing that Mum had taught her was the importance of observational skills: if something looked out of place, make a mental note of it. So Edie did: the man appeared to be in his forties with short hair, possibly balding. He was smartly dressed in an expensive looking dark coat and sunglasses. The car seemed flashy too: a Mercedes or maybe a Bentley. Black, darkened windows, suspicious looking. For a moment, their gaze seemed to meet. Then, quite suddenly, the man turned towards the car, banged twice on the roof with his gloved hand, got in the back and the car drove off.

The car was tracking the circuit of the cemetery and seemed to be getting nearer. Unsettled, Edie quickened her step towards the others. Abruptly, tyres screeched as a left turn was made through the car park, and the car was onto the main road and away. Edie stopped for a second, breathless. She looked up and saw Lizzie waiting by the prayer hall near the main entrance. Lizzie hadn't noticed Edie yet.

The sun had gone in again and Edie felt the chill return. She pulled the sheepskin collar up further and shoved her hands into her coat pockets. The fingers of her right hand came into contact with some paper. Edie explored deeper inside the pocket, suspecting an old cinema ticket or party invitation. But this felt bigger. That was odd, Edie thought. She hadn't remembered putting anything in her pocket. Then again, Edie hadn't put her hands in there since they'd left the house. Maybe not even at the house.

Carefully, Edie removed the object from her pocket and discovered an envelope. She stared at the front and her eyes opened wider. Just one word: 'Edie'. But it wasn't the word that was making her heart race, it was the handwriting. Unquestionably, it was her mum's.

Edie looked up. Lizzie still hadn't seen her. Fingers shaking, Edie tried to open the flap. It was sealed tight and her nervousness wasn't helping. Finally, she managed to pull out the paper from inside. Edie unfolded a single sheet and started reading.

My darling Edie,

If you are reading this now, it means something
dreadful has happened to me. I might even
be dead, most probably murdered ,...

A heave from her stomach, a terrible heat. Edie turned her
head to the side and violently threw up.

CHAPTER 2

THE NOTE

'Get in, sweetie.' Edie's father flung open the passenger door to the Nissan as he spoke. 'Quickly, in you get – I'm not allowed to stop by the school gates.' Edie hopped into the front seat next to her dad.

For the past five days, Edie had been reluctant to open the envelope and look at the note from her mother that she'd resealed inside – perhaps through fear, perhaps fear of disappointment, or perhaps something else. At after-school detention – a result of the sympathetic art teacher, Miss Watson, losing patience with Edie and Lizzie for continually talking in class – Edie had stared down blankly at the lined paper, her mind preoccupied by what was locked carefully away in her bedroom desk. Thankfully, Lizzie had cajoled Edie into finishing the stupid detention task set by Mr Bowling, the maths teacher, otherwise there would have been further punishment. But Lizzie's kindness made Edie feel guilty about not sharing her secret.

'How was it?' Dad asked.

'Okay,' Edie responded flatly. A silence fell as they moved slowly through the Highgate traffic. Glancing sideways, Edie had a moment of affection for her dad, rare over the past year. She noticed how his profile had aged and seemed to be drawn in perpetual sadness, although he remained handsome for a man in his mid-forties.

'How's your day been, Dad?'

Taken aback, Edie's father gathered his thoughts. 'Busy clinic this morning – must have been over thirty patients – then a couple of visits.' After a further pause he continued: 'Dr Martial has asked to see me again on Monday, to discuss "how things are going". He says there have been more complaints from patients.'

'What do they expect?' Edie ventured. 'You've had the stone-setting and now everybody seems to have forgotten that your wife's died!' She calmed down before asking, 'What will you say to Dr Martial?'

'I don't know – same as before, I guess,' responded her dad meekly. 'They're losing patience, though. If a patient is unhappy with me, they just go and see Martial, Friedman or Peters the next day, increasing everybody's workload.'

Edie liked two of her dad's GP colleagues at the practice, but she couldn't stand smarmy Dr Martial, although her dad insisted that Martial – as the senior partner – should act as her and Eli's GP. The traffic jammed to a standstill because of a problem at the pedestrian crossing down the hill.

'How have the nightmares been?' Dad asked. 'Had any more?'

The question jolted a memory of the previous night. In the dream, all the family were on a cruise ship during a terrible storm. As a siren rang and people tore around frantically, one lifeboat was lowered towards the sea, with a single person aboard. Edie had screamed at her mum not to leave without her, but even as the lifeboat neared the raging waves, her mum had calmly replied that she wouldn't. Despite this, the lifeboat disappeared into the distance, tossed about by the dark waters with one woman standing motionless in the middle.

'No, nothing recently,' Edie fibbed.

Back home twenty minutes later, the end-of-the-week routine began. Friday nights at the Franklins' house had always been special. Prayers marked the start of the Sabbath, candles were lit and blessings were said over wine and special bread, challah. They'd done this before Edie's mother had died and had continued since.

After Dad's roast chicken dinner had been devoured and cleared away, the threesome gathered on the sofa – Dad sandwiched between the children – for their Friday night ritual of watching the remake of the 1970s sci-fi show *Battlestar Galactica*. In the middle of an episode in series three, just as Commander Adama instructed the crew to find the Cylon on the ship, Dad noticed that Edie was fast asleep. He gently picked her up and carried her to bed.

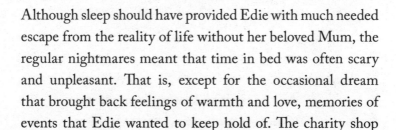

Although sleep should have provided Edie with much needed escape from the reality of life without her beloved Mum, the regular nightmares meant that time in bed was often scary and unpleasant. That is, except for the occasional dream that brought back feelings of warmth and love, memories of events that Edie wanted to keep hold of. The charity shop dream, which came from time to time, was just that.

But not on this occasion. As Edie stood in Shelter opposite her mum, this dream had become as unwelcome as the nightmares. And it didn't make sense: her mum's behaviour had turned from kind to unsettling and she was pressing this odd book, *The Midwich Cuckoos*, urgently on Edie. Even more strangely, the book seemed to be altering in appearance just as her mum's words were changing.

'Read *me*!!' Mum stressed again.

Edie lowered her head: the book had disappeared and, instead, resting on her mum's palm was the envelope – the same envelope Edie had touched a hundred times since finding it in her pocket at the cemetery. Edie looked up and their faces were just inches apart. The message from her mum was becoming clear.

Calmly, Edie opened her eyes, her gaze resting on the darkened ceiling. With her pulse settling, Edie wiped the cold sweat off her face, pulled back the covers and got out of bed. From the top drawer of her desk she retrieved the carefully concealed envelope. Edie returned to her bed, dragged the duvet over her head and turned on her torch. Without giving herself time to reconsider, she opened the envelope and took out the note. Edie carefully unfolded the paper and read.

My darling Edie,

If you are reading this now, it means something dreadful has happened to me. I might even be dead, most probably murdered.

I have been uncovering what I believe to be a major corporate crime and violation of human rights. As I have been getting closer to the evidence, however, the perpetrators seem to have become aware of me. I sense that I am being followed, and in the supermarket last week an unpleasant character coldly but violently threatened me – and our family. I have encountered this kind of thing before, but this time it feels different, more real. And I am scared for all of us.

I have left you a series of clues, five in total, which I hope will help you to complete my investigation and bring these brutes to justice. I couldn't leave the clues for anybody else. I trust you implicitly – we're like peas in a pod – and only you will be able to work out the trail. At the same time, the clues will, I hope, help you in other ways.

Be bold, be brave and carry my life force with you.

With unconditional, ever-lasting love,
Mum xxx

P.S. Almost forgot! Here's the first clue:

Only by working through this clue do you get to the next one.

The moment she reached the end, Edie returned straight to the beginning and reread the letter. Then Edie read it a third time, before sticking her head out from under the duvet for some air, still cool and fresh before the central heating came on. After the unbearable stress of the past few days, Edie experienced a curious sense of release, and she let out a sigh. A knowing sigh. Her mum's death wasn't an accident, one of those random tragic events that people were relieved had happened to somebody else. No, it was cold-blooded murder, and so it had meaning. And that meaning gave Edie purpose. There was a mystery to be solved, and the mystery started with a puzzle.

At first, her head spinning, Edie was unsure what form of clue she'd been presented with. Her mum was a creative thinker, independently minded, a beats-to-her-own-drum kind of person, so the clue could mean almost anything. Was it a riddle? A task to be performed? Maybe even a fake clue, in case it fell into the wrong hands?

Or was the clue a reference to the Three Principles of psychology that had so interested Mum over the past few years? Mum had once described the Three Principles as 'an understanding of how the mind works', and she often brought this understanding into conversations with Edie. Edie loved those chats because they made her feel special (Mum seldom spoke about the Three Principles with Dad or Eli). Mum also shared lots of material with Edie about the principles – web articles, podcasts and books – but Edie didn't often look at them because the learning had been much less important than the private time and closeness with her mum.

Whatever the clue actually referred to, what made things harder was that Edie had no real idea about the direction of travel. Would this clue provide some sort of answer or simply lead to the next clue?

Several hours earlier, unbeknownst to Edie as she slept in front of the TV, her dad closed the lounge curtains, failing to notice the thickly set man lurking outside. Once the lights in the house were out, the former soldier – known to his clients as Zero – made his way back to his flat near King's Cross. Earlier that day, Zero had been forced to call the man who'd hired him over a year ago – Peter Goswell – using the agreed mobile number. At the pharmaceutical company headquarters, Goswell's trusted personal assistant, Margaret, had interrupted her boss, the chief executive, in the middle of an important meeting to take the call. 'It's your *special* phone,' she'd whispered, referring to an old iPhone 6 that was kept carefully locked in the office when not in Goswell's possession.

Goswell wasn't happy as he'd been regaling three of the company's board members – a barrister, an economist and a doctor – with the story he'd told a hundred times: how he had come up with the name Stop It! for the successful anti-diarrhoea drug that had made the company millions, and how he – Peter Goswell – had also suggested Flu-Away for their new antiviral medicine. And Flu-Away, now completing final clinical trials, was going to make them all a fortune.

In the quiet of his office, Goswell saw on the screen that it was Zero calling and, minutes later, had slammed his clenched fist on the desk after the henchman had given him the news about the death of the drug company's director of research and development, Dr Thomas Stephenson. The wallop had knocked over the family photo of Goswell's wife, Jane, two daughters and their beloved black Labrador, Homer, sitting together outside his country home in Cambridgeshire.

'I don't want to watch *Friends*.'

Ignoring her brother's plea, Edie grabbed the two remote controls on the coffee table and made for the DVD player. 'You've already been down here playing games for hours, so I think I'm allowed to watch what I want!'

Eli's tone shifted from defensive to insistent: 'I haven't watched any TV at all. And I hate *Friends*.'

'But you've been on the iPad and that stupid FIFA game non-stop. It's the same thing.'

Their father burst in, his Saturday morning lie-in disturbed: 'What's all this noise about?' he bellowed.

'She always wants to watch *Friends* ... and I hate it!'

'And he's always playing that stupid football game,' Edie countered.

'Enough! Enough! No more television and no more iPad today,' came the unwanted verdict. Flicking the TV off, their grumpy father continued: 'That's what happens if you can't decide together.'

Eli trudged quietly upstairs. With his eyes closed, he counted the six steps from the playroom up to the ground-level hallway. Then, a hard turn to the right, eyes still screwed shut to blot out the next section of fourteen steps up to the first landing. On this occasion, however, Eli stopped exactly halfway up. He waited there, his fingers grasping the bannister. Was it okay to look? He shouldn't really as inevitably it upset him, but he paused and then opened his eyes a crack. Slowly, Eli allowed the framed image on the wall to take shape.

The photograph was taken on Hampstead Heath, the summer before his mum's death. With Edie busy elsewhere, Mum, Dad and Eli had decided to have a picnic on the vast lawn in front of Kenwood House. Eli had played football with his dad on the grass – the first time he'd ever beaten him – then his mum, playfully, had challenged Eli to a wrestling competition. And that was when the photo had been taken, with Eli attempting to pin down her shoulders, their expressions a combination of concentration, joy and elemental love. Looking at the picture helped to recall the day: her smell, the touch of her skin, her giggled but serious declaration of 'I'll never give up!' But then the horrible darkness took hold again.

At the top of the stairs, Eli took in the group shot of his mum's family: Mama, Papa, Auntie Ruth, Mum and her twin sister, Miriam, who'd died from cancer as a child. Momentarily, Eli remembered the 'special' photo of Miriam, as his mum called it: a beautiful black-and-white snap in Papa's study in Hendon.

Soon, Eli's attention drifted towards his sister's bedroom. She'd been behaving strangely, even for her, over the past week. Eli tiptoed into Edie's room, avoiding the squeaky loose plank under the carpet in front of the door. Inside, Eli immediately started poking around, whilst listening keenly for any sign of his approaching sibling. Under the bed – nothing. Behind the bedside table – just a few dusty hairclips. Beneath the small rug that Mum had brought back from India – no joy. The desk, though, might prove more fruitful.

'What are you doing?'

Taken aback, Eli froze. Edie repeated, louder this time, 'What do you think you're doing?!'

Edie's face was red with anger. 'Nothing … I lost my headphones,' he replied softly.

'You're looking through my stuff!' Edie approached and the smaller child cowered.

Dad shouted from the kitchen: 'What's going on up there?'

The interruption provided Eli with the momentary distraction that was needed. He bolted past his sister, up the remaining flights of stairs, turned sharply into his own bedroom at the top of the house and closed the door firmly.

Back at school the following Monday, Edie was in the middle of another argument with Polly when the bell rang at the end of art. Edie packed up her bag and headed for the classroom door, where Lizzie caught up with her. Two periods to go until the end of another long day, although those periods were double games and, in preparation, Edie took two puffs from her blue Ventolin inhaler.

The constant drizzle since morning meant that the outdoor activity had been replaced with dreaded swimming. Together, the two girls did the fifteen-minute walk over to the Atkins Centre pool practically in silence, Edie feeling guilty but also certain that she couldn't share anything yet about her extraordinary discovery.

'Twenty lengths – all of you,' Mr Richards pronounced. 'Three, two, one ...' and he blew the infernal whistle.

After kicking off, Edie was soon into her flow, doing breaststroke up, across and then down the swimming lane. Eight days had passed since she'd found the note, three since she'd read it fully. The written image of the clue was clearly etched in her mind: *Only by working through this clue do you get to the next one.* She repeated it silently in her mind, over and over, as the first length drifted by.

The rhythmic nature of swimming created a kind of semi-meditative state, and Edie recalled the immense mental effort of the days since finding the clue. At first, her analysis had focused on the specific words. It was difficult to see how the word 'only' had special significance, but 'working' seemed important. Edie had wondered whether it was a reference to her mum's job, so she went through her work-related files in the study when Dad was out, but they yielded nothing of obvious relevance. Edie had even phoned her mother's closest work colleague to find out if anything important had been left at the human rights organisation office.

Was 'working' supposed to steer Edie towards her own schoolwork? Again, this was hard to comprehend, but Edie had nevertheless gone through all her own folders, as well as the box file that her parents kept containing information about Highgate Hill School. Nothing. Carefully, Edie had then worked through the entirety of her father's office, rifling through drawers and shelves, being sure to replace everything back as it had been. All fruitless.

Later, Edie had directed her attention at 'through this clue'. She'd held the paper up to her ceiling light and shone a torch straight through it, in the hope that words would visibly materialise as if written with one of those magic pens. Further disappointment. Out of the blue, a thought had then struck Edie that perhaps 'through this clue' was an indication that the whole clue carried the answer. She'd assigned a number to each letter, as per their alphabet position, and had totalled the points for each word: Only (66) by (27) working (97) through (97) this (56) clue (41) do (19) you (61) get (32) to (35) the (33) next (63) one (34). These figures had seemed devoid of meaning, as had the sum for the whole sentence (661).

Edie's arms were flagging from the repetition of the same stroke, so she switched to a front crawl. How many lengths now? The next tack she'd taken with the clue was systematic: over the weekend, Edie had worked her way through the whole house room by room with feverish but careful intent, hoping for some kind of sign. Once again, though, the approach had proved unrewarding.

Four strokes with the arms, sharp head-tilt to the right

and deep inhalation of oxygen to feed the fatigued muscles. Staring at the pool bottom, a particular dark thought re-entered her consciousness. What if she never worked out the clue and was left in awful ignorance of what it all meant? Or, what if her mother hadn't had time to complete the full set? Such bleak prospects weren't to be dwelt on.

With her arms weakening, Edie switched to backstroke. Where was everybody else, she pondered, as her hands touched the end of the pool. On the half-turn, Edie felt a strong pat on her head and a loud whistle in her ear. Pulling her goggles off, Edie surfaced to face the glare of a man crouched at the poolside.

'What on earth are you doing, Franklin?' asked Mr Richards sternly. 'I've been blowing this darn whistle for over a minute. Now get out!'

A ripple of laughter was audible across the cluster of girls and boys from her class, amassed at the water's edge.

Red-faced, Edie clambered out.

Lizzie and Edie, weary from the exertion of the swimming class, slowly climbed the hill back up to Highgate village. Halfway up, Edie stopped and reached into the front pouch of her bag. A combination of the exercise and the cold winter air had made her wheezy. After two deep breaths in, Edie shook the blue inhaler. It was nearly empty and her mum had always warned her never to run out. She made a mental note to book an appointment with Dr Martial.

At the top of the hill, the girls veered right through

the parade of shops, briefly contemplated – and then rejected – the idea of a hot chocolate at Costa Coffee, then headed downhill towards Archway. A left-hand turn at the traffic lights took them onto Hornsey Lane and within a few minutes they were close to Lizzie's house on Stanhope Road.

'I'm off here,' announced Lizzie at the corner.

'I'll come with you,' suggested Edie, 'then take the Parkland Walk back home.'

'Are you serious? It'll be too dark for that.'

'It'll be fine,' Edie countered.

But Lizzie wasn't to be deterred. The Parkland Walk was a tree-lined public path – from Crouch End through to Archway in one direction and to Muswell Hill and Finsbury Park in the other – which had been created from a disused railway line. During daylight hours it was busy with joggers, dog-walkers and parents with bicycle-happy kids. When the light went, however, the path was quickly deserted and muggings were not uncommon.

'Absolutely not,' Lizzie asserted.

Touched by her friend's concern, Edie acquiesced. 'Okay, I'll go home through the streets.' She gave Lizzie a quick hug and set off.

By the time Edie reached her house it was completely dark. She put the keys in the lock and opened the front door.

'Hi, sweetie,' cried her father from the lounge.

'Hi, Dad.' Edie took off her coat and stood in the doorway.

'How was your day?' Dad asked brightly from the comfort of his favourite leather armchair by the window, perhaps after an early whisky.

'Fine, thanks. How was yours?'

'Oh, you know, okay. Martial was up to his usual old tricks.'

Edie thought for a second. 'One day, you should punch his lights out!'

'Hopefully it won't ever come to that … but it does sound appealing!'

Edie felt a loving sadness for the man slumped peacefully in isolation. As she approached, he held out a hand for his daughter to clasp. Edie leant over.

'What are you doing, Dad?'

'The *Guardian* cryptic crossword, but it's too hard for me.'

Something stirred inside Edie as her dad continued: 'Your mum was the one who was always good at these.'

Edie felt a cold chill rise through her chest as her dad carried on: 'Take this clue, for example: "Two lovers in play (5,3,6)." What does that mean?'

There was just a short pause before Edie assisted. 'Dad, it's *Romeo and Juliet*.'

'Oooh, I think you're right. Yes, that fits in. How did you know that, sweetie?'

Edie responded with knowledge and clarity. 'Most cryptic crossword clues need to be split in two, and each side of the clue leads you to the same answer. Here,' she pointed, 'the split comes after "two lovers", who are obviously Romeo and Juliet, and "play", which tells you the answer is also a play. A Shakespeare play.'

'Wow, how did you find that out?'

Edie waited. 'Mum taught me.' Her dad was about to say something but never got the chance as Edie bolted upstairs. 'Sorry, Dad, I've got some homework to do.'

Edie closed the bedroom door firmly behind her, sat at her desk and wrote out the clue on a page of A4 paper. Fired up, Edie applied what she'd explained to her dad by experimenting with different cut-off points in the clue. One possibility was a cut-off after 'Only by working', but the remainder of the clue was convoluted and made no sense. Edie toyed with every other break point in the clue, but in each instance the outcome was meaningless. A glimmer of a memory then surfaced. What had her mum told her? Oh yes. Certain crossword clues didn't follow the normal pattern of splitting into two parts, including a particular kind that Edie's mum had joked were actually the easiest to solve.

The answer to the clue, Edie suddenly remembered, lay in linking together the end of one word in a clue with the beginning of another. And the hint was in the word 'through': indeed, she had to look *through* the words of the clue. Edie jumped up, grabbed the A4 paper and settled on the bed, her head propped up on the pillow.

Only by working through this clue do you get to the next one. Connecting the first and second words yielded nothing, neither did joining the second and third. With a thumping in her chest, Edie's finger continued along the line. At the sixth and seventh words Edie froze. She screwed up the paper, tumbled off the bed and raced downstairs into the playroom. Thankfully, Eli was nowhere in sight.

Edie glanced at the second shelf on the wall, which contained all their family games. Standing on a chair, she reached up and carefully took out the detective game that they would never have played without their mum. In bold red and white letters, the words 'clue' and 'do' were linked on the front of the box: CLUEDO.

Excited by what she might find, but nervous of what she might not, Edie sat on the sofa and cautiously lifted the lid and placed it to the side. Next, she similarly inspected and discarded the board. With shaking hands, Edie picked up the cards consisting of pictures of the playing characters, weapons and rooms. Surely, this was where the search would end? Edie's disappointment, though, rose with the examination of each card. Likewise, the playing pieces and plastic casing.

Edie leant back against the cushions, with all the material of the game strewn around her. A minute passed and then, out of the corner of her eye, Edie noticed the small black envelope in which, at the start of the game, you placed one person card, one weapon card and one room card. Edie turned the envelope over and two words on the front cover stood out starkly: MURDER CARDS. Instantly, Edie knew she'd cracked it, and imagined her mum acknowledging the double meaning as she'd laid the breadcrumb over a year ago.

With determination, Edie pressed the ends of the envelope to widen the opening and looked inside. A piece of folded paper lay in wait, which she pulled out, opened, read carefully, refolded and then held on to tight. Edie's muscles slackened, she closed her eyes and the sofa enveloped her.

And then Edie remembered the last time they'd played Cluedo as a family, not long before her mother's death. She could see the four of them huddled around the board on the playroom floor, an atmosphere of laughter and playfulness tinged with a competitive edge between mother and daughter. But Edie's memories of the good time were just snippets, as if too painful for her brain to allow them back in: Mum moving Reverend Green across the board and asking about the dagger and the billiard room; Eli rolling the dice under the sofa; the Dad-and-Eli team taking the secret passageway to the library just for fun; Dad explaining to Eli that Colonel Mustard couldn't be the murderer if they had his card.

Towards the end of the game, Edie had been ninety per cent sure of the murder cards but held back from naming them since the penalty for getting them wrong was eviction from the game. Edie needed one more turn to be absolutely sure, but before she got her chance, Mum had stepped in, guessed correctly and won: Miss Scarlett, with the spanner, in the conservatory. Edie remembered being annoyed with herself for waiting, and tried to recollect what her mum had said before they'd tussled lovingly on the sofa. Oh yes, Edie could just, achingly, recall: 'You've got to take chances in life, my angel. Be bold. Be brave.'

As Edie had been preparing for swimming, Peter Goswell and Zero were meeting at their usual place, the Rose Garden in Regent's Park. Whilst Goswell's chauffeur, Jack, waited nearby in the Bentley, the chief executive arrived first at the designated bench – next to the 'Santa Fe' roses – whilst Zero appeared silently a few minutes later. Goswell knew little about the hired assassin, except that he used to be in the Special Forces, the SAS, but had been dishonourably discharged from the military a while back following an incident in Afghanistan. Zero's growing reputation as an all-round badass was unquestionable, however, and Goswell was always surprised by the stealth of the muscularly framed man, well over six-foot tall and menacingly dressed all in black with a hood pulled up over his head. It was as if he had appeared from nowhere.

Sitting together on the bench, Zero then elaborated that Dr Tom (as he was known) Stephenson had perished some days back on a holiday to southern Italy with his wife, Claire. She'd found him dead in bed one morning, the sheets soaked with blood; preliminary medical reports suggested pulmonary haemorrhage – or bleeding from the lungs. Apparently, Tom had been unwell for some days beforehand with a respiratory bug. Zero added that Tom's wife had just returned from Italy to the UK, and their sons – Martin, in his second year at King's College university and seventeen-year-old Ethan, on a school trip to Peru – were soon to be joining her at home in north London.

The incident in the Vietnam lab eighteen months earlier flashed through Goswell's mind as he listened to Zero. The nature of Dr Tom's death sounded similar to the poor Vietnamese drug trial volunteers. They'd managed to keep the company's name out of that disaster by burning down the lab, paying off the bereaved Vietnamese families and dealing with the interfering human rights activist. But it didn't make sense to Goswell for the illness to resurface now, as Tom hadn't visited Vietnam for a long time. At this point, Zero dropped the bombshell that Tom had secretly brought some of the deadly virus back to the UK from Vietnam directly after the incident.

Shaken, Goswell asked about the health of Tom's wife, Claire – and not because he cared about her. She was apparently fine, but Zero then conveyed worrying information about the behaviour of an overly inquisitive young girl, Edie, who'd been searching oddly around the house, as well as contacting people from her mum's workplace. (The surveillance equipment and computer keylogger they had installed to track Edie's mother were still active.) On hearing this, Goswell instructed Zero to do something that disturbed even the assassin, who'd never harmed any children.

Irritated by Zero's discomfort, Goswell reminded him who was in charge, handed over a brown envelope filled with £50 notes and walked briskly back to the Bentley, where he tapped on the roof twice – which maddened Jack as he quietly read the *Daily Mail*. 'To Mary's school,' Goswell barked, riled that he had to collect his daughter, Mary, who'd vomited during a hockey match and whose mother couldn't be contacted.

CHAPTER 3

DAVID AND GOLIATH

As she exited the school gates, Edie failed to notice the tall man seated on a low wall on the opposite side of the road. Hunched up against the chill, his face – with its large, circular scar – was concealed behind a dark hood. The stranger stubbed out a cigarette as he caught sight of the two girls. At the meeting in Regent's Park, Zero had been unhappy about the instruction to scare a schoolgirl, and was unimpressed when Goswell shared that he'd watched Edie at the cemetery, keen to see what she was up to: the chief executive was increasingly pig-headed and careless, his curiosity getting the better of him.

Distraction, though, was a problem for Edie. If unoccupied elsewhere, her mind went straight back to the second clue – even when just standing on a street corner – meaning important observations could be missed.

What if Charlie got it wrong?

Edie had played with the words of the new clue over and over in her head in the two days since their discovery. Elation at solving the first clue had soon been replaced with the nervous puzzlement of trying to work out the second. Who was Charlie: somebody Edie knew, a fictional character, perhaps not even a person? And what was the meaning of Charlie getting something wrong? It had to be connected to her mum and their relationship, surely …

'Are you heading straight home?' Lizzie asked her best friend, who was a little too close to the edge of the road.

Lizzie looked good in her Doc Martens school shoes, black leggings, short grey skirt, white shirt, thick sweater and navy blue and maroon blazer. Her naturally straight blonde hair was pulled back in a ponytail by an elastic tie with a plastic skull-and-crossbones bobble. Cool, and just within school regulations. Smart brown-rimmed glasses added to the effect rather than making Lizzie appear bookish.

'Not necessarily,' responded Edie, who then looked down at her watch. It was quarter past three, and those not involved in school play auditions had been allowed to leave early. A couple of hours of daylight remained and some brief sunshine provided a little warmth against the winter cold.

'Although I do have quite a lot to do at home,' added Edie.

'Good afternoon, girls!' proclaimed a loud adult male voice, the teacher not breaking stride as he paced past the twosome.

'Good afternoon, Sir,' replied Lizzie, whilst Edie simultaneously said, 'Good afternoon, Mr Bowling.' They looked at each other and broke into a chorus of giggles.

'Fancy a hot chocolate on the way back?' nudged Lizzie, once the laughter had subsided.

How could Edie refuse?

As Lizzie bought the drinks, Edie sat at a table near the back of Costa Coffee in Muswell Hill; it was a slight detour but they liked the Muswell Hill shops. With the thoughts impossible to shift, Edie appraised her detective work so far. She'd considered a range of Charlies including Charlie Chaplin, Charlie of Chocolate Factory fame and Charles Dickens. She'd checked all the books connected to these figures in the house, including one of her own favourites when she was younger, Roald Dahl's *The Witches*, and her mum's beloved Dickens, *Great Expectations*, but the search yielded nothing. Edie had also considered Prince Charles, whom her mum had met because of his connection with the environment, but no obvious link emerged.

Lost in thought, Edie neglected to notice the imposing stranger who was sitting a few tables behind her, thumbing through a copy of the *Evening Standard*. Lizzie, though, was aware of him as he had inadvertently knocked her arm as she'd been paying – resulting, annoyingly, in her spilling some hot chocolate onto her right hand. She walked over to her friend, tray in hand.

'Wotcha.'

'Hey,' replied Edie, refocusing.

Lizzie placed the two mugs on the table, moved one of them over to Edie and sat down: 'What are you thinking about?' she quizzed.

'Not much,' Edie replied instinctively, struggling with the guilt of not yet sharing the secret with her closest pal.

Edie redirected the conversation. 'Did you see Mr Bowling?' she continued. 'He's got hair growing out of his ears!'

Lizzie looked directly at Edie – their gaze held a recognition that something was amiss – then smiled: 'And there's hair coming out of his nose as well!'

Edie grinned. 'His wife should tell him to do something about it.'

'I don't think he's married,' replied Lizzie.

'How d'ya know?'

'Well, for one, he doesn't wear a wedding ring.'

'So what?' Edie retorted. 'My dad didn't wear a ring, even before ...' she paused and looked down at the table, '... before my mum died.' Edie raised her head and continued: 'It used to annoy Mum. She couldn't understand why he refused to put it on.'

Lizzie was determined on this occasion not to let things get too bleak, so she changed tack. 'Anyway, I think Mr Bowling fancies Miss Watson.'

'Eeeeerrrgh!' gasped Edie. 'That's horrible!'

'Well, she is pretty.'

'I know but ...' she shook her head in violent humour, 'NO, NO, NO, NO, NO!'

Lizzie took a gulp of the frothy drink, which made Edie laugh.

'What is it?'

'You've got foam on your nose.'

Lizzie dipped her finger into the dregs of her cup and planted the scooped froth straight onto Edie's nose. 'So do you!'

After they had cleaned their faces with napkins, Lizzie seized the opportunity.

'So, how are things?'

A dramatic shift in Edie's expression reflected her irritation. 'Fine,' she fibbed. 'I've told you before.'

'It's just that you seem—'

'I'm fine!' Edie interrupted assertively. 'Why do you keep on asking?'

This wasn't going as Lizzie had planned. She'd hoped that a more relaxed atmosphere might help her friend to open up. A different approach was needed.

'How's work going?'

'What d'ya mean?'

'You know, our school projects.' The end of term was only a few weeks away and the class had to complete projects in history, art and biology. Lizzie knew that Edie had missed the last two deadlines.

'I'm building a miniature kitchen out of pieces of things you'd find there for the art project. You've seen it. But it's taking a lot of time.'

'And history?'

'You know what I'm doing for history. It's about the Crimean War – Florence Nightingale. She was amazing.'

'Have you finished it?'

'No!' exclaimed Edie. 'Nowhere near.'

'What about biology?'

'What is this?' countered Edie with rising irritation. 'Why don't you tell me what you're doing instead,' she demanded.

Keen not to inflame things, Lizzie took a moment. 'We've talked about it before – I'm doing a project on evolution.'

'Oh, yes,' said Edie as her mind wandered briefly. 'Natural selection. Survival of the fittest.'

'The Galápagos Islands look amazing!' Lizzie interjected lightly, trying to grasp an opening. 'All the turtles, penguins and … finches.' Suddenly Edie's demeanour changed – the unpredictability that was becoming more commonplace.

'What is it you want from me, Lizzie?' she probed.

Oh dear, thought Lizzie, here we go again.

'It's just that I'm still worried about you, Edie. You seem so … so … troubled at the moment. What's going on? Is it one of the girls at school?'

'I've told you, I'm fine!' Edie shouted. 'Now, just leave me alone!' She shoved her chair back and stormed out of the cafe.

Lizzie sat shell-shocked and still as the man perched a few tables back stood up and made for the exit, walking right past the wet-eyed, blonde-haired girl.

Edie tore down the high street, dazed and confused, dodging surprised shoppers and mothers with pushchairs. She slowed a little by the cinema, then walked briskly down Muswell Hill Road. Ten minutes after abandoning her best friend, Edie stood outside the main entrance to Highgate Woods. Holding on to the gate, Edie allowed her breathing to calm down.

Edie adored the ancient woods, a haven of tranquillity. They were another connection to her mother, for whom the area represented an oasis away from people and cars. The sign at the entrance said the woods closed that evening at quarter past five, meaning Edie still had forty minutes before she would have to leave.

Edie headed past the drinking fountain on the main path before turning sharp right towards the cricket nets. Deep inside the woods it was more shadowy as the gloaming descended. At a bend in the track, she sat on her mother's favourite bench. With its back adjacent to a large oak, the seat faced the beautiful, dense woodland; overhead was a big, grey sky with criss-cross patterns formed by the high branches. A large crow appeared from the holly bush to the right of Edie and squawked loudly.

Edie took out her phone. The light was getting poor, and an older woman with a grey Schnauzer paused and said, 'I wouldn't leave it too long, luv, not if you're alone. It's getting rather gloomy.'

Edie smiled, screwed up her eyes to focus and got back to her text.

Hey Lizzie, sorry about before. In Highgate
Woods now to calm down. Speak later.
XXX

Edie checked the message, pressed 'Send', leant back on the bench and allowed her eyelids to close. A few minutes passed.

All of a sudden, Edie was snapped out of her doze by

the sound of the bell signalling ten minutes until closing. Her head felt stuffy. It was cold and had become much darker. Edie looked back down the path in the direction she'd come from, which was also the quickest way out. She made to stand, but stopped as she noticed something in the near distance. Bearing down the path towards Edie was a tall and broad-shouldered man. He was dressed in black and had a hood pulled up over his head. Edie remembered the security training her mum had been required to do because of her job, and how she had recounted what she'd learned about 'situational awareness' – about living in the present and always being mindful of your surroundings. This felt like one of those moments.

The dark shadow was approaching with menacing speed, hands inside pockets, head and shoulders hunched. Fifty metres. Forty metres. With legs like jelly and a fierce pounding in her chest Edie felt immobilised by fear, but she knew that she had to act quickly. Edie slapped her fists on her thighs to force her lower limbs to get her standing. At thirty metres, the features of the man's clothing were becoming clearer and his speed was increasing alarmingly. The slightest of tilts of his head upwards clarified that he was, unquestionably, heading straight for the young girl.

As she stood up, Edie thought quickly. The one advantage that Edie had, possibly, was that she knew the woods – and the prowler hopefully didn't. If she went left, the path wended its way to a corner of the woods and a side entrance that was quite far off. However, that section of the woods was isolated and unsafe – the chance of seeing anybody else at this hour was extremely remote.

No, Edie had just one option: to delve into the undergrowth behind her and try to weave a route around and back to the main gate. Edie turned on her heels and began to run through the bushes. Twigs snapped underfoot as she pushed aside low-hanging branches and foliage with outstretched arms. Thorns scratched Edie's face but there was no time to pause or cry out. A quick check over her left shoulder revealed that the towering predator had veered off the path and was lurching after Edie. Paying little heed to the obstacles in his way, he was gaining ground.

As Edie battled through the vegetation, she was acutely aware of two noises associated with her progress: the rapid-fire gasps of her own breathing and the trampling of leaves and earth underfoot. But then a third sound began to intrude: the crashing of a person with greater mass and velocity. He was so near now that Edie could almost hear his breath. A realisation flashed across Edie's mind as the park cafe came into view – she wasn't going to make it to the exit so she needed another plan.

The toilets next to the restaurant? But if he located her, she'd be completely trapped inside. What about the seating area beside the cafe building? Again, it was enclosed by fencing and, if he entered, she'd be unable to get out.

Only one other possibility. With the adrenaline-fuelled effort of a life in danger, Edie darted around the cafe towards the shed that contained educational material for children about the wildlife and ecology of Highgate Woods. An unexpected spark of memory brought back a visit with her mother, who'd enjoyed the photographs of how the species and environment of the woodland had evolved over time.

Edie caught sight of what she was looking for and crouched down low behind one of two benches in front of the education shed.

She held her breath.

Despite the terror, the atmosphere of the evening felt impossibly calm. No rain, no wind, no voices. Just a chilling stillness. Apart from the chirping of a bird in the distance, the only sound was the thumping under Edie's sweater; the man who'd been giving chase was suddenly nowhere to be seen. Maybe he'd changed his mind? Perhaps he'd been seen by a walker? A bead of sweat made its way down Edie's forehead and settled in the corner of her left eye. She wiped it away whilst maintaining complete concentration.

Then the predator appeared, with surprising quiet for a man of his size. He was just metres away on the other side of the education shed, but seemingly hadn't seen her yet. He stopped and looked around in an alarmingly measured manner.

What else could Edie do? If she ran now, he'd be on her in an instant. On the earth and gravel around her, Edie noticed a number of stones of different sizes. She silently picked up one pebble and one larger stone. Holding on tightly to the latter, Edie threw the pebble into the bushes well away from her to the right. As the small stone hit the shrubbery, the rustling captured her pursuer's attention. His head turned quickly to the left and he took a couple of paces away from Edie.

Braced to launch herself past the man and up the main path to the gates, Edie waited like a caged animal. A few more of his strides would give her a window of space and time to accelerate away. Devastatingly, though, he stopped and turned towards Edie. He may not have been able to see Edie behind the bench yet, but in just a few steps she would be visible. Threateningly, he took one of those steps and Edie felt sick.

Only one thing left to do now. Fingers curled tightly around the large stone, Edie prepared to throw her only weapon as hard as she possibly could – directly at his forehead. Very slowly, Edie began to draw her arm back over her shoulder. An image of David and Goliath appeared in her mind – she needed young David's luck. The man took a further step and was almost upon her.

Then, on the verge of flinging, Edie's attention was suddenly grabbed by a shadow creeping up behind the ogre. It was Lizzie, out of nowhere, and she had a finger to her lips telling Edie to keep quiet. In her right hand Lizzie was wielding a solid branch, raised up by her ears. When Lizzie brought her finger away from her lips, the left hand joined the right to create a strong grip.

The monster took another step – so close he could surely see Edie now. Lizzie moved even nearer to him as Edie firmed up her hold on the stone. It was all happening in slow motion, as if time was almost standing still, until Lizzie pounced forwards. Having been focused on the bench area, the man was taken aback by the noise behind him, and wheeled around just as Lizzie arced the branch through the air with all the strength she could muster.

A combination of the height differential and the man's turning meant the branch failed to strike his head full on. Instead, the blow landed around his left ear. It was a hefty blow, nonetheless, and after a moment of surprise and recoil, the large man fell to his knees – his head just a couple of metres from where Edie was crouching.

The whack, together with the fall, had dislodged the hood from the would-be assailant's head. Staring at his face, Edie was transfixed by one aspect: the trail of blood from the man's left temple and ear that was settling around a scar on his left cheek. It was the shape of a circle, but with a small piece at the top missing.

'Run!' screamed Lizzie, but Edie was rooted to the spot.

'Run!' Lizzie yelled again, yanking Edie to her feet.

Side by side they hurtled down the path towards the main exit.

CHAPTER 4

BREADCRUMBS

Even at the exit the girls didn't dare to stop. They turned right and pelted up the street towards the busy Archway Road. Lizzie grabbed Edie's hand as they crossed near the lights, dodging by inches a blue Ford Focus, the driver of which glared angrily and sounded his horn.

Next, they shot left down the short section of the noisy main road where the pavement was narrow. A pair of gangly schoolboys from the nearby St Aloysius' College pulled out of the way sharply, hurling obscenities before laughing once the girls were out of earshot. Another left down Shepherd's Hill and the girls were finally able to slow their pace, with regular glances over their shoulders showing no sign of their pursuer. At the corner with Stanhope Road they came to a stop, still gasping, Lizzie leaning forwards with her hands on her thighs. It took half a minute for their breathing to slow enough to allow them to speak.

'What the hell's going on?' asked Lizzie directly, hauling herself upright.

Edie used the excuse of her still strained breathing to avoid answering. Yet, it wasn't what to divulge that was occupying Edie's mind but a germinating seed that might help to solve a clue.

Emphasising each word whilst grabbing Edie's

forearms, Lizzie repeated herself: 'What the hell is going on? That man could've killed you!'

With her friend failing to respond, Lizzie noticed that Edie's right fist was still clenched shut. Lizzie prised the curled fingers open, revealing what was concealed inside.

'What were you planning to do?' Lizzie enquired in a mocking tone: 'Kill him with a stone?' She pointed to her own forehead: 'Right here?'

With her own breathing finally close to normal, Edie turned towards her saviour.

'I'm really sorry,' she said earnestly. 'And thank you.'

This only inflamed Lizzie, however, who exclaimed. 'What do you mean, *thank you*? You could have been dead if it wasn't for me!'

'I doubt it.'

'You doubt it!' she yelled, then carried on sarcastically: 'Oh, big, strong Edie would've killed the giant – with a pebble!'

Lizzie paused, piecing something together: 'You know that man, don't you?' Edie wouldn't acknowledge anything. 'Don't you?!' A slight shake of Edie's head failed to appease her friend's ire.

'Well, if you don't, I do. I'm pretty sure he was in Costa earlier and bumped my arm as I was paying. I would've said something to him but I was frightened by his size.'

Edie gently rocked her head from side to side. She felt wretched, her emotions all over the place: panic-stricken from the experience in the woods, shamefaced about what she was concealing from her closest friend and excitable about her developing thoughts. Edie held Lizzie's shoulders with both hands.

'I'm really sorry but I've gotta go.'

Lizzie couldn't believe what she was hearing and had her mouth half open in astonishment when Edie repeated herself: 'I'm sorry. I'll call you later.'

Before Lizzie had a chance to answer, Edie charged off down the hill towards Crouch End and home.

Twice a week, when their father was doing an evening surgery, Grace worked through the afternoon: picking Eli up from school, making an evening meal and tending to the children. Edie had completely forgotten that it was a Grace day as she came through the front door.

Inside the house, the childcarer greeted Edie with open arms.

'Hello, Edie. You're so late. I was getting worried.'

'I'm sorry, Grace,' replied Edie.

'You're hot and sweaty,' continued the good-natured Filipina. 'And what's all this dirt and leaves on your tights?'

Grace circled around the young girl and started brushing her back. 'Your blazer. It's filthy. What have you been doing?'

'Nothing, Grace. I was in Highgate Woods with Lizzie.'

Just then, her brother ran down the stairs.

'Why are you so messy?' he asked. 'And your face is scratched.'

'None of your business,' replied Edie, patting her brother on the head whilst edging through the hallway and up to her bedroom.

'Beefburgers for dinner,' shouted Grace. 'Ready in twenty minutes!'

Upstairs, Edie headed straight for the study. Maybe it was Lizzie talking about the biology project or perhaps being close to the educational shed in Highgate Woods. Either way, it didn't matter, as Edie was certain that she knew who her Charlie was. And he wasn't a Charlie, he was a Charles – the Charles who'd discovered evolution. Edie's mum had researched him extensively at university and had been fascinated by his ideas and their implications.

The study was where her mum had spent many hours gathering information on human rights abuses and then exposing the wrongdoers – whether individuals, organisations or governments. Torture, child labour and female genital mutilation had all been subjects of her mother's passion for a better world.

Edie closed the study door behind her and, with her index finger, scanned the top shelf, moving quickly past the Greek philosophers, Kant, and John Stuart Mill's *On Liberty*. Midway along the middle shelf, a green hardback cover indicated that Edie had found what she'd been looking for. Carefully, Edie removed an old edition of Charles Darwin's masterpiece.

Edie brushed dust off the spine and noticed, for the first

time, that the proper title was much longer than commonly used: *On the Origin of Species by Means of Natural Selection, or the Preservation of Favoured Races in the Struggle for Life.*

Edie gently opened up the book. Where would the next note be? Evidently not inside the front cover or, indeed, the back cover. Surprise became frustration as Edie frantically thumbed through the central pages. Nothing. She held the book upside down and shook it. Still nothing. Demoralised, Edie placed the book back on the shelf, went into her bedroom and took off her dirty clothes.

'Beefburgers in ten minutes!' shouted Grace from the kitchen.

Ignoring the reminder, Edie stepped next door and into a hot shower. She closed her eyes and allowed the powerful jet of water to warm her skin. Edie should've been more shocked by the encounter in the woods, but she knew the chase wasn't by chance because Lizzie had seen the man earlier – which meant the perpetrators were getting worried. And, as her mum used to say, when people knew you were on to them, they were more likely to make mistakes.

Still, all of that meant Edie must have been followed but hadn't noticed. A good detective needs to pay attention at all times, Edie thought, and she clearly needed to up her game.

'Come on!' she said aloud to herself, returning to the need to maintain momentum and solve the clue.

Edie mentally retraced her steps. Mum was onto something and was killed because they suspected her. Mum didn't quite have all the evidence she needed but realised she was being watched. She must have started saving the information, but where was it? Her mum had left a trail of clues that only Edie could solve and she trusted her daughter to do so. *What if Charlie got it wrong?* Edie was convinced that Darwin was part of the answer but hadn't factored in the 'getting it wrong' part.

Out of nowhere, Edie recalled something her mum had once read her aloud from one of her Three Principles psychology books: that fresh thinking – new ideas or insights – almost never emerge from a busy mind. Edie took a deep breath, in and out. Then another: in and out. With the water pounding rhythmically on her head, Edie's thoughts gradually settled and her hyperactive mind quietened right down.

And then Edie remembered: it was a conversation she'd had with her mum at the cafe near the lido at Parliament Hill Fields, about halfway through her first year at Highgate Hill. They'd just finished a beautiful walk under blue skies and were enjoying a drink together in the late winter sunshine, when Edie brought up something that had been troubling her for weeks. A boy in 7S, Joshua, was being relentlessly teased about his stammer by two other boys, Leo and Max, whom the other children were scared of because of their size and aggressiveness. When Rosie had asked them to stop mocking Joshua, they'd pushed her over on the pavement, causing a nasty gash to her leg that needed stitches. Edie couldn't bear witnessing their behaviour but she wasn't sure what to do.

Edie's mum had sat and pondered for so long that Edie thought she'd lost track of the problem. Eventually, though, her mum came up with a solution which drew on her university studies. She told Edie the story of how Charles Darwin had written down his theory of evolution by 1839 but, for two decades, was too scared to allow it to be published. The reason: if his theory was correct, then all the creatures of the world, including man, were the product of evolution rather than being created by God – a scientific answer that proved religion wrong. Darwin imagined he'd be shamed by the Church and ostracised from his community for these views, and he became ill with worry. Darwin finally allowed his theory to be published in 1858, but only in a joint paper with another scientist, Lord Alfred Wallace. And here was Edie's mum's point. There is power and safety in numbers, so work with others to bring the boys down – which Edie duly did, mobilising a gang of eight girls who'd embarrassed the boys in the playground. Joshua was never bullied again.

With the comforting heat of the water soaking her skin, Edie noticed that allowing the memory back in felt less painful than before, if only by a little. So, was her mum trying to tell her something about it being all right to get help? In an instant, though, Edie's thoughts switched back to the clue. If Darwin *was* wrong (which he wasn't) … then all the animals in the world weren't the result of evolution. They were put on the earth by God, and the Old Testament was correct.

The Bible. The Bible. Unbothered by residual soap, Edie darted out of the shower cubicle and slung on her towelling dressing gown.

'Beefburgers in five minutes! Wash your hands.'

Dripping a trail of water, Edie slipped quickly back into the study. She knew exactly where the Bible was and had been inches from it just a few minutes earlier. Her eyes scanned the shelf underneath the one containing Darwin's gift to the world. In the very middle sat the Bible. Edie yanked it out and her heart leapt. Something had clearly been slipped between the pages in the very early part of the book. With wet fingers, Edie took out an envelope. After glancing over her shoulder, she unfolded the piece of paper inside and read.

Well done, sweetie! I knew you would work it out.

Now, don't forget to check carefully exactly where I placed this clue – it's important.

And, oh yes, nearly forgot again, the next clue is underneath.

Keep at it, my soldier.
Big love,
Mum xxx

There once was a girl called E-D,
Who made it to clue number three.
If she works hard, for sure,
Next is clue number four.
So, snap to the task urgent-ly!

Much relieved, and ignoring the limerick, Edie checked carefully where the note had been placed – at the very beginning of the Old Testament in the Book of Genesis. Of course, Edie thought, if Darwin was wrong then creation was right.

Genesis.

Edie went over to the computer on the desk, typed in the password and googled the seven-letter word. Edie scrolled down through the findings.

Genesis Wikipedia. No.

The band Genesis. Maybe, although her mum hated Phil Collins.

A Christian Society. No.

Genesis cinema in London. Probably not.

Genesis Bikes and various other unassuming Genesis companies. Probably not.

More evangelical Christian references.

Edie took a moment. Something wasn't right. She looked carefully again at exactly where the note had been placed: it was the precise page where creation was described. Creation. That could also be what her mum was pointing to, Edie thought, so she googled Creation. The first two or three items didn't fit. And then …

Creation Pharmaceuticals. Interesting. Odd, too, that it came up pretty high on the search list. Edie clicked on the home page, where the headline of an item of current news appeared, written by the CEO Peter Goswell: 'Creation saddened by tragic death of research director'. Edie clicked to open the piece and skimmed through it. After pressing the

'Back' button twice, Edie then worked her way through the original search list. One news item on the third search page caught her attention. It was from the previous year and was again about the drug company: 'Creation denies links with bird flu outbreak in Vietnam'.

'What are you looking at?' came the question. Edie was startled by the noiseless appearance of her little brother at her shoulder.

'Nothing,' she responded, quickly minimising the screen.

'Yes, you are,' Eli countered. 'I saw it, something about Creation.'

'No, it wasn't.'

'Yes, it was.' Eli tried to reach over to the mouse but Edie brushed her brother's hand away.

'Anyway, Grace has been shouting for ages. Dinner's getting cold.'

'Tell her I'm not hungry.'

'You'll be in trouble.'

'I don't care,' Edie replied determinedly. 'Now leave me alone.'

As Eli departed down the stairs, Edie felt desperately low all of a sudden. Despite solving the second clue, all this effort was taking its toll. And the task felt so huge. Perhaps it was time to get some help.

CHAPTER 5

DETECTIVE WORK

School had become a complete burden and a barrier to cracking on with her investigations. At least, that was how Edie felt on Thursday afternoon as she dozed off in Latin class and was shaken awake by an irate teacher. Edie had been up until late, feverishly looking at websites about influenza viruses, bird flu viruses, epidemics and the drugs used to fight these diseases. All interspersed with browsing intently around the website of Creation Pharmaceuticals.

At lunchtime, Edie continued her research using the computer in the school library, then carried on in the evening at home. Such was the diversion of her detective work that Edie had hardly thought about the latest clue, and its solution came to her out of the blue over dinner when Eli asked her dad what the capital of Canada was. Dad jested that the answer was 'C', inadvertently triggering a lateral thought in Edie's mind – which resulted in her racing upstairs before dessert. Once again, a calmer mind was more open to possibilities.

In her bedroom that evening Edie mulled over her findings to date, like a police investigator taking stock of progress around solving a crime. She was pretty sure that Creation was central to the mystery, possibly in relation to a drug it had produced, and imagined her mum delving into any possible abuse of workers in Vietnam. Edie didn't understand the more technical elements of Creation's work but was repeatedly drawn to the article on the company's website about the unexpected death of the director of research and development. This needed to be pursued, as well as getting some help on comprehending the scientific elements. Perhaps Mr Winter, the biology teacher at school? No, he was so overenthusiastic that discussions inevitably became very drawn out. Her dad? Definitely not, as he would instantly become suspicious. Maybe another doctor, though.

Lying prostrate on her bed at midnight with one of her mum's favourites – Nerina Pallot's 'Coming Home' – blasting through her headphones, Edie planned out her Friday. She would continue to focus on gathering evidence and leave the verifying of the third clue for the weekend. At which time, Edie might need to follow her mum's message from the ether – and get some assistance.

Just before turning the light out, Edie reached into her bedside table drawer and pulled out the golden locket. Edie clicked it open, transmitted a kiss from her lips to her mum's head with her fingers and said goodnight.

Mobile phone in one hand, Peter Goswell used the other hand to open the kitchen back door and enter his large garden. He waited until he'd crossed the grey flagstone terrace and reached the lawn before bringing the handset back up to his right ear and restarting the conversation.

'Okay, I can talk now. What is it?'

'It's the girl,' asserted Zero.

'What about her?'

Goswell listened to the latest developments before stopping in his tracks at the flower bed bordering the lawn.

'Just let me think for a moment,' Goswell said, finding it hard to focus.

As Goswell paced around the garden, Zero sat on a secluded bench miles away in St Pancras Gardens, close to his flat. Zero pondered how he'd got to this sad place, his distinguished military service wrecked by the Afghanistan incident that had left five crack British SAS agents and one innocent civilian dead. It defied belief that Zero hadn't been killed by the Taliban as he'd wandered aimlessly around the countryside for three days before an army patrol had picked him up. He wished he *had* been killed with his comrades because what followed had been worse: a biased military court hearing that found someone to blame (him) and now a pointless life back in London. From building labourer to nightclub bouncer to hired muscle, his brutish strength and combat skills had been noticed higher and higher up the social ladder. Now, disreputable lawyers, property developers and chief executives were prepared to pay good money to have their dirty deeds sorted.

Although the work provided an outlet for his rage, Zero had become increasingly depressed and nowadays the darkness was almost inescapable. The only solace came from his dear sister Katie – a nurse and single parent, who'd encouraged him to go to the GP and then to a therapist – and her treasured six-year-old son Dylan, the apple of Zero's eye, who adored his hero uncle. Still waiting for Goswell to say something, Zero looked out on the large oak trees in the urban gardens and smiled as he remembered the greeting he'd received a few hours earlier in his sister's home: 'Uncle, can I show you my Lego?! Can we play football?! Can we watch TV together?!' Zero made a mental note of his nephew's gift request for his upcoming seventh birthday. 'A watch it is, little fella,' he'd promised.

Goswell approached the summer house on the far side of the lawn that he used as a private office, and finally responded. 'You're sure the girl's started looking into the company?'

'Yes.'

'But how?'

'As I said, through the keyloggers I placed on the two desktop computers in the house. They track the websites that are being searched.'

'No!' Goswell interrupted curtly. 'I mean, how did she know to look into Creation? And why now? It's over a year since the death.'

'That I don't know.' Zero paused deliberately.

Goswell reacted to the unhelpful reply and snarled: 'Well, bloody well find out what's going on! It's what I pay you for, isn't it?'

Zero held his tongue, his nerves steady despite the nauseating client. 'I will look into it.'

'Did you at least manage to scare her, as we discussed?'

'I did. In the woods.' Zero refrained from conveying his own embarrassing injury. And, more worryingly, that Edie may have seen his face. 'But she's tough,' he added.

The kitchen door opened and Goswell's wife, Jane, shouted something about their daughter, Mary, feeling worse. Glandular fever was the GP's diagnosis and, for once, Goswell had been there to assist from the outset. Goswell gesticulated that he'd be over shortly, before turning his attention back to his phone. Homer, his Labrador, had bounded over the grass and was rummaging around in the shrubbery close to where Goswell stood.

'Have a look around her house and see what you can find.'

'Not a good idea.'

'Just do it!' Goswell took his voice down a notch before concluding, 'And then let me know.' He ended the conversation with his right thumb.

'Come on, Homer,' Goswell called, but the dog had become transfixed by something on the earth amidst the vegetation. 'Come on, boy,' but Homer refused. Goswell stepped into the muddy border to see what the Labrador was obsessing about. Nestled at the base of a shrub was a bird, lying on its back, shallow breaths visible through slight body movements. There was a misty glaze in its eyes as Homer sniffed around intently. Goswell looked up at the large oak, presumably from where the bird had fallen. He took a step towards the bird, raised his foot, paused for a moment and then crushed its head with his heel.

On the walk back to the house, Goswell made a further call with the burner phone to the one other person implicated in his malevolent dealings.

After lunch on Friday, Edie noticed Lizzie peeling off the normal route back to the main school building. Having resolved to tell Lizzie the truth about recent events, she collared her friend at the junction of Broadlands Road with Southwood Lane.

'Can you come round at about ten o'clock tomorrow?' Edie asked, concerned that further delay might backfire.

'It's Saturday morning,' replied Lizzie, surprised by the early weekend start.

'I know.' Edie stepped closer. 'I'll tell you everything tomorrow – I just don't have time now. Please trust me.'

'Okay,' responded her confused friend, not obviously placated.

'Oh, and I'll need your help with something important,' said Edie. 'Wear trainers.' She turned on her heels, a girl on a mission.

Skipping afternoon school, Edie took the number 210 bus from the nearby main road to Golders Green station, then two further buses to Mill Hill roundabout. From there, Edie followed Google Maps on her iPhone to find Wise Lane, where she sat on a wall outside number 94. Edie had contemplated telephoning in advance but had decided that it was too risky.

Edie gathered the courage handed down from her mother and rang the doorbell. This was where the serious part of her investigations started, where she needed to behave like a detective but without giving anything away. Over a hundred metres back, the man lurking in the shadows hoped that nobody would answer.

At first, nobody did and Edie pressed the buzzer again. She hadn't noticed the slight shifting of an upstairs bedroom curtain but, peering through an opened letterbox, Edie saw a pair of feet coming down the stairs.

The woman who tentatively opened the door was in a dressing gown, despite the time of day, ashen-faced with bedraggled hair. 'Yes ... hello ...' she greeted weakly. 'I don't buy anything at the door, but ... it doesn't look like you're here for that.'

Edie needed to think quickly as the woman's look was far from welcoming. On a shelf in the hallway in the background Edie saw a set of family photos, one of which looked like a holiday shot of the woman, her husband (now deceased), with two boys between them. Edie took a chance. 'My name is Edie ... Edie Franklin. I'm a friend of your son's.'

'Oh,' came the uncertain response. 'A friend of my son ... which one?' Luckily for Edie, the woman didn't wait before adding: 'Looking at your age, you must mean Ethan ...'

'Yes, Ethan,' Edie replied too rapidly, causing the woman to hesitate.

'Well, he's back from Peru but has just popped out to the shops. Won't be long. I suppose you'd better come in. I'm Claire.'

Orange juice and Jaffa Cakes were placed on the coffee table in front of Edie, although she had no appetite. Edie said thank you and took a tiny bite of the bitter dark chocolate. A small price to pay.

More photographs sat on shelves around the lounge. The walls were an unimaginative shade of beige and the furniture and pictures suggested a desire to conform rather than any genuine style. A spanking new conservatory suggested no shortage of money.

Claire Stephenson sat opposite Edie, folded her legs and then pulled her dressing gown over her knees. She cleared her throat with an unpleasant rasp before restarting the conversation.

'So, Edie … how exactly do you know Ethan?'

Edie lied unconvincingly: 'It's my sister who knows him better, but she introduced us.'

'Right,' Claire said with a deepening frown. 'What school do you go to?'

'Oh, I don't go to the same school as Ethan …'

'You don't go to Mill Hill?'

'No, no. I go to Highgate Hill,' countered Edie, quickly adding, 'But my sister goes to Mill Hill.'

'Okay, and what's your sister's name?

'Lizzie. Lizzie Franklin.'

'Right,' repeated Claire speculatively. 'So, let me get this straight. Your sister Lizzie, who's also at Mill Hill, knows Ethan, and she introduced you to him. But how come?'

Edie felt on slightly firmer footing now, so started to execute her plan.

'I've been doing a school project – a biology project – and Ethan helped me initially, then said his dad knew more about the kind of stuff I was looking into.'

'So, you've been in touch with my husband too?'

'Yes, since last September.'

'That's almost six months,' Claire quizzed. 'I didn't know school projects lasted that long.'

'It's part of the new GCSE biology syllabus,' Edie lied.

'Strange. Tom didn't say anything about it. What was the project about?'

Edie seized the opening: 'The project's about influenza ... Well, about influenza through history ... the flu epidemics. Spanish Flu after the First World War ... Swine flu more recently. And wondering when the next global pandemic will come.'

'And why exactly were you talking to Tom?'

Edie had rehearsed this and had her line of enquiry ready. 'It's because of Creation ...' Claire winced at the name but Edie carried on. 'And how they've developed this new drug, Flu-Away. And your husband was the one who created it.'

'I'd rather you didn't mention that name, Creation.' Claire paused briefly. 'You do know that Tom is dead.'

Edie didn't miss a beat. 'Yes, I do. And I'm *so* sorry. When I read about it on the website I was so upset. You see, he'd been so kind. Helped me with all my questions. He was always very patient. And pleased, I think, that somebody was interested in his work. Which is why I came around … to tell you how sorry I am.'

'That would be Tom,' Claire smiled knowingly. She looked towards the end of the room, through the conservatory windows to the garden, before returning her gaze to Edie. Claire was about to say something when the phone rang. Reluctantly, she picked up the handset and trudged a few steps away from her guest. Although her speech was whispered, Edie listened carefully and could make out most of what she was saying:

'Hello … Yes, I'm okay … Yes, I got the flowers … they're sitting in front of me in the lounge.'

Edie saw no such bouquet on the table and picked up on how agitated Claire was becoming.

'Very little …. not really been in the mood … and I've had a sore throat and cold … No! No need to come around at all, my son's here with me … No, I'm not angry or ungrateful. It's just … I can't really speak as I've got a visitor round at the moment, a young girl … What's her name? What's that got to do with anything! I don't know … Edie … I think she said Edie, Edie Frank … or Franklin.'

Claire stared briefly at the receiver. 'He got cut off. Fine, he's a creep anyway. Keeps sending flowers but I just chuck them in the bin.'

Edie stepped in: 'Has somebody been bothering you?'

'Yes. Peter Goswell. The chief executive of Tom's firm, his boss.'

'Did Tom like him?' Edie asked with deliberate innocence.

With the opportunity to let off steam, Claire couldn't hold back despite hardly knowing her visitor. 'Peter had a hold on Tom. Paid Tom a lot of money ...' She pointed to the refurbishment of the lounge and conservatory. 'But he expected a lot in return. Tom was drawn in by the money at first ... it was way better than at the university ... but then by the lure of success. And he was captivated by Peter's magnetism.'

'But I thought your husband was just helping to make this new drug to beat the flu?'

A resigned expression settled across Claire's face. 'He was ... he was ... but something happened. The glamour of fame ... a contribution to mankind ... I don't know ... the possibility of a fortune if the drug was a hit. Peter promised him all that.'

Claire raised her head to look at Edie. 'I'm sorry, this has nothing at all to do with your school project.'

'Not at all!' replied Edie immediately. She thought about how best to keep the conversation flowing. 'Your husband seemed like such a good person. So caring. So friendly.'

'He was. Tom was such a good man. But he changed over the last year or so.' Claire took a sad, deep breath before carrying on. 'Something happened in Vietnam around a year ago, maybe eighteen months, and he seemed very upset. I read in the papers about the outbreak of bird flu in Saigon ... six or was it eight people dead ... but he claimed to know little about it ... said it was nothing to do with Creation. But they had a lab there and Tom travelled there. Once he even brought back an official-looking briefcase which I'd never seen before … and put something in the fridge overnight, but it was gone by the morning. I wondered if there was something he wasn't telling me.'

Claire became teary-eyed and she took a tissue from her dressing-gown pocket. Edie was about to say something consoling when they both heard keys in the front door.

'Oh, that'll be Ethan back,' Claire observed. Edie's cheeks blushed instantly and her stomach lurched.

'I really am so sorry, Mrs Stephenson, I didn't want to bring back bad memories.' Edie stood up. 'I just wanted to pay my respects. I'll be off now.'

Claire motioned for Edie to stay where she was. 'You can't leave now, honey, Ethan's back. Hold on a moment.'

A few seconds later, Claire returned with her tall, dark-haired youngest son, even nicer looking in person than in the photo.

'Ethan, you know Edie,' she said. 'Lizzie Franklin's sister. She just popped over.'

Bemused, Ethan stared at the young girl on the sofa and was about to respond with a no but held back. As Claire fussed to pour out a drink and put Jaffa Cakes on a plate, Edie silently mouthed one word directly at Ethan, accompanied by her most pleading expression: 'Please!'

Leaning over the tray, Claire sniffled and then suddenly spluttered into a tissue. As she placed the scrunched-up hankie in her dressing-gown pocket, Edie noticed two small flecks of blood.

'Are you okay, Mum?' Ethan asked.

'Yes, fine.' Seated again and composed, Claire

continued. 'As I was saying, Edie, Tom took quite a knock, but after a while – quite a while – he seemed to be getting back to himself, so we planned our second honeymoon in Italy, which is where … well … where he died.'

Edie stood up and came round the table to the sofa. She sat down next to Claire. 'It's awful, I do understand.' Edie waited and then added: 'I'm going to finish this project, Mrs Stephenson, that's for sure. It's a special project. And you'll know when I'm done.' Edie squeezed Claire's hand and slowly stood up, but her exit was unexpectedly interrupted.

'There is one other thing.' It was the voice of the quiet son.

Edie turned towards him: 'What is it?' she asked.

Ethan paused and looked at his mother, who nodded for him to continue. 'It wasn't just the Vietnam thing that upset Dad. It was strange, but he seemed devastated when this woman died a year or so ago, under a train. I don't think he knew her, but he went on and on about it. A tragedy, he said. He collected the newspaper cuttings.'

Edie froze but Ethan wasn't finished. 'I snuck into his study to look at them at the time … and found them again when I was poking through some things a few days ago. What was her name?'

Glued to the spot, a choking sound came from deep in Edie's throat, accompanied by a run of tears. The emotional outburst caught the Stephensons by surprise, and Claire wrapped one arm around the young girl comfortingly.

'What's the matter, luv?'

Edie twisted, politely but firmly releasing herself. 'I'm

sorry, Mrs Stephenson, but I really have to go now.'

Edie grabbed her things abruptly and, at the front door, struggled to open the stiff lock. Eventually, Edie was out and through the front garden. She was a few houses down the road when her arm was grabbed from behind.

'Ow!' Edie spun around.

Ethan handed her a piece of paper. 'It's our home phone number – my iPhone's broken. I think I know who you are … and I can help you. Call me, anytime.'

The sincerity in his eyes softened the young girl, who looked down at the paper. Under the light of a streetlamp Edie noticed what an unusual and memorable phone number it was.

Without looking back, Edie walked decisively down the street.

CHAPTER 6

DOCTORS

Sitting near the back of the 234 bus, Edie considered the findings from her meeting with Claire and Ethan and mapped out the next couple of days: a full-on weekend of gathering more evidence about the drug company and her mother's killers, plus enlisting some help from others. Edie's stomach clenched at the thought of letting her secret out, although she was sure that her mother was telling her something – possibly about collaboration.

As cars and pedestrians and shops drifted by through the bus window, a memory popped into Edie's mind of a book she had sort-of read a while back – the only one of her mum's Three Principles books that Edie had ever looked at. It had a red cover and was called *The Inside-Out Revolution*. Edie couldn't remember much about the book, except that she'd found two of the principles – thought and consciousness – easier to understand, as they were about the psychological link between your thinking and your feelings or emotions. The principle of mind, though, had been tougher for Edie to grasp: it wasn't about the brain, more to do with the connectedness between people and the connection between human beings and something bigger, or more expansive, than ourselves.

Connection. Not being alone in the world. The power

of collaboration. Ideas were germinating inside Edie's head. She definitely needed assistance, and it was a natural part of being human to reach out to others.

Reaching down, Edie took a scrawled piece of paper out of its safe place in the zipped front section of her school bag. This clue, at least on first impressions, had taken only a minute or so to solve. In fact, Edie had been almost disappointed that her mum hadn't entrusted her with something harder. Edie read it again, smirking:

> There once was a girl called E-D,
> Who made it to clue number three.
> If she works hard, for sure,
> Next is clue number four.
> So, snap to the task urgent-ly!

The answer was in the use of capital letters and Edie had drawn a thick vertical line with a yellow marker down the column, spelling a five-letter word, but that only part-solved the clue. On the cramped seat, with a heavily pregnant woman right up against her, Edie reread the limerick. One word in the final line suggested she'd need to visit her grandparents. She wanted to do that tomorrow, but other plans meant it might have to wait till Sunday.

For now, Edie sat back, opened Spotify on her iPhone and listened to Paloma Faith bellowing her way through 'New York'. Edie smiled, remembering when she and her mum had seen Paloma – their second favourite female vocalist – interviewed on TV. They'd laughed at how different Paloma's spoken Cockney accent was to her striking singing voice.

Edie checked the time. It was half past four, meaning she had an hour to get to her next appointment, in which she would try and glean more scientific information to help her investigation – from Dr Martial at the surgery.

Back at home, Edie's dad was seated in the armchair by the window in the corner of the lounge. Friday afternoon surgery loomed and he could barely face the thought of it. Another thirty patients with their moans and groans, expecting a doctor with a smile and a good bedside manner. Not a sad, lonely man in his forties with no desire to hear their ailments.

Although he'd been a GP for almost fifteen years, Dr Mark Franklin had never really understood depression. Patient after patient telling him how they couldn't get out of bed in the morning, their lack of energy and the pointlessness of the world. As a kind physician, Edie's dad had tried his best to listen sympathetically. Deep down, though, he'd been irritated by the wastefulness. Only one life – and this is what you do with it.

All that changed, however, after his wife's death, when the initial shock was gradually replaced by numbness and overwhelming feelings of sadness. Toughest, perhaps, was that the children needed looking after more than ever before: Eli, retracting into a shell of confusion and desperation, and Edie, inconsolable and mad at the world. Dad allowed Mama and Papa to help with the kids, but he didn't understand how Edie's grandparents were able to get through the days: having lost one young daughter, to lose another must have been unbearable. Yet, somehow, Mama and Papa truly did cope, with a fortitude that he saw reflected in his wife and, at times, in Edie.

When the children finally went back to school, Dad had been able to return to work, starting with a few clinics per week. He coped, just about, but in the evenings he turned to the bottle. One whisky became two or three, then whisky was followed by wine. Fuelled by the alcohol, he sometimes lost his temper with the children: over dinner, over which TV channel to watch, over what clothes to wear, over bedtime, over anything.

Edie's dad looked down at the glass of Scottish single malt on the side table next to the armrest. Largely, he refrained from drinking during the day, especially after Dr Martial had smelled it once on his breath, but some days just seemed impossible to get through.

As Dad knew well, the medical term for his feelings was reactive depression, a response to a traumatic incident that usually passes after a few months. But Christmas and the stone-setting had set him back. Tentatively extending his right arm, Dad wrapped his fingers around the crystal tumbler. He drew the glass to his lips and was about to take a sip when he noticed an old primary school photo of Edie. So pretty in bunches and grinning from ear to ear. She'd be dropping into the surgery later on and he didn't want her to sense his state. Dad eased his arm down as his work mobile rang.

'Hello,' Dad answered. 'Dr Franklin speaking.'

It was Nikki, the receptionist at the surgery. 'Oh, hi Mark, sorry to disturb you. It's Olive Prentice. She's fallen over again and can't get up.'

'I'm not on call. It's Dr Martial ... I think.'

'We can't get hold of him,' Nikki added. This was a common occurrence that annoyed the hell out of the other doctors.

'Why not?'

'Sorry, I don't know. But there's nobody else around and Mrs Prentice seemed very upset. Said she'd hurt her wrist.'

Dad pursed his lips and took a deep breath. 'Okay, what's the address?'

After Nikki had given him the information, Dad picked up the glass, walked through the hallway, down the six steps into the kitchen and chucked the brown liquid down the sink. He put on an overcoat, grabbed the book recommended to him by the clinical psychologist at work, placed it in his medical case and closed the front door behind him. Outside, in the shadows, a man with a scar lurked.

An hour and a quarter later, an irritating buzzing sound jolted Edie's dad who, leaning on his forearms, had fallen asleep on his own surgery desk. He lifted his tired head and looked at the complicated telephone apparatus. The 'Line 1' light flashed red, signalling a call from reception, and he wearily picked up the receiver.

'Your daughter's here, Dr Franklin.'

'Send her in please, Nikki.'

'Will do. Oh, how was Mrs Prentice?'

'Colles' fracture, probably ... I mean, I think she's broken her wrist. Otherwise she was fine. I called an ambulance and left her with a neighbour.'

'Oh good, I'm pleased she's all right.' Nikki replaced the handset. 'In you go, dear.'

'Hi, Daddy!' announced a beaming face in the doorway.

'Hello, sweetie. How lovely to see you!' Dad stood up from the swivel chair and embraced his daughter, his mood immediately lifted. The hug went on just a little longer than Edie had anticipated. 'What's going on?' Dad asked, once their arms were back by their sides.

'You know,' Edie shrugged. 'School.' She shrugged her shoulders again. 'Stuff.'

Dad smiled but wasn't to be deterred. 'Can you be a bit more specific?'

'I don't know,' Edie replied unforthcomingly. 'School stuff.'

'Okay, I'll make it easier. What's the most interesting thing you learned – or that happened – this afternoon?'

Edie went cold. Did her dad know something? Had the school called him because she'd played truant from class? Surely not, he was just asking the 'most interesting' question because he couldn't think of anything else. Edie actually quite liked talking through the best part of the day, something she'd done more with her mum than her dad.

'Evolution,' Edie lied. Detectives need to think on their feet, she'd learned.

'Yep, what about evolution? Any particular aspect?'

Now she had to give him something more concrete. 'Our biology teacher, Mr Winter, told us how the Nazis used Darwin's ideas to defend what they did in the Second World War. Hitler said some races were more superior and it was just natural selection to wipe out the inferior people. Like the Jews, like us.'

Dad looked on, astonished. 'You learned *that* in biology?'

Edie perched on the corner of the desk as Dad sat back down. Twisting around, she ran her finger down the clinic list.

'Ooh. You've got Florence Baker at twenty to six. Aged ...' Edie calculated from the date of birth on the sheet. 'Aged eighty-four. I wonder what's wrong with her.'

'I don't know what's wrong with her. That's why she's coming to see me,' Dad responded, clocking that Mrs Baker was one of those 'heart-sink' patients with multiple problems, so-called because of the way they made the doctor feel.

'Constipation, maybe?' suggested Edie. 'Trouble hearing?'

Edie followed the names further down the page. 'Ah, Anna Springer, at twenty past six. Date of birth, ninth of August ... that makes her ... eighteen.' Edie looked up at her father with a smile. 'Contraception?'

'Give me that list!' Dad exclaimed, grabbing the print-out of the evening surgery's twenty or so patients. 'This is confidential, y'know!'

Edie turned her attention elsewhere in the room: scales, height stick, the couch with the large paper roll, medical books and some old-style patients' notes on a wobbly shelf, and the sink with two bottles of pink hand disinfectant. On the desk directly in front of Edie was all the expected medical paraphernalia: stethoscope, sphygmomanometer for blood pressure, torch and a reflex hammer. Edie picked up a metal instrument. 'Have a look in my ears, Daddy. I like it when you do that. And they've been a bit itchy.'

'That's an ophthalmoscope. It's for your eyes.'

'Oh.' They both laughed, but Edie wasn't finished.

'Look at my eyes then. She lifted the device up to her eye and leant in playfully towards her father's face. 'Look into my eyes,' Edie spoke in hypnotic monotone. 'Look into my eyes …'

The odd scene was interrupted by Nikki appearing in the doorway. 'Your first patient is here, Dr Franklin. And Dr Martial is ready for your daughter.' Edie jumped to attention as Nikki disappeared back to reception, knocking a paperback off the desk and onto the floor. Edie picked up the book.

'How come you've got this?' Edie asked, recognising the red cover which, weirdly, she'd been thinking about earlier that day.

'Oh, it's nothing,' Dad replied quickly, reaching for the book. 'Just something someone recommended that might …' he paused, embarrassed, 'might help with my moods … with, y'know … how I've been feeling.'

'Oh,' Edie remarked. 'You know it's one of mum's favourite Three Principles books, don't you?' Dad looked as if he didn't know. 'I've read some of it. Has it helped you?'

'I've only just started,' Dad observed, 'although it's quite interesting so far ...' Then, quite suddenly, his guard was up again and he snatched the book back. 'Anyway, what are you seeing Martial for today?' Dad asked.

'Another asthma inhaler – I've run out,' Edie responded, without revealing the main reason for her visit.

'I have to push on now, sweetheart,' said her dad, smiling sweetly. 'See you later at home. And thanks for dropping in.' Edie waved and his soul felt nourished. Enough strength to get through the clinic.

The door to Dr Martial's room was ajar, leaving Edie unsure whether to enter with or without knocking. Opting for politeness, Edie rapped her knuckles against the wooden frame and stuck her head around the corner. Almost simultaneously a 'yes' was shouted from inside. Ushering her in, the doctor – smartly dressed in a blue striped shirt, white collar and flamboyant navy-coloured bow tie – finished checking a patient's electronic record before looking up from the computer screen. Having closed the door carefully behind her, Edie sat on the chair to which Martial was pointing.

'You seem to grow taller every time I see you, my dear.'

A pause suggested the doctor was expecting Edie to respond, but the unimaginative comment left her with little to say. After an awkward silence, Dr Martial carried on.

'So, what can I do for you today, young lady?'

His patronising manner irritated Edie, but she needed his assistance.

'I've run out of Ventolin,' she said.

Martial's gaze returned to the computer screen and he tapped away at the keyboard, quickly bringing up her medication history. He looked over at the girl opposite.

'I gave you two inhalers just ...' he mentally did the maths on the dates, 'just three months ago. Has the asthma been playing up?'

Edie improvised: 'Not really, it's just that I lost one at school. I took it out for sports ... a hockey game ... and must've left it on the field. It wasn't there the next day. And the other one's nearly run out.'

'Oh dear. That was unfortunate. And do you use the Becotide at all? That's the steroid inhaler, the brown one.'

I'm not an idiot, Edie thought to herself. 'No, Dr Martial. I don't need any more Becotide, just some more of the blue puffers please.' She gave him her best possible smile.

'No problem, my dear. But I do need to examine you and check the breathing is in order. We can't take any chances with asthma.'

'But you examined me last time,' Edie said hastily.

'Indeed. But if you're requiring additional inhalers, for whatever reason, then I'm required to check on your clinical wellbeing.' Dr Martial pulled out from his desk drawer a peak flow meter and attached a cardboard funnel to the end. 'Now, take a deep breath in, then blow into this as hard and fast as you can. You know the drill.'

Edie did as she was asked.

'Excellent,' proclaimed Dr Martial as he inspected the result, before standing up and walking around the desk to stand next to Edie. The doctor was taller than Edie remembered, and the overly neat side-parting of his dark brown hair irritated her.

'Now, take your blazer off and lift up your shirt so I can listen to your lungs.'

Reluctantly, Edie did as requested, embarrassingly revealing one of her new pink bras with a trimming of red strawberries.

'Deep breath in ... then out.' The icy stethoscope was bracing as Dr Martial manipulated it around her back.

'Good, all clear. Now the front, please.'

With deliberate slowness, Edie pulled the shirt up to her neck.

'Okay, and again, deep breath in ... and out.' As soon as he was done, Edie quickly replaced her clothing.

Returning to his seat, Dr Martial printed out the prescription and handed it over. Edie was about to pose her next question when she was caught off guard.

'How is everything at home, my dear?'

Uncertain of his motives, she answered cautiously. 'Fine.'

'Your brother okay?'

'Yes.'

'And your father?'

'He's fine thank you, Dr Martial,' Edie snapped. 'But there was one other thing I wanted to ask you about.'

'Oh yes, what's that then?'

'Well, I'm doing a project at school about flu ... I mean influenza ... and all the pandemics. You know, Spanish flu,

Hong Kong flu ...'

'Right.' Dr Martial leant over, a more serious expression on his face. 'And what exactly can I do to help?'

'Well ... one of the things I want to include in my project is about how they make drugs to treat flu. Antiviral drugs, I think they're called.'

'And what is it about these antiviral drugs that you need to find out?'

'Just ... in order for the drug companies to make the drugs, are they allowed to develop dangerous viruses in the lab? Y'know, so they can test the drugs on them?' A pause ensued, before Martial changed the direction of conversation.

'And which subject is this project for at school?' he questioned.

'Mm ... biology.'

'And who might your biology teacher be?'

Taken aback, Edie had no choice. 'Oh ... Mr Winter.'

'Perhaps I should give him a call? Offer him my medical services?'

'Oh, that's really not necessary,' Edie said defensively.

Martial's glare was disconcerting and made Edie anxious. Amidst the silence that followed, Edie suddenly lost her nerve. Something wasn't right.

'Oh, this doesn't matter,' she blurted out, making to stand up. But Dr Martial was at her side in an instant and had balanced himself on the corner of the desk next to her, far too close for comfort. With his right hand, Dr Martial grabbed Edie's left wrist, firmly but not painfully.

With a steely voice that frightened her he said, 'I do

hope the project goes well, my dear. But take my advice. Don't be an interfering oddball like your mother. If you bite off more than you can chew, things can backfire.'

Edie pulled herself upright, shoved aggressively past the unpleasant doctor and sped out of the room.

CHAPTER 7

BLOOD ON THE TRACKS

Edie had a restless night. Tossing and turning, her thoughts still fluctuated between involving others and ploughing on with her investigations single-handed. Despite Edie's insight about the bonds between individuals, she remained concerned that the more people were in the loop, the greater the uncertainty over what might happen. Maybe it was about the need to be in control.

But in the quiet of the night an image of her mum kept returning: a person who was driven but who encouraged collaboration, a woman who built friendships and networks to help uncover evils in the world. Plus, Edie had to gather more evidence – the essence of detective work – and she definitely needed help to do that.

As the Saturday morning light pierced through the blinds, Edie was dragged from her slumber by a knocking on her bedroom door and a familiar voice.

'Sweetie, it's quarter to nine and I'm off to the surgery. You need to look after Eli, so can you get up please.'

Sleepily, Edie responded, 'Okay, Dad. I'm awake.'

'All right then, see you later.'

'No, Dad! Come in. I want to say goodbye.'

Edie's father ambled into the room and perched on the side of the bed next to his dozy daughter. He grasped her left hand which was resting on top of the duvet, and with his other hand gently stroked the hair away from her eyes.

'Thank you, Daddy. That's nice.' He continued in silence.

'I know you don't like the Saturday surgery, Dad, but I hope it's all right today,' Edie added.

'I'm sure it will be fine,' Dad replied with a smile. 'But I appreciate your concern.'

'Will Dr Martial be there?' asked Edie, and her dad felt the slightest tightening of her grip on his hand.

'No, it's just me. Only one doctor on Saturday mornings.'

Edie waited a little before probing further. 'Did Dr Martial say anything to you yesterday evening after I'd gone?'

Dad looked at his daughter in surprise. 'No, nothing at all. Should he have?'

Edie back-pedalled. 'No, not really, I just wondered.'

Now her dad was suspicious. 'Whatever goes on between doctor and patient is secret – it's confidential – so Dr Martial wouldn't tell me something medical.' He waited a moment before carrying on. 'But is there anything I should know, lovely?'

Edie squeezed her father's hand and looked directly at him. 'No, absolutely not, Dad. I'm just a bit asleep still. When will you be back?'

'Around one o'clock, maybe half past one, depending on any home visits. We can have lunch together.'

'That'll be nice. Is it all right if I go out with Eli whilst you're at the surgery?'

'I thought you would be just hanging out at home.'

'We'll only be going in to Crouch End.'

'Okay, but be careful. Make sure you're home when I'm back.'

'Thanks, Dad. Is Eli up already?'

'What do you think? It's Saturday morning, of course he's up! He's playing on the iPad in the playroom. I've given him some breakfast.' He kissed Edie lightly on the cheek. 'I've got to go now.'

Dad got up, left the room with a wave and, shortly after, the front door slammed shut. For a while Edie lay in bed contemplating the important day ahead. Then, abruptly, she threw off the covers and got up. Lizzie would be round in an hour and Edie needed to prepare.

Jeans, her favourite skinny pair; pale blue Converse trainers; white T-shirt with cool purple geometric cuboid design on the front; navy hoodie from American Apparel – slim-fit with a central pocket; hair tied up, plus the locket – it was one of those days again. The reflection in her bedroom mirror pleased Edie: sufficiently nondescript to look like any other north London teenager, but also adult enough for her needs.

Edie left her room, passed the photos on the stairs that she sometimes noticed Eli dwelling on and went into the playroom. The TV blared out American teenagers screaming rudely at their parents, whilst her brother was simultaneously playing *Subway Surfers* on the tablet on his lap.

With slightly sweaty palms, Edie composed herself: 'Eli, there's something important that I need to speak to you about.'

No answer from her younger sibling. Edie's thumbs fidgeted with her fingertips. She steadily repeated herself: 'Eli, I said there's something important that I need to talk to you about.' Still nothing, so she grabbed the remote control from the sofa, pointed it directly at the TV and brought a swift end to the whining voices.

'I was watching that! What d'ya do that for?' shouted Eli without looking up from the iPad.

'Because I need to speak to you,' responded Edie firmly.

Eli's fingers continued the jerky movements across the screen required to jump a fleeing graffiti artist over a track and oncoming trains in search of some gold coins. 'You're not my boss! Put the telly back on.'

Bracing herself, Edie chose her words carefully for maximal impact. 'Eli, I need to speak to you right now. It's about Mum.' Eli hesitated mid-game, allowing Edie to seize the moment. 'It's about her death. And it's a secret.'

Eli looked up immediately and stared at his sister.

Now she had his attention.

At four minutes past ten the doorbell rang.

'Hey,' Lizzie announced breezily, even in the face of the early weekend hour and confusion over why she'd been summoned.

'Wotcha,' Edie replied as her best friend sauntered into the hallway and looked through the open door to the lounge.

'Is your dad here?'

'No, he's doing the Saturday surgery.'

'Ooh. He hates that.'

'I know,' Edie agreed.

A brief, awkward silence followed as the girls stood in the hallway, Lizzie waiting for some kind of explanation. The text she'd received the previous evening had given little away, but had repeated the necessity of her coming to the Franklins' house.

Lizzie asked, 'So, why I am here?'

'Come into the playroom,' said Edie as she led the way. Lizzie followed down the few steps at the end of the passageway.

'Hi, Eli,' Lizzie said at the sight of Edie's brother on the sofa.

'Hi,' he murmured.

'Have a seat,' commanded Edie, gesturing at the place on the sofa next to Eli. Lizzie complied with a mystified expression, whilst Edie sat on a dining chair across the coffee table and directly opposite them. She'd spent only a few minutes with Eli before her friend's arrival, so she needed to tell the whole story from the beginning. Tentatively and with a shaky voice, Edie began.

'I know I've been a little difficult over the past few weeks ...'

Edie paused, expecting some kind of affirmation of her behaviour, but the audience stayed quiet. So she cracked on with a clear-cut declaration.

'Mum's death wasn't an accident.' Silence, an atmosphere of deadly seriousness. Edie picked at the fraying denim around her knees.

'What do you mean … your mum's death wasn't an accident?' asked Lizzie.

'Mum's death wasn't an accident. She was murdered.' The twosome on the sofa looked perplexed. Edie paused briefly before continuing as she'd rehearsed in her mind.

'At the stone-setting two weeks ago I wore my sheepskin coat. I hadn't put it on since Mum died because it was the coat I was wearing at school when they told me what had happened to her.'

Edie took another moment and glanced at the paintings by herself and Eli that plastered the playroom walls – this was as hard as she'd imagined.

'At the cemetery I found a note in the coat pocket. A note from Mum written … before she was murdered.'

'What did the note say?' Lizzie probed gently.

Edie reached down to the shelf under the coffee table and pulled out a blue cardboard folder from which she extracted a clear plastic wallet that contained the original note. She placed the wallet on the table but carried on talking without sharing it.

'The note … this note …' Edie pointed to it with her finger, 'said … says … that Mum had been investigating some kind of human rights problem, which was her work … but something big, something really serious. She was threatened and thought she was being followed. Mum got so worried about her life that she wrote me this note … just …'

Choking on her words but determined not to break down during the telling of the story, Edie fiddled with the edges of the plastic wallet but persevered.

'Just in case she was killed.'

'Can I have a look at the note?' Lizzie whispered.

Edie pushed the wallet over to Lizzie who took out the note. Eli peered over from his seat on the sofa next to Lizzie; after reading the note she passed it to him. It took Eli a while but he read it through. No tears.

'There's a riddle, a clue, at the end,' Lizzie stated.

'Yes. Can you solve it?' asked Edie.

Lizzie and Eli examined the note again together for a minute or so before shaking their heads.

'What does it mean?' Eli asked.

And so Edie explained how she'd worked out the crossword clue solution after a few days of heartache. With a pencil she demonstrated how the word 'Cluedo' was threaded between two adjacent words. She grabbed a stool and carefully brought the game down from the shelf to show them how she'd found the next note in the small black envelope for the murder cards.

Edie described to her avid listeners how the clues were linked, and how each seemed to be about something special to her and her mum, something only Edie could really work out. From the blue cardboard wallet, Edie presented the second clue and shared how she'd worked out that it was about Darwin and evolution, and how it had led her to the Bible – and to Creation.

With web-page print-outs, Edie then demonstrated how she'd started investigating a drug company, Creation Pharmaceuticals, and the development of their new medicine to treat flu. Edie showed them a news story about the deaths of people involved in a drug trial at a lab in Vietnam and then revealed information both on the recent unexpected death of the company's director of research and development and her trip to Dr Stephenson's family in Mill Hill.

Throughout the conversation Lizzie remained utterly engaged, taking it all in with intense seriousness, whilst Eli listened carefully and softly asked the occasional question. Her retelling of the chase in Highgate Woods was the only element that rattled Lizzie and brought fear into Eli's eyes.

'That monster has something to do with all of this?' Lizzie exclaimed.

'I think so,' answered Edie.' And I may have seen him around elsewhere. Outside school. Perhaps following me.'

After that, the trio were silent, emotionally exhausted from the story and its implications. Eventually, it was the youngest of them who broke the stillness.

'Why didn't Mummy write me a note?'

An hour and a quarter after Lizzie had arrived at the house, the three children walked down Cecile Park towards Crouch Hill. One Edwardian terraced house after another, mostly converted into flats, although some – like the Franklins' – were still family homes. Edie noticed the peacefulness of the front garden at number 46: a small square area covered in slate chippings, interrupted only by a bamboo plant, a rock water feature and a perfectly groomed Japanese maple tree.

After she'd displayed all the notes and other information she'd gathered, Edie faced various questions from Lizzie and

Eli. Had her mother left anything else? Where was Creation Pharmaceuticals located? What did the research director's wife think of it all? Had Edie told anyone else? Did Edie feel she was in danger?

Edie had answered as best she could, even sharing how she was starting to feel differently about her mother's death, as if her mum was trying to show her something through the experience of solving the clues. The hardest question of all was Eli's, which she'd anticipated. All Edie could suggest was her belief that it had all been done in a rush, that their frightened mother had needed to set difficult clues that couldn't be solved by the perpetrators of the crimes should they come across them. And Mum couldn't leave it to Dad as they'd disagreed about this particular investigation, which Dad had concerns about.

After that, Edie had moved the conversation on to why she needed their help so early on a Saturday morning. Lizzie and Eli had listened carefully to Edie's assertion that they needed evidence that her mother's death was murder and not an accident. That was why they were now making their way to Finsbury Park Tube station, the place where her mother had fallen onto the tracks and beneath an oncoming train. The only issue Edie had sidestepped was how she knew that the evidence would definitely be there. The truth was, Edie wasn't sure at all, but she was working on the premise that the police could easily have missed something if they weren't suspecting foul play.

At the W7 bus stop on the corner of Cecile Park and Crouch Hill they sat on the red plastic seats under the shelter.

Edie placed her dark purple rucksack on the ground in front of her. They kept their voices hushed.

'Why don't we just tell the police everything and let them do all this?' Eli asked almost pleadingly.

'All we have so far,' Edie whispered back, 'is a set of odd notes and riddles and no proof at all. The police will just say we're grieving kids and that Mum was a bit eccentric.'

Leaning in closer, Eli added: 'And Dad. Shouldn't we tell him?'

'No! Not yet,' Edie responded forcibly. 'We need proof. I've told you everything but you must trust me. And I can't do this alone. Please.' Lizzie squeezed Edie's hand as the bus appeared.

Out of her jeans pocket Edie pulled her Oyster card, which was inside the plastic card wallet from the Natural History Museum with a picture of an otter on the front. Edie stood up, boarded the bus and presented her card to the electronic reader. As they climbed up the stairs to the top deck, the bus lurched forwards causing Eli to stumble back down a step.

'Are you okay?' Edie asked with concern, looking down over her shoulder.

'Yeah, I'm all right.'

Once all safely up, they headed for the back of the bus and sat down. The journey was only ten minutes so they didn't have much time. Quietly but clearly, Edie reminded them of the plan.

At the Wells Terrace entrance to Finsbury Park station the three children stood under the sheltered overhang. It had started to drizzle, making the winter air feel colder. The W7 bus they'd just dismounted rumbled around the corner in front of them, ready to pick up its next set of passengers and repeat the route back towards Crouch End. Other buses shifted through their lanes. Huddled together, Edie began directing the operation.

'That's the ticket counter over there,' she said, pointing backwards over her right shoulder to the booths inside. People were queuing up to see the agent and buying tickets from the three self-service machines. A stocky man with a shaved head angrily thumped one of the electronic ticket machines.

'Lizzie, your job is to watch the man selling tickets behind the counter, as well as the other person just behind him in the ticket office. If either of them leave, come and tell me immediately.'

'But they might not be coming for you. Even if they leave the room, they might ... be going to the toilet or something,' Lizzie stated.

'Yes,' Edie mused. 'But they might have been alerted and be coming to find me, so you need to let me know, whatever.'

'Okay,' said Lizzie tensely.

'But that's only part of your job, Lizzie, remember.' Edie turned and indicated towards the railings a few metres to her left. 'If you stand just there, you can also see down the ramp to the control room door.'

Lizzie looked worried so Edie held her hands. 'Come on, you can do this. I've shown you the control room – it's just a little bit down the ramp on the left-hand side.' Softly, Edie pressed the important point home: 'Just be sure to come and get me if any of the train people ... the station workers ... are heading towards the control room door. That's where I'll be.'

Lizzie nodded weakly and Edie turned her attention to her brother.

'Eli, are you all right?' He nodded, almost purposefully. 'You know what to do?' his big sister asked.

'I know what to do,' Eli stated.

'Might as well start then.'

At this time on a Saturday morning the number of passengers making for the Tube was relatively light. Edie waited for a gap in the stream of people who'd just been deposited off a 210 bus before taking her younger brother's hand and leading him down the tunnel ramp that led towards the Underground platforms.

About twenty metres down the ramp, a door on the left was clearly marked 'Control Room'. Letting go of her sibling, Edie went about thirty paces further down to a location in which she would be concealed when the control room door opened. Edie's research from two previous reconnaissance visits made the positioning straightforward, and she waved to Lizzie who was just visible in the daylight up by the tunnel ramp exit. Edie then nodded to Eli – the signal that he could start proceedings.

Nervous, the young boy tried to focus. Stock-still with fists clenched, Eli tried to imagine the worst things that had ever happened to him. Breaking his wrist at Highgate Woods playground when he was five – that really hurt. Getting the end of his finger caught in the car door when the au pair slammed it shut without checking. Ouch! That was awful, but the recollection wasn't having the desired effect. Turning his head, Eli checked on his sister but she waved him away.

Burning kettle water accidentally poured onto his hand by his mother … his mother … his mother … Slowly, and with great effort, Eli managed to coax a tear to appear in the corner of his right eye. Then another, followed by one in his left eye that rolled straight down his cheek. No sobs, but sadness dragged to the surface. The moment was upon him: Eli composed himself, took a step forward and rapped his knuckles on the solid door. No answer. Edie was watching carefully but she ignored his mimed plea for guidance. He slapped the door with the palm of his hand.

'Okay, okay!' came a shout from inside. 'Hold your horses. I'm coming.'

The control room door opened and a portly middle-aged man appeared, dressed in a scruffy Transport for London uniform.

'What's the matter, sonny?'

Hands hanging by his side, Eli made himself look as innocently troubled as possible. 'I've lost my mummy,' he squealed. Realising his slip of the tongue, Eli corrected himself clumsily. 'I mean my sister. I've lost my sister.'

'Well, who have you lost, son?' replied the attendant,

placing bear-like hands on his thick hips. 'Your mummy or your sister?'

'My sister. I've lost her and I can't find her,' Eli added more confidently. 'She was with me and now she's gone. And I don't know how to get home.'

'Where do you live, sonny?'

'Crouch End.' Eli squeezed his fingernails into his palms and eked out another tear.

'And what were you doing here with your sister?' continued the man.

Eli knew the script: 'We were at the playground in the park, Finsbury Park. And we were going home for lunch. But now she's disappeared.'

'Well, it's just the W3 bus to Crouch End. Or the W7.'

'I'm not allowed to take the bus by myself.'

Beginning to show frustration, the attendant crouched down and instructed Eli with a pointed finger: 'Just go up this ramp, around the corner and speak to one of my colleagues in the ticket office.'

Once again, his sister had anticipated this, allowing Eli to echo what she'd told him. 'I can't,' he said more loudly. 'I'm scared.'

'Well, I'm a bit busy at the moment, sonny and …'

'I don't like losing my sister!' Eli howled. 'I don't like losing my sister!'

'All right, little fella,' said the man grumpily. 'All right. I'll take you up there.' He grabbed his keys from the table top inside, put a hand on Eli's shoulder and began to lead the lost boy up the ramp.

Swiftly, Edie dashed up from her position out of clear sight. The control room door had a metal closer mechanism at the top designed to make the door close slowly, but she still only had a few seconds. For a moment Edie thought she wouldn't make it but, just in time, she placed her foot in the doorway to avoid the clunk of the door shutting. Thankfully, no passengers were nearby, allowing Edie to step quickly inside and close the door quietly behind her.

Edie knew what Eli would be doing: he would be making as big a fuss as he could, bellowing and pretending to be too upset to even go into the ticket office. Playing for time and keeping the control room attendant occupied. Edie had two, maybe three, minutes: she'd rehearsed in her mind, over and over, what she'd do, but this was now for real. It was different – the stakes were high and her body tingled with the rush of adrenaline.

Heading straight for the desk area, Edie sat down in the large swivel chair. She looked at her watch: 11.52. On the wall in front of her was a bank of twelve security monitors in two rows of six. Each screen had a white adhesive label stuck to the plastic frame indicating the position of the camera that provided the image displayed. The pair of screens on the far left, labelled 'A: Front of station' and 'B: Ticket office', provided live feeds of views from the named areas. The next two indicated 'C: Upper ramp' and 'D: Lower ramp'. People milled around purposefully on both screens, except for Lizzie, leaning against a wall towards the left-hand side of screen C looking nervous.

Right of centre, TV screens G and H showed two ends

of the Victoria Line northbound platform. These did not interest Edie, and nor did the four screens to the far right that were dedicated to the Piccadilly Line. Screens E and F were what she was after – the southbound Victoria Line platform – where, a little over a year ago, her mum's life had ended so cruelly. As Edie stared, a Tube train entered that platform's screen, confirming to the young detective that screen E represented the key camera – situated at the end of the platform near the back two carriages, where her mum always went and where she'd fallen to her death. Edie frowned at the morbid irony: E for Edie.

Directly in front of Edie on the coffee-stained desk was a computer keyboard, with biscuit crumbs trapped between the keys. Just behind it were two monitors, one displaying a data table that looked like train times and the other a home screen showing the perfect Caribbean beach. This was another critical moment that Edie had run through in her mind in advance. If too long had passed since the control room attendant last used the machine, the computer would have auto-locked. Game over.

Quick check of the time: 11.53. Edie twiddled her fingers in nervous anticipation and then thumped the return key with her right index finger. The screen jumped to life and Edie breathed a sigh of relief. Speed was now of the essence. Edie clicked the 'Libraries' icon, then 'Computer' followed by 'C Drive'. A long list of folders appeared, which Edie scanned hastily. There it was – a folder labelled 'Camera Recordings'.

Abruptly, Edie twisted round in her seat. Was that

a sound at the door? She waited a few seconds: nothing. Probably just passenger noise outside. Time check: her watch now showed 11.54. Eli was holding his own. Back to the monitor and Edie scrolled down the list and found a sub-folder 'Cameras', which she clicked to find the alphabetical list. Yes, almost there. She pressed 'Camera E' to reveal the next layer of sub-folders. Two of them, but they were labelled as the past two months of *this* calendar year. Damn! Edie clicked on one anyway and saw a day-by-day calendar list of files. The previous year's recordings were nowhere to be seen.

This time Edie was sure it was a knock. Her state of tension heightened and she stood up from the chair immediately. Anxiety engulfed Edie, not so much connected with being caught – although that would be far from ideal – but in anticipation that she might not achieve her goal. All the planning wasted, and where would her investigations go from here? She put her head to the door.

'Edie! You need to come!' Lizzie asserted. 'He's leaving the ticket office.'

Inside the control room, Edie opened the door a fraction. 'But I haven't got it. The recordings aren't on the computer.'

'Whatever. We've got to go!'

'I need more time,' Edie insisted, allowing the door to close naturally as she heard Lizzie say something about not having more time.

Think! Think! reverberated loudly in Edie's head. Wristwatch: 11.55. She had one more minute, at best. Edie closed her eyes for a moment and let the panic settle. If older recordings were removed from the computer, they might still be somewhere in this dingy office. Edie glanced around. There was a small sink in the corner with a cupboard above, which she yanked open to reveal a variety of mugs, tea, coffee and spilled sugar. Back to the cluttered desktop. Edie rifled around but found nothing.

'He's coming down the ramp!' Lizzie yelled, whilst thumping the door with her palm. 'You've got to come now! Right now!'

'Delay him!' Edie ordered without looking. 'I haven't finished.'

'How?'

'I don't know – just do something!'

Edie refocused and instantly her attention was grabbed by a cupboard in the corner: undoubtedly where the control room attendant hung his wet coat in winter and stored his work uniform.

Outside the control room, Lizzie looked up the ramp towards where she'd been standing on guard. The attendant who'd helped Eli was making his way back down the left-hand side of the ramp, separated from the right-hand side by a metal handrail. Thinking fast, Lizzie started ascending on the opposite side of the handrail to the attendant, together with passengers heading out of the Tube station. After about fifteen metres, head down in mock concentration on her iPhone, Lizzie used a break in the railing to abruptly switch tracks to the side of the ramp reserved for those going downhill. It was too sudden for the attendant to adjust his stride and they collided full on.

'Aah! What are you doing?!' shrieked Lizzie. 'Watch where you're going!'

'You watch your language, young lady. You're walking on the wrong side and not looking where you're going. You could've injured somebody.'

Ignoring him, Lizzie leant down to pick up her phone off the floor. 'Look what you've done. The screen is smashed!'

'Let's have a look,' the attendant replied, attempting to grab the device.

'No! Leave it alone!' she said loudly. 'Don't try and take my phone!'

'I wasn't trying to take anything, it's just that—'

'Ow! My ankle,' faked Lizzie, sitting down on the ramp and placing her hand gingerly on her right foot. 'It really hurts. I think you've broken my ankle.'

'You can't sit here, young lady. Now, come on, let's get up.' The attendant attempted to pull Lizzie up but she brushed his arm off. Other passengers began to congregate around them.

Oblivious to the kerfuffle outside, Edie purposefully prised the cupboard door open and winced at the smell from old boots and stale clothes. In the bottom right corner stood a waist-high metal filing cabinet. A downward push of the metal handle met immediate resistance, so Edie turned the small key in the lock clockwise by ninety degrees. This time, depressing the handle met no resistance and the cabinet door swung open. Inside were four drawers. Edie glanced over at the control room door, fully expecting to be caught red-handed at any moment. No movement, though, just a rising commotion from outside in the tunnel.

Pulling the top drawer open revealed masking tape, packets of spare staples, pencils and other assorted stationery. Edie yanked at the bottom drawer, damaging a nail in the process, but it refused to budge. She closed the top drawer and tried again. Success, but only to disclose a stack of printing paper. 'Oh God!' she shrieked. Another glance at the door, but she was still safe.

Second or third drawer? Edie pushed the bottom drawer closed and opened the one directly above it. In the pit of her stomach, Edie felt the adrenaline surge on seeing a set of plastic storage boxes for DVDs. Each box had a label with a letter and the word 'Camera', followed by the year.

Edie pushed aside 'A', 'C' and 'D' and, from behind them, took the box marked 'Camera E' of the previous calendar year out of the drawer. With shaking hands, she tried to open the catch. 'Come on!' Edie screamed as the fastener refused to yield. Suddenly, it gave and the DVDs tumbled onto the floor.

In a second Edie was on her knees, shuffling the discs around as if playing some kind of game, twisting some over so she could see the label displaying the month. April, January, December, November, July. Where was it? From outside Edie heard what was surely Lizzie's voice at shouting pitch. Simultaneously, Edie located the disc marked March, tucked annoyingly underneath another disc. Edie scooped it up.

Oblivious to the mess, Edie grabbed her rucksack off the ground and headed out the door. A little way up the tunnel a group of ten or so people were gathered around causing a jam. Pushing her way through the small crowd, Edie found Lizzie sitting upright, clutching her ankle and shouting at the control room attendant.

'Come on, you're all right now,' Edie said, supporting Lizzie to her feet.

'I'm her friend,' Edie announced to a bunch of puzzled faces, as she escorted her apparently injured companion up towards the exit – the pretend limp disappearing after a few steps.

'Hey, what's going on?' came a shout from behind them. The irate-looking attendant was gesticulating at the girls, whilst also twigging that something was awry and turning on his heels towards the control room.

'Quickly,' pressed Edie as they hastened towards the exit, her arm linked with Lizzie's. But it took the attendant only a few seconds to reach the ransacked control room where, to his bewilderment, he found cupboards and drawers open and items strewn on the floor.

'Stop those girls!' the attendant screamed from the doorway, his finger pointing up the ramp directly at the offenders. 'Stop those bloody girls!' The level of anger in his voice took everyone around by surprise, and a bespectacled man in a suit and grey overcoat put a hand on Edie's left shoulder.

'Does he mean you?' he asked, overly polite.

'No! Get off her!' Lizzie responded abruptly.

At the top of the ramp, close to the Oyster card reader, Edie noticed a white 'Help Point' fixture on the wall. It had a red glass box covered in glass labelled 'Fire alarm' and a large green button marked 'Emergency'. Underneath, in black capitals, it read '£200 fine for inappropriate use'.

What the hell, thought Edie. Ignoring the suited man, she strode over and walloped the green button. Immediately, a siren started wailing. Edie grabbed Lizzie, turned sharp right and made for the ticket office. 'That's my sister,' Eli shouted from inside, pointing wildly the moment he saw Edie through the glass window.

'What about your mother?' asked the confused London Underground official next to him, distracted by the intense noise and frenetic activity.

'No, I said "my sister". She's here.'

'Off you go then,' he said, allowing Eli to tear out of the ticket office and join his accomplices. There was no time to spare, though, as the control room attendant was heading for them, jostled by the agitated crowd.

'Quick,' urged Edie, grabbing her brother's arm as they ran over the zebra crossing that linked the Underground ticket office area to the bus station, narrowly avoiding an incoming W3. To their luck, a W7 was boarding passengers, the line dwindling before their eyes as they raced across the pavement. As the final person in the queue climbed on board, the driver glanced in his rear-view mirror and noticed the children running at full tilt. He took his hand off the push button that closed the door, allowed the breathless kids to get in, then started the journey back towards Crouch End. Outside, a puffed out control room attendant yelled and furiously waved his arms, but to no avail.

Instinctively, Edie felt going directly home to be too risky, and an easy alternative existed as Lizzie's family were all out. In Lizzie's bedroom, the threesome huddled on the floor around her old laptop. Little had been said on the bus journey back, although Lizzie had checked that the detective thief had the sought-after item. Edie had slowly released her clasped fingers to reveal an indented palm and a DVD.

'You were both brilliant,' declared Edie to her accomplices, who were still shell-shocked from the adventure. 'Thank you.'

'So, how *did* you know it would be there?' Lizzie asked.

'Well, to be honest, I wasn't completely sure,' Edie responded. 'But when the police investigated Mum's death, I overheard a conversation my dad had in our kitchen with an officer who said they'd made copies of the CCTV recordings, looked at them in the station and seen nothing suspicious.' She paused. 'I was just guessing – hoping – the originals would still be there.'

'Can we have a look now?' asked Eli quietly.

'Are you sure you'll be all right, Eli?' his sister probed gently. 'This could be really hard.'

'Yes, I want to see.'

Edie powered up the laptop, inserted the DVD, opened the Windows Explorer folder icon, clicked 'External Disc' and, almost immediately, a list of files appeared on the screen. With a quickening heart, Edie scrolled down the dates until the pointer rested on the file for the fateful day.

She looked over at her brother at precisely the moment that he turned to face her – the unbreakable bond of shared grief alive in their expressions. Eli grimaced and Edie touched his hand delicately. A double-click on the tragic date opened Windows Media Player and, before they had time to compose themselves, camera footage of the Victoria Line southbound platform appeared on screen.

Fixated, they all watched the first few minutes of that awful morning's activity. At such a dawn-of-the-day hour only a handful of people scattered the platform, early birds heading for work in the City. The camera captured the Tube train as it rolled in, almost empty on arrival, picked up the passengers and slowly disappeared into the tunnel. Just a couple of minutes later and the second train of the day arrived, a few more business folk embarked and off it went again.

After a few more trains Lizzie interrupted the group's meditatively observant state and asked softly: 'Can't we fast-forward the film … I mean the footage … to … y'know … to what we're looking for?'

Eli inspected his sister's face, his own giving away the mixed emotions of wishing, like her, to get quickly to what they were seeking, but also nervousness at what they might find.

'Okay,' Edie replied, and pressed the fast-forward button once for 'x2', then repeatedly until it reached 'x32'. People swarmed at impossible speeds around the station, trains were in and out in a flash and the clock in the top right-hand corner whizzed ahead in time, each minute taking just a couple of seconds.

As they approached the deadly hour, Edie slowed down the footage gradually and brought the image back to normal speed at 09:21, just a couple of minutes before the fatal moment. Glued to the screen, Edie felt sick and Eli was as pale as a sheet. Although rush hour had passed, the platform was still packed with people. As the clock snapped to 09:22, Edie moved her head closer to the screen and searched for her mother.

'There she is!' Eli screamed.

'You're right,' Edie replied, identifying the coat and demeanour of her mother. Edie squeezed her brother's hand tighter as they watched on helplessly as their mum allowed the first train to pass and, thereby, progressed through to the front of the crowd and closest to the tracks. Carefully, but definitively, their mother checked that her feet remained safely behind the yellow line. Faces around her started to peer towards the tunnel to their left, necks craned on hearing the recognisable sound of a train approaching.

With heartbreaking fascination the children watched on. Eli stared unblinkingly as Edie began to cry, the tension of the inevitable almost unbearable. And there it was. Amongst the packed masses, a metre or two behind their mother a jostling began – not much more than one might expect on a busy morning, but noticeable. Unbeknownst to their mum, a tall hooded man was persuasively pressing his way through the pack, closer and closer. His movements were performed with calm authority, such that the other passengers hardly noticed, unconsciously adjusting their feet as he pushed his way through.

All of a sudden he was right behind her, and the rest was a blur of horrid happenings. With the crowd at his back, the tall man appeared to stumble, his body barging into their mum, who was forcibly knocked forwards and lost her footing on the platform edge. From the angle of the camera the children were unable, thankfully, to see their mother's face. As if in slow motion, wildly flailing arms tried uselessly to defy gravity, and the body of the woman who'd nurtured Edie and Eli from their first day on earth fell forwards and onto the metal tracks. At the moment she disappeared from the camera's viewpoint, a Tube train swept from the tunnel into the station and pummelled over her helpless body.

Edie screwed her tearful eyes shut, unable to cope with the grizzly image, and her head sank forwards. Eli stared blankly through the screen, his vision and mind seemingly frozen in the middle distance. Only Lizzie paid real attention to the following seconds of footage.

Amidst the commotion, the tall man who'd bumped into their mum manipulated himself skilfully away from the platform edge. His actions had been so subtle throughout that the unsuspecting police wouldn't have noticed anything untoward. Many of the commuters were now covering their faces and turning away from the tracks in shock. Suddenly, one woman thrust her arms into the air as if appealing for assistance and, in so doing, dislodged the hood from the man's head just before he disappeared from shot. Reactively, he turned towards her in anger and, just for a second, revealed the left side of his face to the camera, before pulling his hood back up again.

Unnoticed by Edie and Eli, Lizzie gasped audibly and put her fingers to her lips. She pulled the laptop towards her, rewound the footage by several seconds, pressed pause and took a screenshot. Then Lizzie switched from Media Player to the actual screenshot, moved the focus to slightly right of centre and zoomed the image to 300% of its size.

'What are you doing?' asked Edie.

The image was grainy but just clear enough. 'Look,' Lizzie said, pointing to a man's face, now centre of the screen. 'The circular scar on his left cheek.'

Edie leant in further as Lizzie continued: 'It's him. It's the man from the woods.'

CHAPTER 8

INTRUDER

Walking back down Cecile Park, Edie became acutely aware that they were late. In Lizzie's bedroom, the gruesome video recording had been watched and rewatched, leaving no doubt in Edie's mind as to the identity of her mother's killer. As a result, by the time Edie and Eli were approaching home they were fifty-five minutes past the lunch hour Edie had promised to be back by.

The moment they reached the brow of the ever-so-slight hill halfway down Cecile Park, just before the letter box, Edie knew that something was amiss. Blue and red patterns of shifting light were visible on the buildings around Edie's home, projected unquestionably from police vehicles parked in the vicinity.

'Look!' Eli exclaimed, pointing at the obvious. As the children cautiously approached, it became clear that there were two white Ford police cars parked directly outside their own home. And, from just a couple of houses away, Edie easily picked out her father, standing on the path leading from the road to their front door, speaking to a female police officer.

'Where have you been?' shrieked Dad as soon as he caught sight of his children. 'It's almost two o'clock!' He looked angry but also relieved to see them. 'And why haven't you been answering your phone, Edie?'

Dumbstruck by the activity around them – including officers milling about outside and inside the house – the children walked up the path silently. Crouching down, Dad wrapped his arms firmly around his beloved kids and nestled his head in close to theirs. 'I was so worried,' he stressed with loudly whispered concern. 'I ... we ...' he pointed to the police officer waiting by the front door, 'thought you might have been abducted ... taken ... by whoever burgled the house.'

'What?' said Edie incredulously, as Eli simultaneously exclaimed, 'We've been burgled?'

'Yes, that's what this is all about,' Dad responded, briefly using one arm to indicate the melee around them. 'Somebody's broken into the house ... made a terrible mess ... and you two weren't around. Thank God you're all right.'

Dad buried his face in their necks and squeezed hard again. And, in that moment, Edie understood: losing one person he loved was hard enough but Dad couldn't cope with losing another.

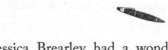

PC Jessica Brearley had a wonderfully calming manner. Shoulder-length brown hair, tied back to reveal an attractive face, sharpened by take-your-breath-away aquamarine eyes, almost out of place beneath the regulation police hat. Without appearing patronising, PC Brearley bent down, just a fraction, to be on a similar level to the children, who were now standing on the pavement outside the house. Inquisitive neighbours loitered nearby.

'In these kinds of situations,' she explained, 'we have to search the house thoroughly before allowing you to go back inside.'

'What kinds of situations do you mean?' asked Edie, feigning innocence.

'Burglaries. Break-ins,' responded the officer. 'Only, what is a little odd in this case is that I'm not sure anything has actually been taken – not even the silver in the lounge, TVs or laptops.'

'Nothing's been stolen?' questioned Eli.

'We can't be sure yet, but it appears not, which is strange – for a home intrusion. The house has been given the all-clear by my colleagues, so the intruder's gone … but they're just checking over the valuables with your father. Won't be long now.'

Whilst Eli seemed excited by the attention and drama, Edie anxiously chewed at the skin around the nail of her left thumb. Blood and pain failed to stop her biting down on an irritating flap. Lost in concern about what might have been removed from the house, Edie failed to register PC Brearley directing a query at her.

'Edie.' More loudly. 'Edie, are you okay?' asked the officer, which brought back the young girl's focus.

'Yes, I'm fine, thank you. Just a little shaken.'

Notebook in hand, the officer carried on. 'I just want to check over some facts with you both, whilst we're waiting.'

'Okay,' the children said together.

'You said you left home at around eleven o'clock. Is that right?'

'Yes, that's right,' responded Edie on behalf of them both, a little too quickly.

'And your friend Lizzie was with you?'

'Yes.'

'All of the time?'

'Yes, all of the time. She came to the house first, maybe an hour earlier, and then we all went in to Crouch End.'

'And did you notice anything peculiar when you left? Anybody prowling around? Or watching the house from the street?'

'No, nothing at all,' said Edie.

'And what about you, little fella?' asked the officer, turning to Eli.

He answered curtly, 'I didn't see anything either.'

'Okay,' PC Brearley remarked slowly. 'This *is* important,' she stressed. 'Think carefully.'

Met with blank faces, the officer changed tack. 'So, you went in to Crouch End?'

'Yes,' affirmed Edie. 'To Costa Coffee.'

'And were you there the whole time?'

Edie glanced over at Eli before answering. 'We walked around the shops a little … as well.'

'Before or after you went into Costa?'

Biting hard on the skin of her right thumb, Edie thought on her feet. 'Before … and after.'

PC Brearley spoke again: 'It's a long time to be out, almost three hours. Weren't you hungry?'

'We had milkshakes,' Eli suddenly offered.

More shuffling of uniformed officers in and out of the

house, some carrying cases and equipment, as a third police car arrived. Looking down at the ground, PC Brearley hadn't quite finished: 'What's in the rucksack?'

Edie's heart leapt. She couldn't lie, since if the woman asked to see inside, Edie's evading of the truth would appear suspicious.

'Just a few bits and bobs,' she replied calmly. 'And my ... and Eli's gloves.'

The officer didn't seem convinced but didn't pursue it either. 'One last question: you didn't put the alarm on. Your dad says you always use the alarm. Why was that?'

'I must've been distracted,' Edie said apologetically. 'I'm really sorry.'

'Not to worry,' the police officer reassured. 'It's not your fault at all. Or yours,' she added, glancing briefly at Eli.

With a maternal manner, PC Brearley put her hand gently on Edie's left shoulder and rubbed up and down the young girl's arm. Out of one of the many pockets in her uniform, she took out a card with her contact details and passed it to Edie.

'Call me if you remember anything,' she said clearly, taking time to look at each of them. 'Or if you're worried. Anytime. Use the mobile number.' A second or two passed as the officer pondered whether to say anything more. 'And I'm sorry about your mum. You dad told me about the accident. I'm truly sorry.'

A nod from the kindly policewoman indicated that it was fine to go inside, allowing Edie to stride up the path. As she brushed past her dad he tried to forewarn her: 'Your room seems the worst, sweetie. It's a terrible mess.'

But by then Edie was in the hallway and soon inside her bedroom. Everything had been turned upside down: the floor was covered in books, games, clothes thrown out of drawers and items from her desk. Edie had her mind on only one thing, though. With her foot, she brushed everything on the floor away from the door so she could close it. She then made her way over to the poster on the wall above the bookcase, a black-and-white image from *It's a Wonderful Life*, bought for her by her mum when they'd trekked down to the National Film Theatre to see the movie one snowy Boxing Day.

Gently, Edie peeled the Blu Tack off the bottom corners and pulled the poster away from the wall. Underneath, in a plastic wallet attached by drawing pins, was half of the material she'd gathered in her investigations. Unfound and unharmed. And, underneath the Billie Eilish poster next to the window was the other half. All placed safely back in their hiding place after sharing them with Lizzie and Eli earlier in the day. It had been worth watching *The Shawshank Redemption*.

A knock at her bedroom door startled Edie. It was both the loudness, knuckles cracked crisply against the wooden panel, and the fact that nobody in the household would do such a thing.

'Edie,' stated a voice from the landing with firm intent. 'Edie.' It wasn't her dad, so it must be a police officer, she thought.

'Just a moment,' Edie replied, promptly restoring all the secret materials to their safe locations. 'I'm changing.'

A few seconds later, Edie opened her bedroom door to be greeted by a face she'd last seen at the stone-setting. It was John, the partner of her dad's oldest medical school friend, Miles.

'Oh, hi,' she said, surprised.

'Hello, Edie. Can I come in?' he asked, but already had a foot in the room.

'What a mess!' John observed with little emotion, casting his eyes across the devastation. 'It's like a hurricane's hit the room.' Sidestepping the debris, John worked his way across to the window opposite the bedroom door, where he stopped to gaze out over the small back garden.

'Yeah,' responded Edie uncertainly.

'You may be wondering why I'm here,' John said with no apparent expectation of a response. 'Well,' he continued, 'your father called Miles and me when he got home and found ...' John paused and gestured around the room theatrically, 'and found all of this.'

Edie said nothing and stayed standing by her bed, unsure where all this was going.

'He was very worried – your father, that is – when he spoke to Miles. Much more than worried, actually ... He sounded ... a little hysterical when Miles put it on speakerphone, about you and your brother ... not being here ... Crazy thoughts going through his mind about what might've happened to you both.'

'Oh,' said Edie, taken aback by the description of her

father's mood. For a reason she couldn't put her finger on, Edie found John's approach unsettling. 'Well, we were fine, just went in to Crouch End and got back a bit late.' She folded her arms. 'Forgot to put the alarm on, that's all.'

'It's not just that, though,' said John, clearly with more on his mind. 'You see, your father's been rather concerned about you, Edie – you, in particular – over the past couple of weeks. He's been speaking to Miles, almost semi-professionally about you.' Realising this needed further explanation, John added: 'Miles is a paediatrician ... a doctor for children ... You know that, I think.'

'Yes, I know that,' Edie retorted. She and her mum loved Miles dearly: he was fun and playful, and he was also Edie's godfather. They were also fond of Miles's partner, John, although he was somewhat cold, seeming to analyse everything in keeping with his professional role as a therapist.

Smartly dressed in black jeans and beige polo-neck sweater, John turned around from the window to face Edie. 'Your dad wondered if Miles could perhaps have a word with you about your state of mind, but we – that is, Miles and I – agreed that, as a family therapist, I might do so instead.'

'Okay,' said Edie slowly and nervously. 'But I don't know what you want to talk about.'

John waited a moment before starting. 'So, how's school?' he asked, rather predictably.

'School's fine.'

'Work going okay? Grades okay?'

'School is fine, as I just said. Grades are fine, maybe could be better, but my mum has died, y'know.'

John waited, not rising to the bait. 'And are you enjoying school?'

'I don't think anybody enjoys school that much,' replied Edie, who took a step backwards and started fidgeting with her mother's scarf which was tied around the post at the head of the bed. After a year, her mum's smell still clung to the scarf – just.

'Children do enjoy school, Edie,' John continued, 'and, of course, I know what an ordeal you've been through ... but your father – and the school – are concerned about your behaviour.'

'How do you know about what my school's thinking?'

'Through your dad, Edie, who's been in regular contact with them. Teachers mention that you're distracted in class ... poor concentration, intermittent rudeness ... and the detentions.'

Taken aback, Edie went into self-preservation mode. 'Just one detention, actually.'

Immediately John countered: 'Just the one you told your dad about?'

John waited but evidently hadn't finished. 'We're all worried about you, Edie. You've had a horrible, horrible time – as have your father and brother. But it's, well ... important to try and make sense of it all and think about your future. Nobody wants you to do anything silly.'

That was the trigger. She needed out, right away.

'You don't know what you're talking about!' Edie shrieked. 'You don't know what it's like for your mum to die ... and ... and ... you're not my father.' She pointed at the door.

'So get out of my room!' John was unmoved. 'Now!' she added.

Again, John stood still, so Edie had only one option left. She grabbed her coat and bag, pushed past him and ran downstairs, where her dad met her in the hallway.

'Is everything okay, sweetie?'

'Dad,' she said pleadingly. 'I don't think I can be here right now. It's just too upsetting ... all the mess and everything. I've spoken to Mama and she said it's fine for me to come over, and Papa will bring me back later. Is that okay?'

'Well, I suppose so. How will you get there?'

'The bus. I'll tidy up my room later.'

'No, let me drive you at least,' Dad proposed. 'It's been a terrible day.'

'No,' said Edie firmly. 'I'll be fine.'

'All right then, but call me when you get there. And keep your phone on all the time – please.'

'Sure,' said Edie gratefully, standing on tiptoes to peck her dad's cheek with a kiss.

'Love ya, Dad.'

After a quick check of Günther, who was mercifully untouched and completely unbothered by all the goings-on, Edie was on her way.

An hour later, Edie stood at the front door of her grandparents' house in Hendon. Her mother's parents had stayed in the family home in Rundell Crescent ever since they'd bought it over forty years ago when Edie's mum, Alexandra, was just a young child. Over the years, they'd paid little attention to updating. As a consequence, the exterior blue paintwork was flaking and the decor inside was jaded and, in places, verging on tatty. Despite this, Edie adored the warmth and good-spiritedness that pervaded her grandparents' home.

For a second time, Edie pushed hard on the bell but, on this occasion, with her ear pressed against the front door. No ringing, no buzz, something else broken, so Edie walked over to the front bay windows, peered through into the lounge and then knocked loudly on the glass. Papa looked up from the dining table, where he was hunched over a large-print book from the library, waved at his granddaughter and stepped into the hallway.

'Hello, darling,' he welcomed her with outstretched arms. She embraced the trim-looking elderly man strongly.

'Wow! Well, it's good to see you too, Edie. Obviously, we'd prefer different circumstances but we're still delighted you've come over.'

He'd hardly finished his sentence when Mama, having bustled out of the kitchen at the sound of chatter in the hallway, pushed him crisply out of the way. After a cursory wipe of hands on her apron, Mama grabbed Edie's outstretched arms at the elbows, eyed her adored granddaughter approvingly, and then pulled Edie in for her own extended cuddle.

'You look lovely, Edie,' Mama said once they'd separated. 'Each time I see you, you're more grown up. Taller than me now, definitely! And – I hope you don't mind me saying this – but as you get older, I see more and more of your mother in your face.' Edie returned a smile.

'Can I get you a drink?' Mama asked as they moved

further indoors. 'I've heard you like coffee now. Is that right?'

'In a moment, Mama, thanks, that would be nice. Could I go upstairs for a few minutes first, though? I have a little reading to do.' Edie turned to her grandfather. 'Would it be okay if I used your study, Papa? It's nice and quiet. I won't be long.'

'Yes, of course,' Papa agreed, allowing Edie to climb the creaking stairs and make a right into the small room that overlooked the front driveway. Her grandfather was exceptionally organised and black box files sat neatly along all the wall shelves, each clearly labelled – savings, taxes, home receipts and guarantees – and dated.

Edie closed the door, sat on the hard-backed chair at the oak desk and leant her arms on the glass top. Underneath the glass, a number of photographs that clearly held particular importance to Papa had been arranged: a small black-and-white image of his own parents in Poland, several from a similar period that included his siblings, and others that were more recent of his own family and grandchildren. But it was the one framed photograph that stood upright on the desk that interested Edie.

She pulled the picture towards her. The photograph was set in a white-rimmed, old-fashioned frame and was bigger than current standard-sized prints, perhaps fifteen centimetres wide by twenty-five high. Edie held the frame up and delicately ran her right index finger over the glass.

The black-and-white portrait photograph was of her mother's twin sister, Miriam, who'd died of leukaemia when she was five. In this picture she was perhaps three or four, showing no visible signs of illness. Miriam was a non-identical twin, but with her pale Eastern European complexion, black shoulder-length curly hair and deep-set dark eyes, Edie could see the similarities with her mother and even herself. This was the photo – or the 'snap' as per the final line of the third clue – that Edie and her mum had spent ages looking at and talking about together. It was also the item Edie had thought of immediately when she realised that if you took the first letter of each line of the limerick it created the word 'TWINS'.

Carefully, Edie turned over the photo frame to reveal the back cover. She undid the four small metal clips holding the backing in place and took out the piece of protective cardboard. Lodged between the photograph and the cardboard was a piece of paper, folded in two, which fell out onto the desk. Mesmerised, Edie stared at the latest puzzle.

I know how hard this must be, my darling, but we're almost there. Listen to your heart – you need to finish what I started.

Mum xxx

121141
4512
18525

- - - - - - - - - - - -
♪ 2294515-7113519 (hint)
- - - - - - - - - - - -

Edie felt a mixture of exhilarating relief and total exhaustion.

She placed her forearms flat on the desk, leant over and rested her head on her arms.

And then Edie remembered, not painfully but with warmth, an event about two months before her mum had died. Edie, Eli and their mother had visited Mama's and Papa's house on a Saturday afternoon. After various group board games, Eli was playing chess – against himself – in the lounge whilst the other four had tea around the kitchen table. They'd chatted about Eli's success in the Under-10s chess team and how he now beat his teacher (Papa), about Edie's school and about Mum's latest 'big' case – although she'd refused to reveal much about it. Edie smiled as she recalled that her grandparents were the only people to call her mum 'Sandy'.

Edie had then asked about Miriam and the photo upstairs in the study. Mama had told her that having the twins was the happiest day of her life, and it was incredible how different they were. Sandy was very organised and determined but also a bit unconventional, surprising her parents with odd remarks and off-the-wall thinking and, when she was older, a penchant for strange clothes. Miriam, on the other hand, had quite a naughty streak, always joking and tricking, but she was just as sharp as her sister. And Miriam loved puzzles, Papa had reminded them, just like Edie.

Then Edie had asked about the illness, and Mama

had explained how it had started quite innocently with an extended cold. But ongoing chest infections finally led to a diagnosis of leukaemia which, back then, few children survived. Tearfully, Mama had related how she and Papa had been holding Miriam's hand when she died, very peacefully, in her sleep. With great care, Edie had asked Mama how she'd coped – losing a child after most of her family had been murdered in the concentration camps. And Edie recalled Mama's response: that her Jewish faith had helped, with its focus on being grateful for all the wonders that life has to offer. Edie had then posed the same question to Papa and, with her head on the desk fourteen months later, Edie allowed his answer to return to the front of her mind: Papa had read in a book about grief that you never really get over the death of a loved one but, over time, you gradually learn to live with the loss.

CHAPTER 9

FROM HERO TO ZERO

'Happy birthday, sweetheart.'

A low-pitched, sleepy mumble met Peter Goswell's softly spoken greeting.

'Happy birthday, honey,' repeated Peter, shuffling over from his side of the double bed. The moment, however, was interrupted by two young girls bursting into the bedroom.

'Happy birthday, Mummy!' they screeched in chorus, as Jane pushed away her husband.

'You've got a lot of presents, Mummy,' announced Mary throatily, relishing the birthday present-giving ritual. The nine-year-old was pale but remarkably perky, given the painfully swollen glands in her neck. At two years younger, Zoe – who shared the same red-brown coloured hair of her sister – was even more excitable. 'Which one are you going to open first?' she asked, grinning.

Jane dragged herself into a seated position. 'Wow! What have we got here?' she said sweetly, taking in the neatly laid out gifts on the floor – all covered in the same pink paper with pale green stars. 'They're beautifully wrapped,' Jane added, turning to her husband. 'Did you do this?' Peter smiled and said nothing, grateful for the assistance of their housekeeper. 'So, which one shall I open first?' Jane asked.

'This one!' screamed the girls in unison, each pointing

at a different object.

However, the magical family moment was interrupted by the muffled ringing of a mobile phone, causing heads to turn and search. Peter ignored the iPhone on his bedside table and opened the drawer underneath.

'That's not your normal ringtone, Daddy,' observed Mary. 'Did you change it?'

'It's my special phone, angel,' he replied flatly. 'A sort of work phone.'

'What do you mean, "sort of"?'

'Okay, my work phone then,' he said dismissively.

'But you said "sort of".'

'Can't you just leave it alone for once?' Peter reacted irritably. 'That's your problem, Mary … once you get hold of something you won't let it go. Like a dog with a bone.'

The drug company boss reached inside the drawer and took out his old iPhone 6, the burner phone that served just one purpose.

'I'm sorry, Daddy,' murmured Mary.

In the bathroom, Goswell spat angrily down the phone: 'What is it? It's Sunday morning and my wife's birthday.'

'It's the girl,' Zero divulged calmly.

'Still? Can't you even deal with a fourteen-year-old schoolgirl, for God's sake?'

'She's thirteen.'

'Even bloody worse!' Goswell grabbed the edge of the sink and squeezed firmly. 'So, what's going on then … Zero?

Or should I say, *Mr Zero?*' he added sarcastically.

'Zero will do fine,' the ex-soldier replied coldly. 'I went to her house yesterday, like we discussed. Looked all over.'

'And what did you find?'

'Nothing.'

'What do you mean, nothing?'

'I mean *nothing*. Nothing at all.'

'Well, that's good, isn't it?' asked Goswell, relaxing his grip.

'No, I don't think so. She's clever. I think she's up to something. She's hidden away whatever she's got – carefully. And there's more.'

'More?'

'Something happened at Finsbury Park station whilst I was at the house. I think she might've been there with her brother – there was an alarm and the place was evacuated. I'm trying to find out exactly what went on.'

'Finsbury Park? The station where we … you … killed the mother?'

Zero gritted his teeth in annoyance: 'I've told you before not to speak like that on the phone.'

'Okay, okay!'

Goswell looked at himself in the bathroom mirror. Haggard and tired. 'We need to meet,' he said. 'Decide what to do. I'm not having my life ruined by this kid.'

'The usual place?'

'No. You come up this way. Do you know the King's Head pub in Ely?'

'I don't like meeting in enclosed places – it's too visible.

You know that.'

Goswell overruled Zero's protestations. 'Christ, it's just a pub on the high street. There's hardly anybody ever there, even on a Sunday.'

After years of being careful to stay in the shadows, all of a sudden Zero felt unsure that it really mattered where they met.

'Okay, I'll find it.'

'Good. I'll see you there at one o'clock.' Goswell ended the conversation, took four brown envelopes packed with fifty pound notes from the wall safe in the airing cupboard next to the bathroom, and made one more call before turning on his heels.

In the bedroom, the excitement had subsided.

'You missed it all, Daddy,' grumbled Zoe, pointing at the mess of torn wrapping paper, tape, ribbon and envelopes on the carpet. 'Mummy's opened all her presents.'

'Oh dear,' replied Peter glumly. 'I'm really sorry. It was a work call …'

'That's all right, Daddy,' said Zoe with undeserved understanding. It saddened Peter and he walked over, sat on the edge of the bed and reached for Mary's hand.

'I'm sorry I shouted earlier, gorgeous. I didn't mean it.'

'I know, Daddy. That's all right.'

Peter pulled his girls towards him. They sat on one leg each and he wrapped his arms around them. 'I just didn't sleep well last night. You know I love you both, don't you? More than anything – whatever happens.' His daughters didn't know how to respond, so Peter re-emphasised: '*Whatever* happens.'

Concerned, Jane came over. 'I think you might be scaring the girls, Peter.' She turned towards the children: 'Nothing's going to happen. Why don't you two watch the telly downstairs,' she suggested, and the girls duly disappeared.

'Is everything okay, Pete? I mean, really okay? It's just that you've been so stressed recently.'

He hardly dared look at her. 'It's just some stuff at work.' Peter waited but knew she needed more. 'Our new drug.'

'What? Flu-Away?'

'Yes. Sort of.'

'Well, I've never seen you this bad before.' Jane cupped her hand around his cheek affectionately. 'Try not to take things too seriously. I'm sure it'll all be fine.' She waited a moment for a response that didn't arrive. 'And, by the way, thank you for my beautiful necklace. You know I love pearls.'

Peter wished it would all be all right, but feared it wouldn't.

'I'm very sorry,' Peter said. 'But I'm going to be really late for your birthday lunch today. Perhaps dinner instead?'

Zero made his way from his Somers Town flat to nearby King's Cross, then took the Underground to Finsbury Park station, where a number of lads were milling around in red and white Arsenal scarves and shirts. As he bought a train ticket, Zero cautiously questioned the man in an official rail uniform behind the Perspex screen.

'Return to Ely.'

'Same day?'

'Yes. Back this afternoon.'

The seller punched some buttons and tickets slid out of a slot on the machine's side.

'I hear there was a bit of trouble here yesterday, mate?' Zero probed innocently.

'Yeah. Bloody annoying. Station was closed for an hour whilst they checked everything.' He looked upwards: 'That'll be £34.60 please, Sir.'

Zero pulled out his wallet. 'Do they know what happened?'

The ticket seller took the cash and returned the change with the tickets. 'Couple of young girls, it seems. Maybe a little boy too.' He waited but the large man's silence suggested his response wasn't sufficient: 'Ruined my day – made me an hour late home. Bloody kids pressed the station emergency button and legged it.'

'What?' posed Zero innocuously. 'Just for laughs?'

'I guess, though the boss said they might've nicked something from the control room. Mind you, I don't know what they'd want in there …'

Zero nodded, put the tickets in his pocket and made his way towards the overground rail platforms. He boarded the on-time 11:36 to Cambridge, taking a forward-facing window seat. As the train made its way out of the London suburbs, Zero turned to his private, dark thoughts. He knew he was on the edge: on the edge of destroying himself, on the edge of destroying others. Sleep was his only solace from the black clouds, but it was getting harder and harder to come by, despite all the tablets from his GP.

Just one thing kept Zero going, an anchor to reality: his loving sister, Katie, and her beautiful son, Dylan. It was a week until his nephew's birthday but Zero had already bought the gift that would spoil the boy immeasurably: an Omega Seamaster Chronometer wristwatch. Black face, illuminated numbers, chunky stainless steel case and strap, waterproof to two hundred metres.

Katie, dear Katie: it was only because of her that Zero bothered to keep seeing the psychotherapist, although the session earlier that day had been different. With little left to lose, Zero had finally felt able to open up – to somebody, anybody – about the incident in Afghanistan. Staring blankly into the therapist's garden outside the lounge, Zero had started at the beginning, when the major had given Beta team a 2200 hour briefing in the ops room about the location of a kidnapped female British aid worker from Save the Children. She'd been snatched in Kandahar and was now supposedly held captive near the village of Shah Karez, around a hundred kilometres from the team's location at Camp Bastion, the British army base shared with Afghan security forces. The mission was simple: go in, extract the hostage and get out. Hostiles to be killed on sight.

Zero had described to the therapist how it was the last week of Beta team's four-month deployment and nobody wanted a tough mission at the end of a tour of duty: it felt like bad luck. But the six highly trained SAS soldiers – Zero and his friends Smith, Wooding, Nolan, Carruthers and Blackstock – were professionals and had a job to do. Zero had hesitated at that point, then clarified to the silent therapist that during the mission these names were never used, and instead they referred to each other by numbers: One to Five – and, of course, Zero. He'd noticed the slightest of flinches as the therapist realised that the circular scar on his left cheekbone, upper segment missing, was not the basis of his nickname.

They were up at 0400. An hour of preparation involved putting on full combat gear, checking all the equipment and then double-checking it. Inside the Snatch Land Rover, four of the soldiers were seated in the rear section, plus the driver and navigator in the front: Zero was closest to the back. The team were unhappy using the Snatch, a very lightly armoured vehicle, but the army had removed all the newer and better protected Foxhounds. Little was said during the journey, each man going through his mental routines and staying focused. At one kilometre from their destination, they made a sharp left turn onto a dirt track, surrounded by wasteland. The edge of the village appeared out of nowhere: a few ramshackle huts, not a person in view. Nods went around the team: they were ready.

At this point of the story, Zero had struggled, before finally sharing how that was the very last thing he remembered from inside the armoured vehicle. When Zero recovered consciousness, he was at first completely disorientated. But he'd been trained for this kind of thing and soon checked himself over quickly: his arms were still attached to his body and were moving normally; next he wiggled his toes and managed some shuffling movements against the ground with his legs. He noticed a fifteen centimetre piece of metal embedded in his left thigh, blood soaking into his khakis, and was surprised that it didn't hurt at all. Amazingly, he was otherwise okay.

It must have been an improvised explosive device, or IED, as there was smoke and dust everywhere, swirling around in the hot air. Gradually, the Snatch, from which Zero had been thrown, came into view, upside down and ablaze about twenty metres away. At first glance things didn't seem too bad. But then Zero glimpsed a foot with a boot on – just a booted foot with nothing attached. Next, another leg and an arm with a watch still wrapped around the wrist. Closer, much closer, was his best friend, or what was left of him: Blackstock's head, with the upper half of his torso still there – but only that half – plus his helmet, hanging at an angle. Blackstock looked astonished. In the vehicle, the two bodies in the front seats were blackened and charred.

Zero had taken a breath before recounting to the therapist that, despite the terrible ringing in his ears, he'd heard screaming and shouting penetrating through. Villagers were approaching from their huts and homes, bearing down from all directions, with the one nearest – a young girl, maybe thirteen or fourteen, an emerald hijab setting off her sea-green eyes and dark skin – standing just ten metres away. A few wisps of brown hair, which had escaped from her headscarf, blew gently in the breeze. Her appearance was serene amidst the chaos.

Sitting on the comfortable sofa, Zero only just managed

to complete the dreadful tale. He'd been scared, he told the therapist, the kind of fear he'd never experienced before. The girl was wearing a light blue robe and was clutching something in her right hand, thrust slightly forward as if showing it to the wounded soldier. He shouted at her to stop but she came closer, quietly holding out her hand. Wind blew the smoke back into Zero's eyes, blurring his vision. His mind was spinning. Suicide bomber. Suicide bomber. It had been drilled into him in training: bombs strapped under clothing and a detonator in the hand. He drew his pistol from the holster attached to his thigh and demanded again, in English and Pashto, for her to stay still and put her hands in the air.

But she didn't: the young girl moved two steps closer and their eyes locked, both staring intensely. The kindness in her face was confusing. Zero levelled the gun at her forehead – between the eyes – and took aim.

'Last chance,' he screamed. The girl flinched and … and …

The memory was almost too much to bear. A single tear had rolled down Zero's cheek.

'What happened next?' the therapist asked sympathetically.

So he told her.

***

'You need to lighten up,' Goswell advised his unhappy accomplice.

'I told you,' Zero retorted. 'I don't like meeting where we can be seen together.'

'Relax,' responded the chief executive arrogantly. 'Nobody's going to recognise you here.' Goswell downed the last drop of beer from his pint glass and placed it firmly on the wooden table, next to the small tumbler that had contained a whisky shot.

'What can I get you, then?' he asked.

'Half of lemonade,' Zero responded blankly.

'Come on! You can't let me drink alone.'

Zero pondered his own rationale: 'Okay. Double whisky, one cube of ice. And a half of lemonade.' Smiling, Goswell ambled over to the bar.

It wasn't the old-fashioned pub that bothered Zero, the kind of place he'd yearned for when stationed in Iraq and Afghanistan. It was the people who were problematic – too many for his liking. And the Arsenal vs Chelsea game on the TV in the opposite corner was attracting a noisy crowd. He should've realised when he'd seen through the train window the hordes of fans close to the Emirates Stadium.

'Here you go,' announced Goswell as he placed the tray with the collection of glasses on the table. 'I got us some crisps too.'

'So, how's your Sunday going, big man?' Goswell asked, the alcohol fuelling his overly friendly manner.

'I didn't come here to chat,' Zero responded. He took a sip of the pale brown liquid which bit into his throat pleasantly. 'This is business.'

'All right, all right. You think I don't know that?' countered Goswell, his mood suddenly switching. 'I've got more to lose than anyone.'

Zero was about to respond when a bespectacled man in his forties approached: professional looking, casual jeans, smart brogues and a stylish check jacket.

'Good afternoon, gentlemen. Mind if I join you?' the newcomer posed rhetorically, as he took a seat next to Goswell.

'Please do,' said Goswell, shuffling over.

Cheers erupted from the far side of the room: men in red shirts jumped up and those in blue remained seated. Zero gave Goswell a stern look to reflect his dissatisfaction that somebody else had been invited to the meeting, then chugged back the remainder of his whisky and made to leave.

'Where are you off to?' demanded Goswell. 'We haven't even started yet.'

'It's too busy here,' Zero responded. 'And I like to know who I'm meeting.'

Goswell put a hand on Zero's sizeable forearm as the big man started to stand up. 'Come on. I'm sorry – I should've mentioned it. Stay a few minutes.'

Zero contemplated briefly and then sat down.

'Thank you,' said the chief executive, who looked around his immediate surroundings carefully, checked for eavesdroppers and then continued softly.

'Okay, this is the situation. As you both know, Dr Tom Stephenson, our research director, is dead. His wife woke up next to his blood-soaked body in their hotel bed in Italy a couple of weeks ago. Is there any further news?'

'Difficult to find out much,' Zero said. 'But from my contacts, I understand the post-mortem has been completed and they're awaiting further test results.'

'What do you think was the cause of death?'

'Still not clear, although the Italian doctors have apparently been in touch with health officials here in England.'

'What does that mean?'

'Don't know. Could be routine. Could be something else.'

'And Tom's family? His wife?'

'She's been a bit unwell – she's been to see her GP. The sons have been around the house.'

'Yes,' said Goswell. 'I spoke to her on the phone the other day. She didn't sound great.'

'You shouldn't keep calling her,' Zero reminded him. The third man nodded. 'It looks suspicious.'

Goswell ignored them. 'And the Vietnamese families? Anything from them?'

This time the well-spoken third man responded. 'I haven't heard anything or seen anything in the press. Seems they're content with their pay-offs.'

'Or Zero scared them shitless,' Goswell commented tersely, turning to face his frightening accomplice. 'You must be about twice their size!' he joked, then added, 'And you saw them all? In Saigon?'

'It's not called Saigon any more. It's Ho Chi Minh City. And yes, I saw all six families, as I've told you before. Ten thousand pounds buys a lot there.'

'And the lab?'

'Burned to the ground,' said Zero assertively.

'Okay,' Goswell countered, then turned to the other

man. 'And what about Flu-Away?'

The man in the check jacket replied. 'Everything's been submitted and is going through the regulatory authorities. It's close to the next stage of approval.'

'And they didn't notice anything in the experimental data?'

'Nothing at all, apparently,' responded the late arrival confidently.

Goswell turned back to Zero: 'You destroyed all Tom's records? His computer at work ... all his files and folders?'

'All done.'

Suddenly, Goswell's steadiness dissolved and he barked an angry question: 'So, what the hell's going on? What's this stupid little bitch doing? She's obviously got something on us, or her bloody mother did. Tell me! That's what I pay you both for.'

After a few seconds of silence Zero spoke. 'Well, she's got some information, for sure. That's why she's been doing the internet searches on Creation, on Vietnam and other stuff linked to us. And it's been recent, even ...'

'Since when exactly?'

'Since the stone-setting of her mother in the cemetery.' A pause, then in an unimpressed tone: 'Where you saw her ... and she may have seen you.'

'All right! Lay off that for Christ's sake,' Goswell reacted belligerently. 'She didn't even notice me.'

More silence, ended again by Zero in a hushed voice: 'And I'm suspicious about this Finsbury Park incident. If it's connected to her mum's death ...'

'If that comes out we're all in for a long prison stretch,' declared Goswell, and then checked himself. 'Only, I'm never going to end up in prison – I tell you that.'

All three were unsure where to go next with the conversation, so Goswell led them: 'We need to put an end to this stupid little girl's detective work ...'

He stopped and waited. 'Meaning what exactly?' asked Zero.

'You know perfectly well what I mean ... another accident ... just like we did with her mother.'

The ensuing silence grated on Goswell's nerves, unsure if it represented agreement.

Eventually, the conservatively dressed man, not out of place in a Cambridgeshire pub, piped up: 'I've got an idea. I think you can leave this with me.'

On the train back from Ely, Zero nodded off briefly, the product of whisky and a warm, quiet carriage. He awoke just as the train pulled into Finsbury Park, jumped out a moment before the doors closed and made his way down the stairs to the Underground platforms.

What a bloody mess, Zero thought, as he boarded the crowded Piccadilly Line Tube to take him the few stops to King's Cross, Arsenal fans in celebratory mood everywhere. He'd left the Ely pub shortly after the idiot in the brogues had offered to take care of the girl. He decided to let the moron try something out and allow the chief executive to stew in the consequences.

Now, compressed amidst sweaty bodies in the packed carriage, Zero just wanted to be in the peace of his own home. That still felt a little way off, though, with the atmosphere in the tight space becoming more raucous by the minute, football fans fuelled by beer and a win against their London rivals. It wasn't those wearing red and white shirts that bothered Zero, however; it was a group of five Chelsea fans, clad in blue, standing just a few metres away.

Zero was positioned close to the electric double-doors at the centre of the carriage, holding on to the vertical pole. To his left, along the length of the carriage were two rows of seats, one facing the other, and in-between these stood the five Chelsea fans, the loudness of their voices a deliberate show of macho fearlessness to the opposing fans.

From all around, Zero heard the rise of chanting from the Gunners fans, spelling out where their loyalties lay:

And it's Aaaaaaaarsenal,
Aaaaarsenal FC,
We're by far the greatest team,
The world has ever seen …

Two of the Chelsea supporters were tall men – over six foot – and the others were average height, all in their twenties or early thirties. Tattoos adorned fairly muscular arms but nothing Zero recognised as a military affiliation; oversize bellies suggested more time in the pub than the gym. Three of the five sported shaved heads. The group responded to the Arsenal voices by singing their team's name over and over:

'We are the Chelsea ...
We are the Chelsea ...
We are the Chelsea ...'

All of this Zero could put up with, but he was troubled by the leader of the small pack in blue, who had turned his attention to a dark-skinned teenage girl in a hijab seated directly in front of him.

'What ya reading, luv?' the fan asked nastily.

The girl had her nose in a book and didn't even realise the question was directed at her. The failure to reply prompted a more aggressive approach.

'I'm talking to you, luv.' He flicked the side of her head with the back of his fingers. 'Don't ignore me, it's rude. I asked what you're reading?'

She looked up nervously and glanced around for support, but soon realised she was alone: 'I wasn't being rude, I didn't hear you. It's just a book.'

The fair-haired aggressor now had the attention of the rest of his troop, who stopped chanting and smirked in anticipation of what might happen next.

'I can see it's a bloody book, luv! D'ya think I'm stupid?' He looked over his shoulder to check his mates were watching before thwacking the book, which fell to the floor: 'It's probably the Koran! Don't you think so, Jimmy?'

The shortest of the group, all nervous energy, grunted back in agreement: 'Probably is, Bob. Go on, you show her.'

Zero felt his temper rising. He knew of the brutish, racist reputation of some Chelsea fans, yet nobody in the carriage was prepared to do anything. The Tube pulled out of Caledonian Road station; just a few minutes until they reached King's Cross. Zero took a step towards the gang, made sure of his footing and waited.

As the girl reached down to pick up the book, Bob tugged her headscarf away, revealing long, dark hair. She looked up, clearly very scared.

'When you live in England, luv, you need to wear what we wear and follow our rules. No need for this rubbish scarf.'

Calmly, audibly and with authority, Zero uttered his short instruction: 'Leave the girl alone.'

A hush fell across the carriage. Those in the immediate surroundings drew back in concern for their own safety. Slowly, the leader of the Chelsea pack turned around and squared up, full height, to Zero.

'What d'ya say, mate?'

Unflinching, Zero repeated his point: 'I said, leave the girl alone.'

Bob moved even closer to Zero, their faces just inches apart. His friends braced themselves: 'And what are you gonna do about it, pal?'

Steadily Zero replied, 'All I'm asking is that you leave her alone.' He paused. 'Otherwise, I'll make you.'

To Zero's right, Jimmy stepped forwards. Special Forces training and combat meant that Zero was used to this kind of situation and had already assessed the danger of all five men: their physicality, their concentration, their nerve. In Jimmy, Zero saw a vicious unpredictability, and the rule was always to take the most dangerous out first. Shaven-headed

Jimmy moved closer and stared up at Zero.

'You and whose army, mate?' he asked through pursed, angry lips.

'Just me,' spoke Zero, and on the second word thrust his large hand, fingers extended and locked together, hard into Jimmy's windpipe, catching the unsuspecting man off guard and leaving him doubled over, clutching his throat and gasping for breath.

After the most dangerous, next get the leader and don't hold back on violence. Zero had little space, but in one motion he drew back his right arm and delivered a full force jab direct to Bob's chin, knowing that the impact of such a crunching blow rattled the brainstem. Distracted by Jimmy's plight, Bob had no time to adjust and the powerful punch sent him tumbling to the floor, knocked out on top of the girl's book.

But it certainly wasn't over and Zero switched to the remaining three. The crowd had pulled right back, leaving the space between the doors clear for the final assault.

'You bastard!' screamed the third lout and drew a knife from his inside pocket. Zero assessed it: solid looking eight-inch blade, good handle, possibly ex-army. Taking up the stance of one unaccustomed to a knife fight, the Chelsea ruffian held the weapon out in front and bellowed: 'Come on, then!'

Zero kept his eyes on the deadly blade. It was simple really, if you had confidence and knew how. The fan lunged without skill or plan, and Zero took a half-step to the left, closer to the knife hand, and wrapped his own massive left fist around the assailant's right wrist. Zero yanked outwards, snapping the bone at the elbow as the man in blue shrieked in agony. With his right hand, Zero ripped the knife from the man's flailing hand, got on to one knee and plunged the razor-sharp blade into the inside of the man's right thigh.

Blood instantly blotted the man's jeans, and Zero felt arms from behind locking around his chest, attempting to keep him close to the ground. Zero pushed himself back up to a standing position and with his left elbow thrust backwards into the solar plexus of the man behind him, who let out a winded gasp. Zero spun around and viciously headbutted him, the crack of a breaking nose heard by all around.

Just one left standing. Zero closed in, intense concentration accompanied by a madness in the ex-soldier's eyes. This fan was the youngest and looked terrified. From behind, Zero heard a voice, spun round and was about to hit, but saw it was an older man in red and white, his arms raised submissively.

'I think they've had enough, mate,' he said quietly. 'That's enough now.'

Breathing loud and fast and with adrenaline at maximum level, Zero twisted again to check on his adversary, who'd stepped as far away as he could. Like a cornered animal, Zero took in the watching faces around him, unsure what to do next.

'It's okay, pal,' came the quiet voice again. 'It's okay. They've learned their lesson.'

The Tube train pulled into King's Cross station and Zero tumbled out.

CHAPTER 10

COLLISION COURSE

Monday morning and she'd had just a few hours' sleep: two reasons making the loud knocking on Edie's bedroom door even more of an irritant.

'Come on, luv! It's gone seven o'clock and you'll be late for school.'

'I'm up!'

'No, you're not,' Dad insisted. 'The light's not even on.'

Edie clicked the switch on the lamp on her bedside table. 'Yes, it is!'

'Shall I open the curtains?'

'No! Don't even come in, I'm getting dressed.'

'Okay. Just make sure you don't fall asleep again.'

'I won't. I told you, I'm up.'

Dad must have twigged that continuing this line of conversation was pointless, as Edie first heard his footsteps trundle down the stairs and then, barely audible, offering Eli a choice of either cereal or toast with peanut butter.

Throughout the previous evening and the early hours Edie had battled with the latest clue. Her mother said in the note that she was almost there, but the mathematical conundrum was making Edie feel anything but close. Although logic was one of Edie's real strengths, whether in debating or reasoning, she was medium-good at maths rather than top of the class. So, why would her mum create a clue full of numbers now?

121141
4512
18525

- - - - - - - - - - - -

♫ 2294515-7113519 (hint)

- - - - - - - - - - - -

As a pure calculation, the figures didn't seem to stack up in terms of reaching the supposed total. Edie had tried adding them, subtracting them and every plus and minus combination of the three lines. Division or multiplication also failed to work, and even if the figures had somehow meshed together, what would that mean? Just one set of numbers leading to another. Was it binary code? No: not even in the bottom row. It just didn't make sense.

So, what of the 'hint'? Clearly, her mum was trying to assist, but was the apparent tip a stand-alone solution or a separate way to get to the answer? And how exactly did it help?

Furthermore, what on earth did the music symbol denote? Music really wasn't one of Edie's good subjects, and she wasn't even sure whether the symbol was a quaver, semi-quaver, crochet or treble clef. Looking that up on the internet provided the answer but also seemed to lead nowhere. And, of course, she'd tried the obvious – that each number represented a letter in the alphabet – but 'ABAADA' in the top line was devoid of meaning.

Edie's mum was certainly prone to lateral thinking, but this clue seemed to be taking things too far. Hence, another night of frustration.

Eventually, Edie threw back the duvet and hauled herself to a sitting position on the edge of the bed. As her dad pleaded again from downstairs, Edie pulled on her school clothes and checked that her bag contained what she needed. After replacing the original fourth clue in her secure hiding place, and a copy of the clue in her zipped pocket, Edie shuffled down the stairs.

As Edie entered the kitchen, the clock on the oven showed 07:55. Ignoring Dad and Eli at the table, Edie scooped some cornflakes into a plastic sandwich bag, filled up her water bottle and exited without Dad even looking up from his newspaper. Edie pulled on her coat and opened the front door, to be greeted by drizzle and a bitter wind. That kind of day, she thought.

'Have a good, day, luv,' boomed Dad from the kitchen.

'Thanks,' Edie returned, unsure if her day would meet her father's hopes. 'You too.'

As Edie crossed over Crouch Hill and cut through to Hornsey Lane, she tried to focus her attention back on the current clue. It was hard, though – perhaps due to tiredness, perhaps the bitter weather – and her mind wandered. In a few minutes, at five past eight, Lizzie would be waiting for her at the corner of Stanhope Road. Maybe Edie should draw her friend in deeper. Since the Finsbury Park incident and sharing the detective work with her best friend and her brother, Edie had kept both of them at a distance. She'd sworn them to secrecy but now felt conflicted about their ongoing involvement.

On the incline up Hornsey Lane a cold, gusty blast caused Edie to slow her pace and then stop. She coughed. After a few more paces uphill, Edie was forced to halt again. Out of breath, she reached into her rucksack and retrieved the blue inhaler. As advised by Dr Martial, she took two additional puffs, inhaling deep and holding each breath for five seconds. After a minute or so Edie felt a little better. If she was coming down with a bug it would at least explain why she was feeling out of sorts.

As the road levelled and Edie began to get back into her stride, her iPhone rang from inside her red and blue school blazer. Probably her dad reminding her of arrangements for later. Edie unbuttoned her black padded raincoat and was surprised to see the phone display show a number rather than a name – a number she didn't immediately recognise, although it seemed vaguely familiar. Short of time, Edie was about to press the red circle and reject the call when, inexplicably, she changed her mind and touched green instead.

'Hi, is that Edie?'

Holding the mobile close to her right ear, Edie cautiously responded, 'Who is this?'

'Is that Edie? Edie Franklin?' repeated the young sounding voice.

'Yes, who's speaking?'

'It's Ethan here.'

Flustered, Edie wracked her brain. Picking up her failure to recognise his voice, the boy helped her out: 'Ethan Stephenson. Dr Tom Stephenson's son. You came to visit my mum in Mill Hill.' He paused. 'My dad died a few weeks ago.'

'Oh, yes. Hi. I'm just on my way to school,' Edie replied cagily.

'You sound breathless. Are you all right?'

'Yes. Fine, thanks. It's just my asthma and the cold weather.'

Awkwardly, neither of them said anything for a few seconds, allowing Edie to sit on a front garden wall. 'It must feel a bit odd, me ringing you like this.' He waited but Edie said nothing so Ethan continued. 'It's to do with my mum. She's been taken to hospital.'

'Oh dear,' Edie responded sympathetically. 'What's wrong with her?'

She could hear Ethan take a breath before answering: 'You remember she had a bad cold when you were here?'

'Yes.'

'Well, the GP thought it was just that – a cold – due to being exhausted and run down since my dad died. But it wouldn't go away and she got a fever … started feeling terrible … so the GP gave her antibiotics.'

'Did that help?' asked Edie, concerned.

'No. Not at all. Then she started coughing up blood and the doctor got worried.'

'Was that what happened to your dad? I mean … with the blood.'

'Yes. Exactly. They took Mum into hospital – into isolation – and some other people came to see me … infectious disease experts from Public Health England. They told me they were worried that Mum might've caught what Dad had.'

'Really?' Edie put on her most concerned voice. 'What did your father have, anyway?'

'From the post-mortem in Italy, they thought he had some kind of severe viral infection … viral respiratory infection, I think they said.'

'What?' said Edie, her anxiety rising.

'Influenza, possibly,' continued Ethan. 'They're still waiting for the results of all the tests.'

'Influenza?' repeated Edie, astonished. 'Like, the flu?'

'Yes, I think so. But a severe kind. They're not sure. Anyway, they asked me like … loads of questions, and I'm not allowed to leave the house until they tell me I can.'

'But you're okay, yeah?'

'I feel fine. Absolutely fine.'

In the back of her mind, Edie was piecing bits together: Creation working on a new antiviral medicine, Ethan's dad working for Creation, the Vietnam connection. Edie also remembered that she was getting later and later for school, and that Lizzie would be standing on the street corner.

'I'm so sorry about your mum, Ethan, but I'm not sure what this has to do with me. I have to be at school in a few minutes.'

'I know. Sorry. It's just that they asked me … the public health people … if I'd been in contact with anybody else.' Ethan paused.

'Right,' interjected Edie.

'And I gave them your name.'

'You gave them *my* name?'

'Yes, of course,' stated Ethan. 'Mum's only seen a few people since she's been feeling ill – which is when they think she would be infectious – and one of them is you.'

'I see.'

'So, are you feeling all right?' Ethan asked with concern.

'Yes. Just my asthma playing up a bit as I said.'

'Okay, good. Well, I've given them your name and phone number so I guess they'll be in contact soon.'

'And how did you get my phone number?' Edie asked with interest.

'Aha,' the older boy quipped. 'I have my sleuth-like skills too!'

Edie was mildly impressed but her mind was racing, and not with thoughts about her own wellbeing. 'Did you tell them anything about … well … about … your dad's work and what he did?'

'Not really. I mentioned it but they didn't seem very interested, more focused on telling me what to do and when to call them. Plus all the other people they needed to follow up.'

Edie felt her fingers getting numb from the cold, so she stood up from the wall and walked. Something still didn't feel right but she needed to find Lizzie, who would be mad with her. Also, Edie had another detention after school today and if she turned up late for register she'd be in even more trouble.

'Well, thanks for letting me know, Ethan, but I've really got to go to school now. Perhaps we can talk later or tomorrow?'

Silence.

'Ethan? Are you still there? Is everything all right? I said can we speak ...'

'There's one other thing, Edie,' the older boy interrupted.

'I've really got to go, Ethan,' Edie repeated, quickening her step. 'What is it?'

She heard another sharp inhalation of breath before he whispered: 'It's my dad. I found something.' Suddenly, he had Edie's complete attention and she pressed the phone close to her ear to hear Ethan's quiet voice against the wind.

'I was in the attic yesterday. Not sure why I went there, I think just to be in the space where he spent a lot of his private time. To connect in some other way with him. I miss him so much ... still can't believe he's dead. Sorry, you know all about that, of course.'

Edie waited patiently but said nothing.

'My dad made his plastic models up in the attic,' Ethan continued. 'It was, like, his workspace. Aeroplanes, ships, cars, tanks ... that kind of thing. He was actually really good at them – there's hundreds up there.'

'Did something happen?' Edie probed.

'Sorry, I'll get to the point. When I was a little boy and made models up there with him, I once saw him go into a tiny latched space behind his worktop area, concealed by various books and boxes on the floor. He didn't know I was watching but it was obvious that it was like ... a secret place that nobody else knew about. When he was out the house I had a peep, but I couldn't really understand the stuff that was in there, so I forgot all about it.'

'Right,' said Edie definitively, urging Ethan to get to the point.

'Until yesterday, that is. I was up there and suddenly remembered, so I moved all the junk on the floor out of the way and crawled into the space. There were a couple of plastic model boxes in there – Mosquito and Messerschmitt planes from the Second World War. They seemed out of place, so I opened them.'

'And what was inside?' Edie asked anxiously.

'Papers. Lots of papers … about his job, about Creation, results of the tests on a drug against viruses, I think. Stuff about some lab in Vietnam. And a copy of a submission for the drug to get a licence, with certain parts highlighted in yellow marker pen. I don't know what it all meant but … Edie … I'm worried. It felt like Dad might have been in some trouble.'

Edie had a terrible sudden sense that she was being followed and abruptly looked over her shoulder, but there was nobody there.

'Ethan,' she said as calmly as she could. 'Keep it safe. Photocopy it all if you can … if you have a machine at home. And don't tell *anybody* about this.'

Out of nowhere came a high-pitched yell: 'Edie! Edie! Get a move on, we're going to be *so* late!' Just up the road, Lizzie was looking furious, although her anger was also about Edie still refraining from telling her the truth.

'I've got to go,' Edie repeated. 'I'll call you later.'

'But ...'

Edie didn't hear the end of Ethan's sentence as she pressed the red circle that thankfully she'd not touched ten minutes earlier.

Twenty-two minutes was the average amount of time that it took Edie and Lizzie to get to school from their meeting point, allowing three minutes to grab books from their lockers, deposit unwanted coats and be seated in class ready for register.

They often cut it fine but never quite as bad as this. With only fifteen minutes to complete the journey, most of which was uphill, the two girls had to run up Shepherd's Hill, stopping only for the traffic lights at Archway Road. Lizzie was pretty enraged throughout. With a minute to go, they bombed through the front gates, disregarded their lockers until after assembly, legged it up the stairs to the form room and grabbed their seats as Miss Watson, head of the art department, paused from completing the register – a task she was doing for the absent Mr Hollister. The girls' laboured breathing was evident to all.

'Edie, are you okay?' asked Miss Watson. 'You look a bit ... well ... peaky.'

'Just been running, Miss. My fault, not Lizzie's. Sorry to be late.'

'All right then, just calm down. You too, Lizzie.'

After completing the register, Miss Watson had news:

'I'm afraid that Thursday's trip to Cambridge, to visit the History of Science Museum, has had to be cancelled. They've had to do some emergency renovations. Shame, I know.'

'Can't we do something else that day, Miss?' asked Allegra from the front row. 'It's like … well … everybody's been looking forwards to that trip. Getting out of school for the day, seeing something interesting, doing something different.' A background hum of soft 'yeahs' indicated general assent.

'It's very hard, Allegra, to organise these things at the last minute, without much preparation.' The teacher paused then recalibrated: 'Unless someone has a good idea, that is.'

'What about Chessington?' joked the good-looking, self-assured Callum. 'Chessington World of Adventures.' A chorus of laughter and approval greeted his suggestion.

'It's not a holiday, Callum. Any other suggestions?'

Edie's mind ticked over rapidly. Just before Miss Watson moved things on, she announced: 'We could visit one of those pharmaceutical companies … drug companies … where they, you know, make medicines and do research on new drugs.' Then Edie lied for effect: 'My dad, who's a doctor, says it's really interesting.'

'Not a bad idea, Edie, but that kind of thing does need some planning.'

The teacher had barely finished her sentence before Edie jumped in: 'There's one company I've heard about that does school trips. It's located near Cambridge, I think, so would be the same distance for the coach.'

Although the idea didn't garner universal endorsement

from the class, there certainly wasn't any disagreement, and Miss Watson responded favourably. 'Nice suggestion, Edie. I'll look into it.'

And she did.

The school day drifted by in something of a haze. Plant photosynthesis in biology, more strange adventures of the Cazorla family in Spanish, followed by double history in which they were learning about how public health laws were passed in the Victorian era to improve sewage and sanitation and keep the streets clean, which in turn reduced mortality from infections.

Fatigue was taking its toll, compounded by the thought of an extended day because of detention. All Edie wanted to do was go back home to bed. She chose pea soup and chicken pie for lunch but ate little and, during the afternoon, fell momentarily asleep as Mr Bowling was explaining simultaneous equations. Ethan's comments sat in the back of her mind and she noticed two missed calls on her iPhone from unknown numbers.

By quarter past four, as school began to empty, Edie felt completely exhausted.

'I hope it goes okay,' said Lizzie in reference to the detention. The morning's irritation seemed temporarily forgotten in the face of Edie's obvious discomfort.

'It'll be fine,' Edie replied. 'Thank you. See you tomorrow.'

Edie watched through the classroom window on the third floor of Building C as pupils dispersed into the courtyard below. Heads were shielded from the drizzle and Edie was envious that they'd soon be in the warm in front of the TV. It was extraordinary how quickly the school emptied, from a sea of noise to almost devoid of life, all in a matter of minutes. Occasionally a teacher crossed the courtyard, and Edie spied the head, Mr Pennant, eating a biscuit on the go. She looked again at the clue, which intuition told her must be connected with music, but her mind wasn't clear enough to engage.

At twenty-five past four, Edie descended the three flights of stairs, entered the main quadrangle and, in an archway between courtyards, slammed straight into an adult coming from the opposite direction.

'Watch out, young lady,' came a vaguely familiar voice. 'Steady as she goes.'

Winded, Edie leant her hands on her knees.

'Oh, it's you, Edie,' continued the out-of-place voice. She looked up.

'Ah, Dr Martial,' Edie said, surprised.

'Yes, indeed,' the GP affirmed, brushing himself off and adjusting his jacket and tie.

'What are you doing here?' Edie asked warily.

The doctor paused, momentarily uncertain over what to divulge, before deciding to grasp the opportunity. 'Well, as you know, I'm the school doctor, so I come here from time to time. But this visit is actually about you, young lady.'

'About me?'

'Yes, indeed. You see, I've been to see your head teacher today, as a concerned physician and your doctor. I spoke to your dad beforehand, who also mentioned the concerns of a family therapist friend ...'

'You spoke to my dad about this?' said Edie indignantly.

'Naturally. My duty, as well as my responsibility to you, my dear.'

Edie's anger was brewing as Dr Martial continued: 'Anyway, I've been to see the head – confidentially, of course – to tell him of my concerns that you may have a psychiatric condition, a personality disorder, that has made it especially hard for you to cope with your mum's death. And that your behaviour has become irrational and we may need to put you on medication or even admit you into hospital for a period ...'

Edie couldn't believe what she was hearing from the smarmy, so-called professional. But Dr Martial wasn't finished. 'And the school will be keeping a much closer eye on you – on what you're allowed to do. Enhanced supervision ... reduced time alone—'

Impulsively, Edie screamed in the doctor's face: 'You can't do that to me! It's a lie and you know it!' She clenched her teeth. 'There's nothing wrong with me ... you're not even a proper doc—'

'What exactly is going on here?' intervened an assertive male voice.

'Ah, Mr Pennant,' said Dr Martial. 'Just the man. As

162

you can see, this is precisely what we are dealing with here …'

'Well,' responded the head teacher. 'I'm not sure what this shows but—'

Edie had had enough: 'It's all lies …' she shouted, then stormed off towards the school underpass that took her below busy Southwood Lane and to the art block where the detentions were held.

Inside the art department building, Edie stumbled through the first door available and collapsed onto a bench next to a large wooden table used for painting. She started bawling her eyes out, uncontrollable tears of exhaustion and distress, accompanied by loud groans of fury at a world that seemed stacked against her.

'Is everything okay, Edie?' asked a kind voice a minute later, as a hand gently touched her back.

After a moment, Edie looked over her left shoulder to see Miss Watson, who appeared genuinely concerned.

'NO!' Edie spluttered, cupping her face in her hands.

A further minute passed without a word, after which Miss Watson handed Edie a tissue, which she gladly accepted. 'I can't do detention,' Edie mumbled whilst blowing her nose.

'Don't worry about that, Edie,' the teacher replied. 'It was only you today, in any case. Let's get you home.'

'Thanks,' said Edie with surprise and gratitude. 'I'll get the bus back to Crouch End.'

'No, you won't,' countered Miss Watson sensitively. 'I'll give you a lift in my car. I live near there anyway.'

Little was said in the small Fiat 500. Miss Watson opted for the narrow Highgate backstreets in an effort to avoid the clogged main roads, requiring her full concentration to slalom past cars heading in the opposite direction. Intermittently, she glanced over and gave Edie a comforting half-smile. At Archway Road they hit solid rush-hour traffic.

Edie leant forwards to turn on the radio, checking with the driver first who nodded, tried a few channels and settled on Heart FM. Edie closed her eyes and sat back in the seat. A combination of the music, in-car heating and purring of the engine helped Edie to calm down and relax. With her eyes closed and mind wandering on the edge of awareness, Edie wasn't initially sure about the words she was hearing. But gradually they took a stronger form – lyrics from a familiar song about hanging out in the backyard with a boyfriend.

Comforted by the melody, Edie's lips stretched into the beginnings of a smile as recognition of the song surfaced. Underneath the sweet-sounding tune was a sadness that Edie, and many others, found so engaging. The image from an album cover flashed across Edie's mind: a beautiful young woman getting out of an old American car, long brown hair trailing across a pretty white summer top. Lyrics came to her, too: the woman's boyfriend opening up a beer, calling her over and asking her to play a video game. Video game. 'Video Games' …

All of a sudden Edie's heart thumped in her chest. She opened her eyes wide, reached into her school blazer, unzipped the inside pocket and pulled out the note. The answer was indeed music related. With a sense of what the answer might be, Edie turned away from Miss Watson and stared searchingly at the paper, willing the solution from the ink. Then it dawned on her: it didn't have to be one number per letter: the first two numbers could provide the first letter. On her fingers Edie counted out the twelfth letter of the alphabet, 'L'. The following two numbers provided a 'K' so that couldn't be right, so she needed to interpret the clue more flexibly. If the next number, '1', was a letter it would be 'A'. Then, with fingers again, the next two letters meant 'N', followed by an 'A' again.

Together the letters spelled a word: 'LANA'.

A tear appeared in the corner of Edie's left eye, and she sped through the remainder of the cryptic sum to confirm that she'd solved the latest clue. With the traffic beginning to clear, Edie rested her head back and closed her eyes again.

And then Edie remembered when she and her mum had gone to see Lana Del Rey at the Camden Roundhouse just a few weeks before her mum's death. As they exited the venue she'd teased her mum about calling it a 'gig' rather than a concert. Although it was late, her mum had wanted to show Edie one of her old haunts, so they'd walked down Chalk Farm Road to Marine Ices – open until midnight because of the live music – where Edie had chosen chocolate and pistachio and her mum had ordered hazelnut and melon.

Seated in the old-fashioned ice-cream parlour, they'd chatted intensely about the amazing gig: Lana's effortless beauty, her cool name and silky, melancholic voice. As their bowls emptied, her mum had asked Edie what her favourite Lana song was, which was easy: 'Blue Jeans'. When Edie had posed the same question back, she was surprised by her mum saying 'Video Games', so had asked her why.

Sitting in the car over a year later, with everything in her life so different, Edie recalled vividly her mum's explanation, which had to do with the lyrics of the sad song: lyrics that her mum had sung quietly in Marine Ices, much to Edie's embarrassment.

At first, Edie hadn't understood why the lyrics made the song so special, so her mum had explained that, to her, the words were about what we give up for those we love. With her ice-cream spoon licked clean, Mum had said something to Edie which was still crystal clear: 'The reason why I love the song so much is because of its poignancy. Love is what makes life worth living. It's worth living if you've got somebody that you love and who loves you. That's the magic of life. And I have that with you, Edie, and, quite extraordinarily, with Dad and Eli too.' Then her mum had smiled before concluding: 'Lana says the world is built for two, but I have three sets of those loving relationships! How lucky is that!'

Edie remembered feeling strangely unsettled at the time. The relationship she had with her mother was completely special, of that there was no question. Yet her mum's comments had made Edie understand, for the very first time, that her mum also had truly special relationships with others – with Eli and Dad, in particular.

And as Miss Watson pulled up to the family home in Cecile Park, Edie realised – also for the very first time – that those two people were hurting, hurting deeply for their own loss, just as much as Edie was.

CHAPTER 11

THE PUBLIC'S HEALTH

Outside the house, Dad arrived home just as Edie got out of the car. The teacher and doctor exchanged pleasantries before Miss Watson drove off, then Dad told Edie that Eli had felt sick at school so Papa had picked him up.

At the open front door, Mama grabbed her precious granddaughter, pulling the youngster close: 'So nice to see you again, Edie!'

Papa emerged from the lounge, babysitting duties now over. 'I'm not sure I can watch *Taken* again,' he joked, before turning to the grandson trailing behind him: 'I have a very particular set of skills,' Papa mimicked in jest. 'I will look for you, I *will* find you and I will kill you!'

Eli replied with a poor imitation of an Eastern European accent, enhanced by a croaky, sore throat: 'Good luck.'

'Isn't Liam Neeson about my age anyway?' said Papa with a smile.

'Thank you both so much for looking after Eli,' Dad said to his in-laws, 'and at such short notice. I couldn't have done it without you.'

Mama replied earnestly: 'You don't have to, Mark. We're always here for you. I hope you know that.'

Dad acknowledged their kindness and politely escorted them down the front path. The Honda Jazz was soon heading back to Hendon. In the lounge, Edie grabbed Lana Del Rey's *Born to Die* CD from the rack, told her dad in passing that she was feeling exhausted, and withdrew upstairs. On her bed, Edie quickly opened the plastic case and, inside the coloured insert, found a piece of paper which she carefully unfolded and placed on her pillow, revealing a different kind of clue.

Don't smile
Don't smell
Don't hear
Don't grow
Don't think!

Edie grinned at the picture. It was awful and Edie imagined the time her mum must have spent preparing it: she was terrible at Word Art and Paint, despite her daughter's lessons. Anxiously, Edie read through her mum's words in her familiar handwriting.

My darling Edie,

This is indeed the final clue. Solving it will take you to the evidence which, I hope, will bring the criminals to justice. If you have got this far, it means that I am surely gone, and you have been putting together the jigsaw, piece by piece. Locate the evidence and the puzzle should be complete – and I know how much you like solving puzzles!

I know how very hard this will have been for you. You will be navigating your own journey now – one without me – but time is a great healer and slowly you will learn to live with the loss. Trust me on this, as I have entrusted you.

Edie, you and I have had something special – truly special – that can never be taken away, and I have thanked God for every moment of that. But you have two other very special people close to you, Dad and Eli, and together you can be even stronger.

Look out for them, look after them and remember: you don't need to do this alone.

You are my shining star – shine bright.

With all my love,
Mum xxx

Edie returned to the computer-sketched face and giggled aloud.

'Everything okay in there, luv?' Dad asked as he emerged from the bathroom adjacent to Edie's room.

'Yes, fine,' she responded swiftly.

'It's just that I thought I heard you crying.'

'No! I'm fine, Dad!' Then more gently: 'I'm okay, Dad, really, just feeling a bit run down.'

'Can I get you anything? A cup of tea?'

'No … thanks. But I'm not sure I can go to school tomorrow if I still feel like this.'

'Okay, well rest up and we'll see.' Fatherly footsteps withdrew up the stairs, and Edie heard the click of his bedroom door closing.

Without making any attempt to decipher the clue's meaning, Edie allowed the words of the latest note to settle peacefully inside her. No tears.

After a few minutes, Edie checked her iPhone on the bedside table. Two missed calls from an unknown number and one answerphone message. She pressed the icon that connected to voicemail and heard a doctor from Public Health England enquiring about Edie's health and asking her to call back. Ignoring the request, Edie turned on her iPad. The final clue had steeled her resolve – especially in light of Dr Martial's annoying interference. Edie needed to accelerate matters.

After the burglary, Edie was sure her desktop computer had shifted position slightly and possibly been tampered with judging from scratch marks on the side, so she worked again through all she knew about Creation using her tablet. According to internet reports, Creation was a medium-sized pharmaceutical company, employing around five hundred people at their headquarters near Bourn in Cambridgeshire. Although established almost two decades earlier, Creation's rise up the industry ladder had coincided with the appointment of a new chief executive, Peter Goswell, five years ago. Since then, Creation had produced three successful new medicines – most notably the anti-diarrhoea drug Stop It!, which had made Edie laugh when she'd seen it in Boots.

According to the Creation website, their drug testing laboratories were part of the Cambridgeshire site and the home page had a leading article about their new product Flu-Away, summarising the excellent progress with trials and anticipating the antiviral medicine being on the market within the next two years. Shares in Creation had increased in price and, elsewhere, Edie found that the company was now valued at over £2 billion.

Edie stumbled around the website fruitlessly for half an hour then returned to the main page about Dr Thomas Stephenson. She took time to read again about the collective grief in the organisation over the sudden death of their director of research and development. A dutifully written obituary by the chief executive emphasised how much he would be missed by all his friends at Creation. At the very bottom, Edie then noticed something she hadn't seen before, which must have been newly added – a web-link to staff tributes for the deceased director. Edie followed the link.

On the screen appeared a stream of warmth and appreciation from people across the organisation. Edie scrolled down the list, which went on for over three pages:

Thank you, Dr Stephenson, for all your support and help. You will be terribly missed. (Gillian Davenport, R&D)

You were the best boss I've ever had and were always a pleasure to work with. Your life was taken away too early. My heartfelt condolences to your lovely family. (Becky Myers, PA)

A great colleague. Always a pleasure to work with. (Matt Hughes, HR)

Scanning down the list, Edie was touched by the esteem in which Dr Stephenson was held and, by the third page, she was about to move off this track of web investigation when her eye was caught by an unusual message:

Tôi sẽ bỏ lỡ năng lượng và niềm đam mê cho nghiên cứu của bạn, và cả tình yêu Việt Nam mà chúng ta cùng chia sẻ! (Nguyễn Văn T, senior researcher)

Delicate images of flowers supplemented the beauty of the letters and characters, clearly prepared with considerable care. But what did it mean? Edie copied the sentence, opened Google Translate in a new browser window and pasted in the Vietnamese text, receiving an almost instantaneous response:

I will miss your energy and passion for research, and the love of Vietnam we share!

A jolt surged through Edie's body. Was Vietnam the key to it all? She remembered looking into the Vietnam issue when she'd solved the first clue about Creation, which seemed an eternity ago. She'd printed out an article and hidden it in the secret stash behind the poster. The piece covered an outbreak in the country's largest city. Was it bird flu? A connection to Creation was suggested but never proved.

Her thoughts racing, Edie suddenly recalled her last phone call with Ethan. He'd mentioned finding some papers of his dad's in the attic which were also connected with Vietnam. Edie needed to speak to Ethan but, all of a sudden, she felt absolutely drained, like a blanket of tiredness had been wrapped around her. She remembered her mum explaining, from a Three Principles perspective, that overthinking and a hyperactive mind causes mental exhaustion, which Edie had experienced over the past week or two. But this felt different – worse.

Edie thought she should probably eat something, but all she really wanted to do was sleep. Before that, however, one thing had to be set in motion, which involved taking the investigatory work to another level. She texted Lizzie who, thankfully, was still bearing with Edie despite everything:

Hi. At home now, very tired but OK. Going to sleep soon.

A few minutes later, the reply came:

Lizzie: Hiya. Will you be in school tomorrow?
Edie: Probably not tomorrow, not feeling well.
But I need a favour.
Lizzie: What is it?

Edie: Remember how Miss Watson said our trip
to the medical history place was cancelled
on Thursday?

Lizzie: Yeah, coz of a flood in their building. And
you suggested a drug company.

Edie: I need you to be more specific. Suggest
we visit Creation Pharmaceuticals.

Lizzie: What are you plotting?!

Edie: On their website it says they like school
visits. Educating the next generation.
Trust me.

Lizzie: OK, I'll try. But will you be back in school
by Thursday?

Edie: I wouldn't miss the school trip for
anything! XXX

Lizzie: XXX

A combination of the emotional strain and physical exertion had taken their toll. For fourteen hours straight Edie was immersed in a deep, dream-free sleep, interrupted eventually by a rhythmic banging sound. As if pulling herself out of a vat of treacle, Edie gradually surfaced to the noise of someone knocking on her bedroom door. Not gentle, just-checking-on-you style knocking, nor in-two-seconds-I'm-coming-in angry knocking, but somewhere in-between.

'It's me, Dad. I need to come in.'

'Okay. I've just woken up!'

The door opened abruptly and Dad moved quickly into the room, looking taller than usual and not particularly happy. Cursorily, he checked on his daughter's wellbeing: 'How are you feeling today, luv?'

'Fine. All right. I've just woken up, though. What's up, Dad? You seem upset. And how come you're not at work?'

'I've taken the day off to be with you,' Dad paused. 'Martial wasn't happy about it at all.'

Edie was about to say something but Dad, still upright, had more on his mind: 'Edie, I've just got off the phone to a doctor from Public Health England, Dr Montgomery, who says he's been trying to contact you for days … got your number from a boy called Ethan … that he needs to speak to you urgently and that you haven't returned any of his messages on your mobile.'

Edie's heart sank and she felt the blood drain from her cheeks.

'Oh that, yeah. I was going to call him back but forgot,' she answered unconvincingly.

Visibly annoyed, Dad pressed further: 'Dr Montgomery said it was important … that he'd had to get the police to track your mobile to the owner's address … to here … and then get BT to give them our landline number.'

A more remorseful and defensive tack was needed, so Edie softened her tone: 'I'm sorry, Dad. Really sorry. I hope I didn't get you into trouble.'

It worked, as her dad sighed audibly and his anger came down a notch. He took a few steps across the room and sat on the edge of the bed.

'No, I'm not in any trouble, sweetie, but I'm worried about you. You seem not quite yourself – and then there's been the break-in. And now this public health thing.' He took Edie's hand from underneath the duvet: 'I'm worried, lovely. Is everything okay?'

Edie waited and then placed her left hand on top of her dad's: 'Yes, everything's fine, Dad,' she managed to reply.

'You would tell me if something was wrong? Something important?'

'Of course I would, Dad,' she said and tried to draw her father in close, but he wasn't quite ready.

'If any of these things were connected, for instance?'

Momentarily lost for words, Edie pulled her father towards her again, and this time he didn't resist. But just before the embrace, their eyes met and they both knew that there was more to this story than was being told. After the hug, he didn't press further: not being pushy (or even nosey) had always been part of Dad's personality and had enabled Edie to get on with her investigations unhindered. So far, at least.

Edie decided to change the subject. 'Dad, you know that book you were reading ...'

'Which one?' Dad said, sounding surprised.

'The one in the surgery that I knocked onto the floor – the one you said was helping you ...'

'Oh, yes. *The Inside-Out Revolution* by Michael Neill.'

'Yeah,' said Edie. 'That one. Well, I was wondering ... in what ways do you think it's been helping you?'

Dad paused, then enquired gently, 'What makes you ask, sweetie?'

'I dunno,' Edie responded. 'It's just that I've been

thinking quite a bit recently about Mum's Three Principles psychological stuff and the conversations we had together about it ... when she was alive.' Edie paused to catch herself before continuing: 'I didn't pay much attention then ... but now ... now it feels more real, more relevant.'

'I agree, sweetie,' Dad added sensitively. 'At least you listened back then ... and discussed it. I didn't give it any consideration at all! But now ... well, the book's been helping me to understand the connection between my thoughts and my feelings ... So, when I'm feeling low or down about things, I recognise that it's just my thoughts creating those feelings ... my thoughts are responsible for my low mood.'

Edie looked on with real interest, so her dad continued: 'And I know those thoughts will pass, so I try not to take my thoughts too seriously. Sometimes it works and sometimes ...' Dad smiled and shrugged his shoulders.

'Thanks, Dad. I'm glad it's helping,' Edie affirmed. 'That's good to know.'

After a short silence, Dad added, 'About what we were talking about just before. You'll call Dr Montgomery back later today?'

'Yes, I will, Dad. I have his number.' Edie waited a few seconds then quizzed: 'Did he tell you what it was about?'

'A little. Something to do with a possible disease outbreak and they were tracing the contacts of a woman in Mill Hill who's unwell.' Dad stood up, took a pace towards the bedroom door then turned around with a frown: 'Although I don't know what connection you'd have with a woman in Mill Hill.'

Ninety minutes later and Edie was back on her bed, rejuvenated. After a long hot shower she'd had a smoked turkey sandwich for lunch, then thoroughly cleaned out Günther's cage. Seeing her pet's home tidied with fresh hay and a full bowl of food always made Edie feel good. Before she placed the guinea pig back inside, Edie held her neglected furry friend on her lap and fed him cut-up carrots and broccoli – his favourites.

Edie washed her hands, marched upstairs, closed her bedroom door and, seated at her desk, dialled the number left on her voicemail.

'Hello.'

'Oh, hi. Is that Dr Montgomery?'

'Yes. Can I ask who's speaking?'

'This is Edie Franklin. You left messages on my voicemail. Sorry it's taken so long to get back.'

'Oh, good. Hi. Just give me a moment so I can get somewhere quieter.'

Background chatter softened then stopped. 'Okay, I'm in a private room now. Thanks for calling back. Did your father mention why I've been trying to speak to you?'

'Just a little,' Edie said tentatively.

'All right. I need to check a few details with you first.'

'Okay.'

'Your name is Edie Franklin.' The doctor paused as if writing something. 'Your address?'

Over the next couple of minutes Edie provided her

home details, date of birth, phone numbers, next of kin and other personal information for Dr Montgomery's form. Eventually he moved on: 'And is your father in the room with you now?'

'No, I'm on my own, in my bedroom.'

'Fine. Your father has already told me he was happy for you to talk to me alone. He said you're very sensible and he trusted you.' The comment warmed Edie.

'Right, let me get to the point,' stated the doctor, suddenly keen to crack on. 'I'm a consultant in public health medicine and I work at Public Health England.'

Edie's mind began to whirr with interest. 'Sorry, Dr Montgomery, but I don't really know what that means. What is public health, actually?' she asked politely.

'No problem. Public health is about the health of the population, the community, and we deal with things like outbreaks of diseases. Infectious diseases.'

'Outbreaks?' Edie quizzed. 'Like Ebola?'

'Well, yes, Ebola would be an extreme example. But we deal with an outbreak of any kind of contagious disease – from head lice to meningitis or, a few years ago, swine flu.'

'Right, swine flu,' Edie piped in.

The doctor carried on. 'About three weeks ago, a British man died suddenly in Italy, despite being fairly fit and well previously. He was on holiday with his wife who found him—'

'That's very sad,' Edie interrupted inappropriately. 'But I'm not sure what this has got to do with me.'

'This is serious, Edie,' emphasised the undeterred

doctor. 'The woman found her husband in a pool of blood.'
He waited, but Edie remained silent.

'Does anything so far sound familiar, Edie?' enquired
the doctor.

'I'm not sure what you mean,' Edie blanked.

'Well, I'll get to the point then.' He pressed on: 'At first,
the Italian authorities believed the death was probably due to
something called a pulmonary embolism. The man had been
climbing a mountain the day before and it seemed consistent.
But at the post-mortem – and I'm sorry if this sounds a bit
gory – his lungs were found to be full of infection.'

Information whirled around in Edie's mind. 'That's
horrible, Dr Montgomery, but I still don't understand what
this has to do with me.'

'Let me help. Do you recognise the name Dr Thomas
Stephenson?'

'That sounds a little familiar,' Edie admitted nervously.

'Edie, I believe you visited the Stephensons' house in
Mill Hill last week,' the doctor said.

The silence that followed was as good as an admission
of guilt.

'It's important that you answer my questions honestly.
You see, although we're still waiting for the final test results,
we believe that the infection that killed Dr Stephenson was
caused by a dangerous virus.'

'What kind of virus?' Edie asked, diverting the
accusation.

'Well, we're not sure yet,' answered the public
health physician. 'But it could well be a new form of the

influenza virus.'

'Influenza,' said Edie sharply. 'You mean the flu? But that's not dangerous.'

'It can be very dangerous,' corrected the doctor. 'The Spanish flu after the First World War killed more people than the war itself. And also caused people's lungs to bleed.'

'Like Thomas Stephenson?' prompted Edie.

'Possibly,' said the doctor. 'What's important is that the virus, if it is indeed a virus, appears to be contagious. Mrs Stephenson is now in intensive care at the Royal Free Hospital.'

Edie became acutely concerned. 'She didn't seem well when I saw her,' she admitted. 'She was coughing all the time.'

'There's more,' said Dr Montgomery seriously. 'In Italy, one hotel worker from where the Stephensons were staying has already died with similar lung problems … and two others are fighting for their lives. The Italian medical authorities are tracing all other contacts of Dr Stephenson and we're doing the same here.'

'But I never even saw Dr Stephenson.'

'But you met his wife, didn't you?'

'Yes, I did,' Edie agreed. 'How's Ethan?' she asked, worried. 'I mean, Mrs Stephenson's son.'

'He seems fine at the moment but we're monitoring him carefully. But how are you, Edie? We're tracking all the people Mrs Stephenson has been in contact with since she started feeling unwell – and you are one of those contacts.'

'I'm fine,' Edie replied. 'Just been tired.'

'Since you saw Mrs Stephenson have you felt hot or had a fever?'

'No.'

'Sore throat?'

'No.'

'Runny nose?'

'No.'

'Any coughing?'

'No. Well, I have asthma so I always cough a little.'

'Have you had to use your inhaler more than usual?'

'I've been fine,' Edie answered again robustly. She was conscious that the crime-solving would be over if she did become unwell and that she had to be in school for Thursday.

Dr Montgomery waited a moment before adding, 'I understand from your dad that the house has been burgled recently and you've had some difficulty at school, which was why we couldn't speak yesterday.'

Cornered, Edie felt attack might be the best form of defence. 'Why are you questioning me like this?' she shot back. 'I mean, you're not the police, you're just a doctor!'

'Okay,' he conceded. 'It's just that I'm concerned about your wellbeing.'

The doctor took a breath. 'The important thing is that I want you to be very careful about your health over the next few days. You need to take your temperature three times a day and if you have any symptoms of illness – cough, cold, sore throat, bad tummy or, of course, fever – you must stay at home and contact me. Your dad has all the numbers. We'll be sending you a temperature chart and symptom diary by email – and a colleague of mine, a public health nurse called Vicky, will be following up with you by phone in a couple of days. Is that all clear?'

'Yes, very clear,' but Edie had only one thing on her mind. 'So, can I go to school?'

'You need to take a second day off school, Edie,' came the precautionary response. 'Both for monitoring and for your own recuperation. After that you can return to school, but only provided you stay symptom-free throughout.'

'Thank you,' said Edie, relieved. 'Is there anything else?'

Composing himself, the doctor had one further question. 'Oh yes, I meant to ask: what exactly *were* you doing at Dr Stephenson's house?'

'At the Stephensons' house?' Edie repeated.

'Yes, in Mill Hill.'

'School project,' Edie stated. 'On drug companies … and the drugs they make. I read about Creation on the internet and about Dr Stephenson's work.'

'A school project,' Dr Montgomery reflected back, unconvinced.

CHAPTER 12

SCHOOL TRIP

Amazingly, Edie's plan had worked.

Lizzie reminded Miss Watson how upset the class were to miss the school trip (a bit of an exaggeration), informed her about Creation Pharmaceuticals and let the schoolteacher do the rest. In turn, Miss Watson spoke on the phone to Creation's director of communications, Liz Burrows, who said that they would be delighted to host a visit from Highgate Hill School this Thursday. As Miss Watson was unable to accompany the children, their maths teacher, Mr Bowling, was assigned to lead the reinstated trip instead.

Liz Burrows didn't bother to discuss the proposition with her boss, chief executive Peter Goswell, as the policy of public engagement had already been agreed by the board. Creation was determined to reach out to the community, especially younger children, to encourage careers in science and medicine, and school visits were a key component. Mr Bowling was more dubious about Creation's motives but the opportunity gave him a welcome break from the classroom.

Edie spent a second day at home, although it felt more like isolation than recuperation. With no symptoms of illness and her regularly taken temperature always normal, Edie felt fine – as did Eli, who'd gone to school. Although the public health nurse, Vicky, hadn't yet called, Edie diligently completed the charts sent through by email, not least because she didn't want the cautious Dr Montgomery causing any trouble.

As Dad was at the surgery, Edie was alone for most of the day. Mama and Papa phoned twice to check on her and even visited briefly, but Mama's famous home-baked apple pie was left on the doorstep as her grandparents preferred not to enter the house. Left to her own devices, Edie turned swiftly to trying to solve the final clue. Gone was Edie's amusement about her mum's Word Art skills, however. It was replaced by mounting frustration – bordering on fury – over her own inability to finish the puzzle.

The following day, amidst the clamour of excitement associated with a school outing, forty-six Highgate Hill schoolchildren boarded the Greenways coach parked next to the ornate, nineteenth-century metal school gates at the top of Hampstead Lane.

'I feel sick,' Lizzie said as she settled into her aisle seat, two rows from the back. 'My dad made me eat breakfast.'

From the adjacent window seat, Edie turned her gaze away from the cars negotiating the mini-roundabout.

'Sorry about that, Lizzie. Do you want some water?'

'No, I'll be fine. I just don't like starting the day so early.'

Jittery, Edie looked at her watch. It was ten to eight and they'd been told to arrive by half past seven as the bus would leave at quarter to eight. But the children were still boarding – seemingly oblivious to the instructions.

'Looking forward to the outing, girls?' asked Mr Bowling, prowling down the aisle. He paused at the row in front. Don't sit near me, don't sit near me, Edie thought.

'Yes, Mr Bowling,' Lizzie replied agreeably. 'Should be interesting.'

'Good idea of yours, Lizzie, visiting Creation. They were apparently very welcoming on the phone. Well done.'

'Thank you, Sir.'

'And how are you today, Edie? It's good to have you back.'

Before the teacher had a chance to claim a seat, Allegra and Ella brushed past and claimed the row in front of Edie and Lizzie. They looked odd together: Allegra with her mop of curly black hair and Ella with her straight strawberry blonde hair. Neither of them, though, was to be completely trusted. With Mr Bowling distracted, Allegra spun around and peered over the top of the headrest.

'Are you feeling okay, Edie?' she asked.

Edie nodded reluctantly. She knew there would be more to come.

'It's just we heard you'd been unwell ... and got into an argument with some visitor after school.'

Edie looked out of the coach window nonchalantly.

Failing to get the hint, Allegra continued: 'Is that right?'

Outside, a speeding silver Range Rover almost hit a two-seater Smart car on the mini-roundabout, the smaller vehicle's irate horn oddly high-pitched. Edie turned towards the questioner.

'I'm absolutely fine,' she said sternly.

'Okay, Edie,' Ella chipped in defensively. 'She was only asking. You've been behaving really odd recently anyway.'

Edie was about to respond but Lizzie prodded her in the ribs. 'Ow!' Edie exclaimed. In front, the two girls had twisted around, their interest elsewhere. 'What was that for?'

Leaning in, Lizzie whispered, 'They're not worth it.'

The journey allowed the girls to go over their plans once again, fine-tuning their phone discussions of the previous evening. To Edie, this day felt like a real test of her abilities as a sleuth. The plot that Edie had concocted involved evasion, going undercover and being prepared for various eventualities. All with the intention of finding a missing link.

Almost two hours after departure, the coach came to a stop at a guardhouse in front of double barrier gates on a private access road in the Cambridgeshire countryside. To the left and right of the first barrier was high metal fencing which, as far as the eye could see, surrounded the whole giant complex beyond. Regularly placed yellow and black signs indicated, with the familiar zigzag image of a lightning bolt, that it was an electric fence. From the grass verge to the left of the guardhouse an enormous sign protruded from the ground. It had been changed a year ago, when the chief executive had dreamt up a new catchphrase for the organisation:

CREATION PHARMACEUTICALS
Proud to be saving lives

Inside the vehicle, Edie reached into her rucksack for a water bottle to help with her dry mouth.

'Are you all right?' Lizzie asked.

'Yes,' Edie replied, and then thought again: 'A bit nervous, maybe. It's just that I feel this is the one chance I'll get ... and I'm not even sure what I'm hoping to find.'

'It'll be all right,' Lizzie reassured, uncertain what else to add.

'And you'll cover for me, if anyone notices?'

'Yes, I've already told you I will.'

From his tiny workspace, the guard pushed a button and the barrier rose. Shortly after, the automated steel bollards sunk slowly into the ground allowing the coach to progress. Once the coach was between the two sets of barrier gates, the first one closed behind it and the second one opened up in front.

About half a mile later, the coach rounded the final bend and brought the school party to the car park by the main entrance. Glass and steel glimmered coldly in the damp winter sunshine, and Edie was taken aback by the size of the complex.

'It's so new,' she said to Lizzie as the coach stopped and Mr Bowling asked the children to disembark. 'And so big.'

Lizzie leant over her friend to glance through the back window. 'And in the middle of nowhere,' she commented. 'There's just fields all around.'

'Apart from the electric fence,' Edie observed.

The group gathered next to the coach as Mr Bowling – accompanied by the young new French teacher, Miss Danes

– checked inside the vehicle for any left-behind items.

'It looks like everyone drives here,' said Edie, looking at the lines of cars that filled parking bays stretching out for hundreds of metres.

'You can't get here any other way, I guess,' remarked Lizzie. 'Not good for exercise.'

'Unless you're parked way over there,' Edie pointed. 'And then you've got to walk all the way over here to get in.'

Lizzie turned her attention to the area of the parking lot right next to the main entrance, covered with a fancy blue and white striped canopy. 'I'd prefer one of these spaces,' she said, indicating the half a dozen or so parking bays just thirty metres from where the girls were standing. 'And I'd like one of those,' Lizzie continued, her gaze fixed on a luxurious, shiny black Bentley with tinted windows.

'It's a cool car,' commented Edie. 'Could be in a James Bond film,' she added, but her stomach was beginning to twist.

'Not the car, silly,' Lizzie chipped in. 'One of those,' she repeated. 'The guy next to the car.'

Edie had clocked the chauffeur already, but she was more struck by a sign on the wall above the swish car indicating to whom this particular bay was assigned. It read 'Chief Executive Officer'.

At that very moment, a tall, lean, dark-haired man, impeccably dressed in a grey suit with an unbuttoned navy-blue overcoat and brown scarf, came striding purposefully out of the front entrance doors. The capped and uniformed chauffeur hurriedly opened the driver's door, sat behind the

Bentley's leather steering wheel and inserted the keys, ready to follow his boss's orders.

As the chief executive reached the car he stopped abruptly, put on a pair of sunglasses from his inside pocket, then turned to examine the source of the commotion from the coach parking bay. Another bloody school party, he thought, scanning the jabbering children.

Edie couldn't take her eyes off him. Then, in an instant, the chief executive spun around, banged twice on the roof of the car with his gloved hand, got into the back seat and off the car sped.

'Ouch,' said Lizzie, but Edie was unaware that she'd grabbed her friend's arm and was squeezing it tight to keep herself steady.

Once inside the huge super-modern building, each pupil had to sign in and be issued with a named visitor's pass. As planned, Edie immediately gave hers to Lizzie. Next, the children gathered in the atrium where they were greeted by the company's director of communications. Liz Burrows clapped her hands loudly to bring her troops to attention.

'Welcome to Creation,' she announced. 'We're delighted to have you all here today, and hope that you will have an enjoyable and educational experience. Now, before we get going, a few pieces of "housekeeping".'

'I hate it when people do that quotation mark thing with their fingers,' Edie whispered from the back of the throng. 'It looks really stupid.'

Lizzie was about to agree but was interrupted by Miss Danes: 'Shush, girls. This could be important.'

Speaking in a preachy tone, the director of communications continued: 'Through the morning we'll be doing a tour of the building, including our labs, our clinical suite where we do new drug trials and our animal facilities – yes, I'm afraid we do undertake tests on animals, so those who wish to skip that bit can stay outside. Then we'll have lunch in the cafeteria, take a quick look at the boardroom, before a question-and-answer session with our top scientists in the auditorium. I'll point out toilets on the way. We're not expecting any fire drill tests today, so if the alarm goes off it's for real – just follow me or my deputy, who will be your guide for the day. Listen, learn and have fun.'

The director was about to finish but then remembered one final, crucial thing: 'Most important, please don't wander off. This is a secure facility with areas that are strictly out of bounds, so stick close and pay attention.' She clapped her hands together: 'Now, off we go!'

When the pupils reached the labs, the deputy director of communications, who'd taken over from her boss, split the large group into their two forms. Whilst Edie and Lizzie's form went into the labs first, the other form started with the clinical area.

'Come on, girls,' said Mr Bowling as he guided them from the back of the pack into a large room filled with workbenches, Bunsen burners, sinks, test tubes and numerous women and men in white lab coats. On the glass entrance door it read 'Product Testing'.

'It's just like TV,' said Lizzie quietly as the deputy director ran through a dull PowerPoint presentation about lab safety.

'We should get out of here,' yawned Lizzie.

'Not quite yet,' replied Edie.

Next, the group were led to another cordoned off laboratory area with a more interesting sign on the door: 'Research and Development'. Inside, a youngish woman – who introduced herself as the interim head of R&D, Lucy Fotheringham – gave a brief overview of how this team's task was to develop and test new ideas, after which she asked the class if they had any questions.

'How many ideas do you have that actually become products – I mean, things we buy?' asked the bookish, sweet-natured Benedict.

'That's a very good question,' Lucy responded. 'And not an easy one to answer. Pushed, I would say only about five per cent of what we test here ends up as either medicines that doctors prescribe or as other drugs you can buy at a pharmacy.'

'That's tiny,' Benedict commented.

Lucy countered immediately: 'It is, but when we get it right, it's big bucks.' She paused and was about to wrap up when a female voice chipped in from the back.

'Do you ever do any research work outside this country?'

Initially, Lucy treated Edie's question dismissively: 'Not really. Our scientific research is primarily done here.'

'What about Vietnam?' Edie continued, wary of the risk she was taking.

Now Lucy Fotheringham was becoming more wary. 'As I said, we don't really do any research out of the UK,' she added firmly.

'Didn't Dr Stephenson, Thomas Stephenson, do some research in Vietnam? I read something about it on the internet.'

'I'm not sure why you're bringing this up,' Lucy retaliated. 'Dr Stephenson died recently – a tragedy – and we need to respect him.' Brusquely, Lucy marshalled the children out through the doors of the R&D lab: 'Now, let's move on.'

'What was all that about, Edie?' Mr Bowling asked sternly once they were in the corridor.

'Oh, nothing, Sir,' Edie answered coyly. 'I'm just really interested in this subject and wanted to know more about how it all works.'

'Well, behave yourself.'

Over lunch, Edie and Lizzie talked privately in the far corner of the large canteen. When Liz Burrows announced that it was time to reconvene for the question-and-answer session in the lecture theatre, Edie slipped innocuously into the lavatories located directly behind their seats. Lizzie loitered briefly in the canteen to ensure her friend's absence wasn't noticed, then joined the others in the auditorium. Sitting in a comfortable cinema-style seat in the back row, she texted Edie.

Lizzie: All safe, just arrived in lecture room.

Edie: Thanks. Wish me luck! XXX

After waiting a further ten minutes, Edie quietly opened the toilet door and peered outside. Not a classmate in sight, but a few members of Creation staff were grabbing a late lunch. A short while later and the coast was almost clear, except for one woman paying for a pot of salad and a coffee. From the cash register at the far end of the room Edie could just make out the conversation.

'Good afternoon, Margaret. A little late today for lunch, aren't we?' asked the cashier.

Margaret leant over so she didn't have to speak too loudly: 'He's been in a strange mood today, Angie, so I had to wait till he left the office, then sort out everything in his room for the afternoon. That's why I'm so behind!'

'Oh dear,' Angie replied as she punched in the price of the food items. 'That'll be three pounds and—'

'I don't know what's wrong but he hasn't been himself at all recently,' Margaret continued. 'Maybe something's going on at home – I know his daughter's not been well.' Angie stopped what she was doing and listened to Margaret. 'He's become so impatient, gets angry in a beat. I've heard him shouting at his wife on the phone. It started, I think, after Tom died but it's got worse.'

As Margaret paused, Angie intervened: 'I'm sorry to hear that, Margaret. That's three pounds sixty, please.'

'And all these secret calls he's been making ...'

Margaret paused and took her purse out of her

handbag: I'm sorry, Angie, rambling on like this ... Here you go.'

It was now or never, Edie realised, so she slipped out of the WC, made a sharp left through the canteen exit and into the atrium on the south side of the building. Having concentrated hard on the layout of the building during the morning tour, Edie orientated herself quickly. The main corridor linking the two ends of the building, north and south, was out of bounds – just too busy. But Edie knew there were other, more concealed connecting routes.

Two important things crossed Edie's mind as she took her initial, uncertain steps across the pristine marbled floor. First, confidence. She needed to feel, and more importantly look, confident. Without that she'd be rumbled quickly. Second, Edie still didn't know exactly what she was looking for. But she had a hunch – no, more than just a hunch. Edie had faith, deep down, that she'd know what she was looking for when she saw it. A faith that, increasingly, Edie associated with her mum's Three Principles understanding of the world.

The good signage was helpful. Edie didn't want the Finance Department or the Human Resources Department, and dismissed Public Relations, Marketing and External Communications. Walking swiftly across the atrium, Edie eyed other silver signs fixed to the wall providing directions, one of which stood out: Scientific Research Laboratories.

Due to the post-lunch-hour time, very few staff were milling about, and after ten minutes of careful navigation, Edie reached the laboratories located near the centre of the complex, which she thought was where they'd been earlier –

but this looked different. Through a glass wall, Edie could see two researchers inside a large room, sporting long white lab coats and oversized goggles; one was carrying a pipette and test tube and the other was hunched over a wooden bench analysing a data sheet. Scientific equipment sat in various places: box-like machines with flashing lights.

Edie knew entry into the lab was out of the question, so she moved towards the more promising door marked Research Administration, where she was confronted unexpectedly.

'Can I help you?' asked a young woman, whom Edie recognised from earlier in the day.

Surprised, Edie floundered before dredging up the answer she'd prepared with Lizzie: 'I've lost my coat and think I might've left it in here,' Edie responded meekly.

'Well,' answered the woman quickly, whose name tag identified her as Sharon Johns. 'Nothing's been handed in and you shouldn't be walking alone around here anyway.' Sharon frowned then briefly inspected her surroundings as if to check for onlookers. 'Hey, aren't you the girl who asked that question earlier about Dr Stephenson?' she quizzed.

Cornered, Edie felt she had no option: 'Yes, I did.'

Suddenly, and unexpectedly, Sharon ushered Edie along the corridor and into a small empty office. Inside, Sharon headed to a desk in the corner, took a key from her pocket, unlocked a drawer and removed a small, stapled set of papers.

'Listen,' she whispered anxiously. 'I'm a college graduate and I've been here less than a year ... working for Lucy and ...

for Tom too, before he died. He was so nice but something funny's going on.' Sharon appeared worried and was about to hand the papers over. 'They cleared out all of Tom's scientific research immediately after he died. His lab work, papers, everything. I was told not to talk about anything to do with Tom with anyone. His secretary, Phoebe, was paid off … well, fired, really … and I was told I'd lose my job if I spoke to anyone about Tom.'

'So, why are you giving these to me?' asked Edie. 'And what are they?'

'I don't know,' Sharon replied abruptly. 'But Phoebe gave them to me just before she left – said Tom had given them to her to keep safely "in case anything happened". Tom was scared … Phoebe was scared … and I'm scared. I think the papers are to do with Vietnam, which none of us are supposed to know much about …'

Edie was about to ask another question but Sharon finished the conversation: 'I sense you're onto something, so please take them. Now go. And we never spoke.' And with that Sharon led Edie out of the door, checked the corridor was clear and pointed the schoolgirl in the direction of the main lobby.

Edie set off but soon found herself confused. After taking random turnings, her head spinning, she ducked into the women's loos and locked herself in a cubicle.

Sitting on the toilet seat, Edie took several deep, slow breaths then pulled out her iPhone and texted Lizzie.

I have something.

Seconds later came Lizzie's reply:

Lizzie: Good, come back now as the talk's
finished and we're leaving soon!
Edie: On way. Don't leave without me!

Edie composed herself, hid the papers in a concealed pocket in the base of her bag and opened the cubicle door. At the sink, she stuck her hands under the tap and splashed water over her face. Come on, Edie urged herself: Mum wouldn't waver now and neither can you. Carefully, Edie opened the main door and peered outside. Not a soul in sight, but she was disorientated. Looking to the left and right, Edie was unsure which way to go when, above impressive wooden double doors twenty metres directly ahead of her, Edie noticed a sign saying Corporate Headquarters.

Fuelled by a sensation deep inside that her mother was guiding her, Edie inched towards the sign – her destiny – like a moth to a flame. After what felt like an eternity, she reached the doors.

In the canteen, down one flight of stairs in the opposite wing, Margaret finished her last mouthful of salad, placed her knife and fork tidily on the plate and stood up. After putting her book back in her handbag, she walked over to the collection area in the corner and carefully deposited the plastic salad container in the large recycling bin and stacked her tray on the trolley.

'How was it today?' Angie asked, leaning over from the cash register.

'Perfect, thank you. See you tomorrow.' Margaret smiled and headed back towards the office where she spent so many hours of her life.

A gentle push revealed that the entrance to Corporate Headquarters was locked, something that didn't surprise Edie as she'd already noticed the magnetic card-activated strips to the right of the doors, similar to those they had at school. Inside her jacket pocket the iPhone, turned to silent, vibrated.

Lizzie: Come now! Have handed in your badge
      so they think we've all left the building.
      About to get on coach.

Biting the skin on the side of her left thumbnail, Edie was reluctantly about to turn on her heels when the doors burst open towards her.

'Oh!' exclaimed a smartly dressed woman. The name tag card on her lanyard identified her as the deputy director of finance. 'And who might you be?' she asked.

Calmly, Edie responded as planned: 'I'm the boss's daughter.'

Frowning, the female executive questioned: 'Who? Do you mean Peter's?'

'Yes,' Edie agreed clumsily, then defended her lie: 'Dad.

I mean Peter. Peter Goswell, the chief executive. I went for a walk around.'

'My ... you've grown,' replied the woman uncertainly. 'Well, you'd better go in then. He's down the corridor on the left ... Margaret will help.' And with that, Edie was in, just as the aforementioned secretary was waiting for the lift to bring her back up.

With her mind focused and eyes alert, Edie set off down the corridor, acutely aware that at any point she could be exposed. Edie walked past the first door – open and labelled Director of Finance – unnoticed by a secretary busy at her computer inside. To the right, Edie passed the closed office doors of the Director of Human Resources and Director of Communications. Next, on the left, was the wide-open door to the Medical Director's office, where Edie faltered. A pretty woman in her twenties in a black pencil-skirt and crisp white shirt was pouring coffee. Their eyes met. Instinctively, Edie spoke first to minimise suspicion.

'Is my Dad's office next along – Peter Goswell, the chief executive?' she asked with a forced smile.

'Oh, hello luv,' the medical director's assistant replied perkily. 'Yes, next door on the left.'

Onward Edie walked and was about to arrive at the CEO's door when she noticed two frames hanging on the wall. Edie leant in to look at the first – a set of passport-like photographs of various people mounted on a black background. Bold white letters at the top described the group as the Senior Executive Team; the image at the apex was Peter Goswell. Edie stared intently at his eyes, drawn by their calculating and callous intensity. The rest of the faces and job titles underneath were unassuming, although Edie clocked that Dr Stephenson had already been removed.

Edie moved to the next frame, the Creation Board, and took in the inconspicuous looking chairman, a similarly nondescript vice chairman and worked her way around the ten bland faces labelled non-executive directors. At the penultimate photo, Edie took a sharp intake of breath and gasped audibly. It was an old photo that must have been taken years ago, but her anger was confirmed by the name underneath. Through pursed lips Edie exclaimed: 'You …!'

Face ablaze with rage, Edie stood motionless until she was jolted by her phone vibrating again with another text.

COME NOW! WE'RE ABOUT TO LEAVE!

Not quite yet, Edie thought, as she moved with resolve down the quiet corridor to the last port of call. Outside the next doorway a sign left nobody in doubt: Office of the Chief Executive. With her back to the wall, as if she were a secret service agent, Edie peered cautiously around the open door. Inside, she saw a modern office suite with a small beige sofa, two leather armchairs, glass tables with neatly stacked magazines and a water dispenser. To the right was a smart, dark oak desk, perfectly tidy, with a silver tabletop sign indicating that it was the workspace of Margaret Gardiner – Personal Assistant to the Chief Executive – the woman Edie had seen at lunch, but who was now absent from her station. Directly opposite Edie was a further door, closed, with an embossed gold plaque informing visitors clearly that this was Peter Goswell's private domain and Margaret was the guardian of that space.

Edie's quick glance to the left and right revealed that nobody was around, allowing her to tentatively step inside. Silently, she crept over the varnished wooden flooring onto the safety of a deep pile maroon rug. Edie stroked the pristine glass coffee table, for no particular reason, before proceeding to Goswell's door. Certain she'd seen him leaving the premises earlier, Edie was still anxious at the prospect of what lay behind the door. Was it fear of being caught? No. Fear of meeting her mother's nemesis face to face? No. Fear that maybe the evidence she needed wasn't there? Maybe.

With the tips of the fingers of her right hand Edie pushed the door, but it didn't budge. More firmly, she pressed with her whole hand, but the solid door failed to yield an inch. Undeterred, Edie turned the polished brass doorknob anticlockwise, but the door was securely locked.

Frustrated, Edie turned around and examined the immaculate office suite. She had a sudden desire to damage the gleaming, modern furniture. A black marker pen across the sofa or scratch marks on the glass tabletop. But voices from the corridor – two women talking openly about their lunch – distracted Edie and the inclination faded.

Dispirited, Edie was about to leave, but her eyes – for some reason – settled on Margaret's desk. Undeterred by the talking outside, Edie walked quickly over. She scanned the desktop for documents but saw only regular office equipment and neatly placed stationery: computer screen, keyboard, printer, stapler, sticky tape, paper clips, hole-punch.

'Doing anything nice tonight, Margaret?' asked a barely audible female voice from down the corridor.

'I might go out with Henry for a bite locally, then watch *The Crown* on Netflix.'

'Ooh, sounds like a good evening.'

'What about you, Helen?'

Focus, thought Edie. Focus. If they catch you now it doesn't matter, but this could be your last chance. The drawers: two sets of three plus a longer central drawer. Edie tried the large one first but it was locked, then the three to the left of it, but all were similarly impenetrable. Edie scanned the desktop for a key but none was visible.

With nothing to lose, Edie tried the other set of three, from the bottom up. The first two were shut tight but, to her amazement, the top drawer opened immediately with a gentle swish. Inside sat one item: an old iPhone 6, looking small in comparison with newer models. Edie lifted it out: a sticky label on the back revealed what she needed: 'PG – private'. Edie quickly pocketed the phone, closed the drawer and made straight for the door.

Edie peeked out into the corridor, where the two women were still gossiping about ten metres to the left. Calmly, Edie walked out of the office to the right, away from them and towards the set of electric doors. Please, please let there be an exit button, like at school, Edie thought. Every step seemed to take an eternity, but as she neared Edie spied the green button on the wall next to the double doors. She reached down to press it but was startled by a shout from behind her.

'You there! Can I help you?'

Edie stopped and slowly turned around.

'No thanks, I'm fine. I'm with the school party. Got a little lost.'

'Well, you shouldn't be here,' continued the younger of the two women. 'This is a private area.' Taking a step forwards, the woman beckoned: 'Come over here and I'll escort you back to your group.'

'Oh, it's okay,' said Edie and immediately pushed the button. The doors slowly opened towards her and she squeezed herself through whilst calling over her shoulder, 'I'm fine, I know my way back.'

Nimbly, Edie made her way forwards, turned left around a corner until she was out of sight, then pelted in the signposted direction of the lifts. As she approached the lifts, Edie skidded to a halt by the nearby loos, which she entered tentatively. Inside, Edie was relieved to be alone and went straight into a cubicle and locked the door. An idea had come to Edie earlier out of nowhere, or seemingly nowhere, which she felt compelled to follow. In a flash, she removed her right earring and got to work. The task took less than a minute and, once completed, Edie smiled to herself. But this was no time to loiter, and Edie was quickly out of the cubicle and exiting the toilets.

Not bothering to check if she was being followed, Edie made for the doors adjacent to the lifts marked emergency stairs. The elevator was too slow and risky, but with her mind all over the place, Edie took too many flights down and ended up in the basement area. Breathless and disorientated, she doubled back up to ground level, where she burst out of the stairwell and bumped into a member of staff.

'I'm so sorry,' Edie exclaimed. 'Which way is the main entrance, I mean exit. My school coach is there.' A bemused looking young man pointed her in the right direction. And Edie ran as fast as she could.

At the same time, it was dawning on Margaret that something was wrong, she just wasn't sure what. Had the youngster come out of her office suite? Had she remembered to lock Peter's office door?

'Excuse me, Helen,' Margaret interjected and scuttled down the corridor towards the chief executive's domain. Methodically, she walked around her working space, taking in every aspect. At first everything seemed perfectly normal: chairs and sofa were fine, magazines in order and she breathed a sigh of relief when she confirmed that Peter's private office was closed and locked. But her own desk didn't look normal. Something seemed out of place.

Adrenaline fuelled, Edie had finally reached the main lobby. Meanwhile, Margaret checked each drawer in turn, her own pulse beginning to rise with anxiety. Margaret suddenly doubted if, earlier in the day, she'd remembered to lock the drawer when she stored her boss's treasured phone. Margaret gently pulled out the drawer. It opened, and the iPhone was missing.

Panicked, Margaret started shaking, beads of sweat breaking out on her forehead. She didn't know what to do: ring Peter or call through to the security guard? Her boss would want to know immediately, she decided, so she called him.

'Hello, Margaret. What is it?' her boss asked.

Nervously, Margaret struggled to get the words out: 'It's your phone, Peter, your special phone.' She waited.

'What about it?'

Margaret was so troubled she could barely speak.

'It's gone. Stolen from my drawer, Peter.' On edge, Margaret added her suspicion: 'I think by a schoolgirl on today's tour.'

Silence.

Complete silence.

CHAPTER 13

KIDNAPPED

Edie's lungs were bursting as she reached the atrium, where she steadied her pace to avoid looking suspicious. At the reception desk, a security guard, who'd just replaced a telephone handset, noticed Edie and shouted something in her direction – to which she paid no attention. Despite her breathing being laboured and wheezy, Edie had no time to use her inhaler as she pushed through the revolving doors. Outside, the cold air hit her throat hard.

And then the bombshell struck: the coach was nowhere to be seen. Unbeknownst to Edie, Mr Bowling hadn't bothered with another headcount as all the pupils' visitor's passes had been accounted for and safely returned. Lizzie clearly hadn't said anything – presumably to avoid getting into trouble – though trouble now looked inevitable, one way or another.

Edie had missed the ride back and was well and truly stuck. Anxiety surged through her body as she imagined the inevitable: in no time, Goswell's secretary would notice the missing iPhone and come running down – and Edie would be caught.

Think! Think! Edie urged herself, but she was beginning to feel light-headed from all the frenzied activity. Semi-consciously, Edie's hand went to her school bag and she pulled out the stolen phone, desperate not to be caught red-handed. A flower bed to the right was the obvious place to hide the mobile, but a glance over her shoulder revealed the security guard inside moving towards the revolving doors. Edie needed to act quickly so, reluctantly, she chucked the phone into a bushy part of the bed – a spot from where she could retrieve it at some point in the future. Looking up, Edie was pretty sure that the guard hadn't seen, but a new sight – directly ahead – filled her with dread.

From around the bend in the road, approaching Creation, appeared the black Bentley that had left the premises that morning. Inside the ominous vehicle Edie imagined her nemesis, smug on the leather seats.

'Excuse me. Are you okay?' shouted the guard from just a few metres away, having exited the building.

Edie turned to look at him, but then twisted sharply back when she realised the car wasn't turning left into the chief executive's covered parking spot but, instead, was heading straight for her.

'If you're with the school party, I'm afraid the coach has gone,' the guard continued, almost upon her now.

Sweat began to break out on Edie's forehead with the realisation of being cornered. The car was nearly upon her from one direction, as was the guard from behind. There was no escape. Suddenly the dizziness worsened and a black curtain descended. With legs of jelly, Edie crumpled to the floor.

Inside the Bentley, Peter Goswell couldn't believe what

he was seeing as the car approached the building's main entrance. Just a few minutes before, he'd taken Margaret's distraught call, her voice trembling as she'd conveyed that his personal phone was missing and her suspicions of the culprit. A minute later, Margaret had texted him – after checking with the front desk security guard – to let him know that the school coach had already left. Margaret had wanted to call the police but Peter had told her, calmly but firmly, not to do so. At that point, the information felt to Peter like the last straw: his own demise seemed nigh. Yet now this: the girl had come to him and everything was changed. It was as if God was on his side.

Goswell flung open the car door as Bill, the kindly security guard who'd worked at Creation for years, held Edie under her arms. He'd caught her as she'd fainted, so avoiding her head hitting the concrete.

'Well done, Bill!' Goswell exclaimed, certain of the identity of the troublesome teenager from the photo on her Facebook page.

'She missed the coach, Sir, I think. She was leaving the building in haste … looking worried … and must've fainted. If you hold her, Sir, I'll call an ambulance.'

'No need, Bill,' said Goswell quickly. 'She's one of Mary's friends from school. We'll drop her home in the Bentley.'

'But she's still out cold, Sir. Wouldn't it be better if I got a doctor?'

'I said I know who she is, Bill,' Goswell replied crisply, with no intention of negotiation. 'And I know where she lives. Thank you, but I'll take it from here.'

'As you wish, Sir.'

'Just help me lie her on the back seat,' Goswell commanded as he grabbed Edie's legs and the two of them awkwardly shifted her horizontally into the vehicle. The chauffeur, Jack, tried to assist but Goswell ordered him back into his front seat, and as soon as the doors were closed, barked at him to drive.

In the car, Goswell immediately pressed the button that brought up the darkened glass partition between the front and back seats. Jack's head moved a fraction to the left in recognition of the imposed separation, then returned to the road ahead. Jack was accustomed to unusual happenings but this was particularly strange.

Tapping his fingers agitatedly on the door armrest, Goswell calculated what to do. Was this a final opportunity to set things straight, to tidy up the murky affair and avoid the finality of what he'd figured out overnight? Or was he simply out of control – self-preservation at all costs? Grabbing Edie's school bag from the floor, Goswell rummaged through it. Nothing of interest to be found. Then Goswell saw the shape of a phone in an inside blazer pocket. He reached for it, but Edie suddenly stirred and, in that moment, Goswell lost sight of all the damage she'd caused him and was struck by how young Edie looked. He thought of his daughters and recoiled, just briefly, before snatching the phone from the insensible girl.

'Is everything all right, Sir?' Jack asked cautiously, alerted by Edie's soft grunt.

Goswell noticed the red light on the side panel which indicated that the rear intercom was on, enabling communication between him and the driver, even when the screen was up.

'Yes, fine,' Goswell responded abruptly. 'Just drive.'

'All right, Sir. But where to? The girl's home or Accident and Emerg—'

'Just bloody drive!' Goswell yelled. 'That's your job! I'll tell you where to in a minute.'

'Okay, Sir,' Jack acquiesced, but Goswell couldn't hear as he'd already turned off the intercom.

It was a good question, though. Where to? Goswell looked down at Edie's iPhone and pressed the central button, but the locked keypad required a code. He swore as he shoved the mobile into his coat pocket. Bewildered by the turn of events, Goswell texted his wife, Jane, to ask when she'd be back at the house. He waited impatiently, Edie's dirty shoes brushing against his trouser leg, but Jane responded quickly. The kids – with Mary now improving – both had afterschool activities, Jane reminded him, so they were all out until around six o'clock. Another three hours, at least.

Goswell turned the intercom back on so he could advise the chauffeur. The red light reappeared.

'Take me home, Jack,' he directed, just as Edie opened her eyes.

Instantly, Goswell switched the intercom off again and leant over Edie menacingly.

'Don't say a word,' Goswell insisted unnervingly through gritted teeth, his face just inches from the girl's.

Edie could smell the chief executive's breath and was terrified by the savagery in his voice and the feverish look in his eyes. Goswell raised a finger to his lips, then cupped his hand in front of Edie's mouth to show he would muzzle her if she disobeyed.

'Not a word!' he repeated.

Gradually, Edie began to regain her senses. She was lying on a sofa in what looked like a summer house – a glorified garden shed with exposed wooden beams which housed an office and lounge area. Through a large window she could see the main house about a hundred metres away and the extensive gardens within which her prison was situated. Across her chest, Edie's hands had been tightly bound together with thick, sticky tape and her mouth was covered with similar material. She tried to scream but her lips wouldn't open – all that came out was a low-level murmur.

'Nobody will hear you,' said a voice from behind, startling Edie.

'Mmmmm!' she attempted again from the back of her throat, as she tried unsuccessfully to twist around.

Goswell approached slowly and stared disdainfully at the troublemaker. Getting her into the building had proved easier than he'd anticipated. Goswell knew about fainting, having had episodes himself as a child. Remaining horizontal makes it easier for the heart to pump blood to your brain, enabling you to regain consciousness – but, if you got up too soon, the same thing would happen. Goswell had been worried that Edie would plead to Jack for help when they reached Goswell's home but, as it happened, she tried to sit up too rapidly when the car stopped and had promptly collapsed back onto the seat. With Edie still unconscious, Goswell ordered his driver back to Creation whilst the chief executive had carried the young girl into the summer house.

'Are you going to behave yourself?' Goswell asked patronisingly.

Edie's eyes darted around fitfully, taking in the space. She nodded.

'Are you sure?' he questioned. 'And I've taken your iPhone, in case you're wondering, and turned it off.'

This time Edie bobbed her head even more purposefully, so Goswell ripped the tape away from her mouth, causing Edie to grimace. He then sat in the armchair opposite and just watched. In turn, Edie studied the expression of the man she suspected of organising her mother's murder. It was strange to be so close to him, not as she'd imagined. In his eyes, Edie saw a combination of desperation and resignation.

'Where's my phone?' he asked.

There were so many questions Edie had planned to ask him, but now that the opportunity was upon her they seemed irrelevant. Pent-up fury was replaced with a kind of calm.

'What are you going to do with me?' Edie probed evasively.

'Just answer the question,' Goswell ordered. 'Where's my phone?'

'I don't know what phone you—'

'Don't play games with me!' Goswell exclaimed, his

face reddening. 'You know exactly what I mean. The iPhone from my office. From my secretary's drawer.'

In one corner of the room, beside the desk and next to her school bag, Edie spotted a length of thick rope on the floor. Her stomach tightened when she noticed that one end seemed to be arranged or tied into a circle. Was it a noose? Or was it a trick of the angle she was observing from?

'It's gone,' Edie replied, unsure of her tack.

'Gone where?' he responded immediately.

'My friend Lizzie's got it. I gave it to her.'

'That's not possible,' Goswell insisted, picking up something in Edie's eyes that suggested she was lying. He stood up. 'You were in my office minutes before you fainted. The school coach had already gone.' Goswell moved towards the sofa and raised his arm upright, showing that he was prepared to hurt Edie. 'So,' Goswell spat. 'I'll ask again. What did you do with my phone?'

'I gave it to Lizzie earlier, quite a bit earlier,' Edie lied more convincingly. 'Then went back again afterwards to look for more. Which is when your secretary saw me.'

Edie could see Goswell mentally going through the timings, working out whether she was telling the truth. In that moment, Edie's eyes strayed subconsciously to the hem of her jacket, an innocuous movement that was keenly noticed by her edgy kidnapper.

'Okay then … so *why* were you looking for my phone?' he questioned pointedly, realising that he needed to find out more.

Edie had to think quickly, and she knew there was no

space for any further slip-ups. She was alone, in the middle of nowhere, with a desperate man who could be capable of anything. 'I like to steal things,' Edie fibbed. 'In shops ... pens, chocolate, gum ... stuff from school ... sandwiches from Starbucks. It started after my mum died. I don't know why I do it but I don't seem to be able to stop.'

'Nonsense!' Goswell snarled. 'Don't take me for a fool! You think you've found something out ... about me ... about the company ... and you're searching around. You looked in my office deliberately.'

'No,' Edie replied instantly, hoping that calm certainty would help her cause. 'That's not true. I've been in trouble at school and with the police for my stealing – check if you like.' She paused for a moment before taking a calculated risk: 'Anyway, what exactly would I be looking for about you, or about Creation?' She knew it was a gamble, but putting the ball in Goswell's court offered Edie some time.

Goswell remained completely still, looking Edie straight in the eyes, a stare that seemed to go on forever. Although he was fairly sure that Edie had been trying to gather evidence against him for several weeks – the smartphone being just the latest piece – he couldn't admit to anything or give out any more information, and he certainly didn't want to raise suspicion further.

Goswell's uncertainty was her chance. Edie didn't need to mention anything about her detective work, not for the time being at least.

'Look,' Edie prompted confidently. 'The school will start looking for me soon when they realise I'm missing, and that security guard – and your chauffeur – saw you take me in your car. You don't want to get into trouble for kidnapping, and I *really* don't want to get into trouble for stealing the phone. The school said they'll expel me if there's another incident, and my dad will go mad. Please let me go and we'll just forget that any of this happened.'

Goswell brought over the desk chair and sat at the end of the sofa. For over a minute, he chewed silently over Edie's proposition, but ultimately wasn't convinced.

'No,' Goswell said finally. 'It doesn't add up. I know you visited the house of Dr Stephenson, and it was probably you who suggested the visit to Creation today. 'No,' he repeated, 'you know something – or think you know something – and you're not letting on. So, I've got an offer for you, young lady: tell me what you know and I'll let you go.'

Edie bristled at the 'young lady' phrase, which she hated, and was about to react when a mobile phone rang. Goswell rummaged around in response to the ringtone, then stood up and answered his phone. 'Yes, Margaret,' he said before reaching the window, at which point he went very quiet and just listened.

Margaret, though, had a very loud voice and Edie, with her excellent hearing (like a bat, as her dad said), could make out some of the words from a panicked woman's voice. It seemed that the coach had indeed returned to Creation, and Bill, the security guard, had explained to the teachers what had happened with Edie and the chief executive. It sounded like the school might have even called Edie's dad, but he was doing a surgery. There was something else that Margaret said, which Edie couldn't quite make out, which seemed to lighten Goswell's expression.

As the call ended, Goswell looked less troubled, although Edie was unsure whether that made him less dangerous or not. Edie felt that she had to act quickly, but she also needed to soften her approach: she needed to give in order to get.

'You're right,' Edie began, taking the initiative. 'I did find an old notebook of my mum's that had some scribbles about Creation and Dr Stephenson. But it didn't say much, and mainly I couldn't read mum's terrible handwriting. So, I went to talk to Dr Stephenson's wife to find out more, but she was grieving and exhausted and hardly able to talk. And, yes, I thought a school trip to Creation might help, but I didn't have any plans ... and just stumbled on your office when I got lost. It seems like the phone's important to you but I've no idea why.'

Edie noticed how intently Goswell was listening, so she paused deliberately for effect.

'Listen, I don't think we've got long so you've just got to trust me. I'll call my friend Lizzie from your phone and you can watch. I'll ask her to tell the schoolteachers on the coach that I'm fine ... that my phone died ... that I'm with you, the helpful chief executive, and that you've kindly offered to take me home. I'll talk to the teachers if they want. That way, neither of us gets into any trouble and – I promise – that'll be the end of it.'

It didn't take Goswell long to agree, although for the wrong reason (from Edie's perspective).

'You're a lucky girl,' he announced with a slight smirk. 'That was my secretary, Margaret. It appears that my iPhone has been found ... by the security guard. Apparently, he ... Bill ... noticed you behaving strangely outside the main entrance before he caught you as you fainted. Later, he went back out there with Margaret ... they searched around and found my phone in the bushes. Wet, muddy and scratched, but at least they've found it.'

Edie sat stony-faced and Goswell felt he could sense her deflation.

With his phone now safe, Goswell's main concerns were allayed. He still didn't trust or believe Edie, but he was going to have to take a chance on the girl – that she was telling the truth. Otherwise, things could get even worse for him.

So, a little reluctantly, Goswell agreed to Edie's plan. He grabbed a pair of scissors from the desk drawer, cut the binds to Edie's hands and allowed her to make the agreed call under his watchful gaze. To Goswell's relief it went more smoothly than he'd anticipated.

Afterwards, Goswell instructed Edie to stay in the summer house whilst he looked for the car keys. Goswell's wife was using the main vehicle, a Range Rover, but Goswell hardly ever used the second car, a Mini Clubman. After ten minutes he returned to tell Edie that he couldn't find the keys. They discussed how to get Edie home, but with the chauffeur now finished for the day and not answering his phone, Goswell was stuck. Eventually, Edie shared an idea which, as she spoke, seemed – to Edie at least – better and better.

'I can call Ethan Stephenson,' Edie hinted gently. 'Dr

Stephenson's son … if you don't mind. We've become sort-of friends … y'know, his dad died and my mum died … and I'm sure he wouldn't mind.'

By now, Goswell just wanted Edie out the house before his wife got home and started asking questions. Begrudgingly, Goswell gave Edie his phone to make the call. Edie had noticed that Ethan's home phone number was unusual when they were outside his Mill Hill home some time back and when he'd called her the other day. But she still had to drag the number from her memory.

It was an outer London number beginning, for sure, 0208, and then 201 for Mill Hill. The rest had double digits, and she'd thought at the time how easy it was to remember. Now, what were those numbers … Yes, that was it: 1144. The first number was 1, as she recalled, and the fourth was 4. It was a great telephone number. She dialled and, to her relief, Ethan answered almost immediately.

'Hi, Ethan,' she began. 'It's Edie here. This is important – an emergency. I haven't got long, so please just listen.' Then Edie explained, in outline, what had happened and that she was now at Peter Goswell's home – in the summer house in the garden – and needed a ride back immediately. 'Do you know where he lives?'

'Yes, I think so,' responded a bemused Ethan, before composing himself. 'I've been there before with my Dad. I'll find the exact address, don't worry. I'm on my way. I'll be about an hour.'

'Thank you *so* much. Be careful, please.' Goswell grabbed his phone back just as Edie heard Ethan's final words.

'Don't worry, I will.'

Goswell stood up and walked to the window, where he looked out at the spot by the oak tree where Homer had noticed the helpless bird, whose life Goswell had stamped out with his heel. Goswell inhaled deeply and sighed, aware of the precariousness of his situation. He said nothing, headed to the door and disappeared, leaving Edie alone in the summer house. In the main house, Goswell went upstairs to his and Jane's bedroom and took all their family photo albums out of the cupboard. On the bed, he leafed through each one slowly, absorbing the snapshots of moments, filling his mind with memories of better times.

A black Renault Clio pulled up slowly outside Goswell's house – at the very edge of the main driveway. So immersed was Goswell that, although he registered the sound, he had little interest in checking its origin. Ethan got out, examined his surroundings with great care and then stealthily made his way across the lawn. Through the window of the summer house, Ethan was surprised to see nobody within except Edie on the sofa. He crept inside – a sight that delighted Edie so much that she emitted a squeal of joy.

'Are you okay?' Ethan asked as he moved quickly over to her.

'Yes. Let's get out before he comes back,' Edie responded, leaping to her feet.

Edie grabbed her school bag from the floor and, hand in hand, they tore out of the door, across the lawn and into

Ethan's car. Nobody came after them as Ethan put the keys in the ignition, sparked the engine to life and headed off down the windy country road. Only when they were safely on the M11 motorway did he speak.

'Are you sure you're all right?' Ethan posed gently.

'I'm fine,' Edie replied. 'And thank you so much … *so* much … for coming for me.'

'Any time,' Ethan said supportively and with real heart.

Several minutes passed in silence before he made a suggestion: 'We should go to the police.'

'Not yet,' Edie countered, pointing to the Welcome Break sign on the left of the road. 'Pull over into the service station here instead, please,' she instructed.

Ethan brought the car to a stop in a quiet corner of the motorway services car park. Now in safe hands, Edie enjoyed a moment of stillness whilst Ethan sat in silence and waited.

Once her mind was settled, Edie gathered her strength and recounted the full story of the day. Ethan listened respectfully, not interrupting until the young detective had finished.

'Wow!' he exclaimed, blowing air out forcibly from puffed-up cheeks. 'That's quite a day you've had – and what you've done is … amazing.' Ethan turned to look directly at Edie in the passenger seat. 'I guess it's just a shame that they found Goswell's phone – it's the crucial evidence.'

Staring ahead at the cars filling up with fuel, Edie allowed herself the tiniest of grins, almost imperceptible. 'Can you give me your phone, please?' she asked quietly. Bewildered, Ethan reached into his pocket and pulled out his recently fixed device.

Edie laid Ethan's iPhone carefully on her lap before reaching up with both hands to remove her right earring. Delicately, Edie then used the end of the earring post to prise open the small compartment on the side of Ethan's phone.

'Hey, what are you doing?' Ethan exclaimed with concern.

'It's fine,' replied Edie calmly. She'd read somewhere that this part of the earring was strangely called the 'finding' and, as the compartment clicked open, Edie wondered what indeed all the day's efforts would reveal.

'Take this,' Edie said, placing the SIM card from Ethan's phone into his outstretched palm. Deftly, she popped the earring back into place.

Next, Edie undid the clasp of a thin gold chain around her neck and slipped off the pendant. She placed the chain with the SIM card in Ethan's palm and held aloft the small, heart-shaped locket.

'This was my mum's locket,' Edie explained. 'And it belonged to her mum before that. Somehow Mama managed to keep it hidden from the German soldiers in the camp.' Ethan looked on uncertainly. 'I keep this inside,' Edie added as she popped open the catch. Ethan peered in and could just make out a black-and-white image of a girl around Edie's age. But what lay on top of the image interested him more.

'And this ...' Edie proclaimed proudly. 'This is the SIM card from Goswell's phone.'

Although some of the phone tech stuff was a bit fiddly, it took Edie and Ethan around forty minutes to complete the task. Using Goswell's SIM card they were able to access old voicemail messages and strings of text messages.

Edie stared blankly at one of the most incriminating messages, sent quite recently:

> Scare the girl. If you need to go further, like you
> did with her mother, then do it. You'll get the
> usual payment.

Edie took screenshots of text messages and made audio recordings on Ethan's phone of the voicemail messages. Once she had enough material, Edie put Ethan's SIM card back in and logged in to her own Facebook, Instagram and Twitter accounts. She posted a range of photos and recordings, accompanied by written explanations where she could, then called Lizzie to start sharing the information and spreading the word. Finally, Edie rang Creation and left a message on Margaret's office phone, alerting Goswell's personal assistant to what was now out in the world.

'Can you take me home now, please?' Edie asked finally. 'I'm really tired.'

Without a word, Ethan started the car, made his way out of the services car park and back onto the motorway. For several miles he silently kept his focus on the road. No probing. No further questions.

Then, after a while, Ethan spoke, surprising Edie with his thoughts: 'My dad wasn't a bad man, y'know. He was a good person – a good father – who somehow got mixed up in something bad. But I miss him. I miss him terribly. Like you must miss your mum.'

Edie touched Ethan gently on his arm. She glimpsed a tear forming in his eye as he glanced over fleetingly at her. His grief was fresher but it was something they shared.

A few minutes later, Ethan turned on the car stereo, fiddled with the Bluetooth settings on his iPhone and the car was suddenly filled with music. It was a song Edie recognised, and liked, but couldn't quite place.

'What is this? she asked. 'Haven't I heard it on the telly?'

'It's by Santigold,' Ethan answered as he turned up the volume. 'The song's called "Disparate Youth", and I love playing it loud when I'm driving. That's probably why they've used it for a car insurance advert!'

Edie smiled, sat back and let the electro-instrumental opening fill her head. When the first verse came, with lyrics about roadblocks in your life path, Edie couldn't help a wry smile, which was mirrored by Ethan.

Then the chorus arrived and the words reached deep inside Edie, bringing an image of one person to the fore: a beautiful, committed woman, who was also the best possible mother. Edie's own tears flowed as she thought of what meant so much to her mum. And what meant so much to her now too.

Santigold got it right: it was indeed a life, and a world, worth fighting for.

CHAPTER 14

RESOLUTION

'What the hell is going on, Edie?!' screamed her dad, the moment Edie walked through the front door. He'd been waiting for her and was furious.

'I don't know what you mean,' Edie answered as she tried to brush past her father in the hallway. Behind her pretend sheepishness, though, Edie was scared by the force of her dad's wrath and the veins bulging on his forehead.

'No you don't! Not so easy!' Dad shot back, grabbing Edie's left upper arm in his right hand.

'Ow!' Edie reacted instinctively, noticing Eli perched at the top stairs on the first floor landing, just past the photographs on the wall. 'You're hurting me, Dad!' she cried.

Although he lessened his grip slightly, Edie's father didn't budge: he had no intention of letting his daughter through. 'I'll repeat myself,' Dad said sternly, 'but I don't intend to do so again. What the hell is going on with you?'

Panicked, Edie tried to think of a way out, but she felt cornered and shaken by her dad's insistence. She hadn't seen him this angry before and a different tack was called for. 'Dad,' Edie said quietly, putting her right hand on top of the fist that was squeezing her left arm. Dad relaxed his grip further as Edie looked him straight in the eye. 'If you tell me what's wrong ... what you want to know ... I promise I'll answer.'

Visibly, Edie's dad's tension melted a little and he let go of her arm, but there was no change in his seriousness: 'I've had the school on the phone, Edie, twice, then the police. And that Dr Montgom—'

'The police?' Edie quizzed. 'What did they want?'

'I don't know exactly.' Her dad exhaled, as if just starting the conversation had released an outpouring of worry. 'I'm not even sure if it was connected to the school problem.'

'School problem?' asked Edie anxiously. 'And what problem is that, exactly?'

'To do with today's trip, Edie, and I think you know what I'm talking about.'

'Today's trip? I don't know what—'

'You know what I'm talking about, Edie! No more lies.' But it was the word he added when repeating the sentence that really got her: 'No more lies, *please.*' The love and concern, from father to daughter, that filled the emphasis on that last word struck Edie right in the chest. The game was up. She knew it, and he knew it from the look in her eyes.

'The school called me late this afternoon,' Dad continued, 'whilst I was doing a surgery. I was distracted with patients and missed the first call, but they caught me later on.'

'What did they want?' Edie asked sheepishly.

'It was Mr Bowling. I think he's your maths teacher?' Edie nodded.

'Well, he said there'd been a complaint from the PA … the secretary of the chief executive of the drug company you visited with the school today. This secretary left a message at Highgate Hill saying that there'd been a theft from her office during the trip, and that she'd seen a girl in school uniform coming out of the office. Later in the afternoon she apparently retracted her accusation ... said she might have made a mistake.'

Edie reddened.

'And Mr Bowling suggested that you were the only one not with the group all the time. Apparently, you missed the coach back.'

Edie felt hot under the collar as her dad continued.

'Mr Bowling was apologetic ... embarrassed actually ... and he should've been when he explained that he hadn't realised you were missing until the coach was almost halfway back to London. He said – I think, although it's all so confusing – that the coach returned to the drug company but you were gone. And that he spoke to you using Lizzie's phone and you were making your own way back home.'

Edie said nothing, so her dad pressed her: 'Did you steal something, Edie? And why did you miss the coach? And who exactly brought you home?' Again, Edie was silent and she could sense her dad's frustration rising. 'Tell me, Edie.'

'I will, Dad, I promise,' she said submissively. 'Can you just tell me what the police wanted?'

He waited a moment then acceded. 'Well, I don't know exactly. It was that nice woman officer, PC Brearley, the one who was around when we were burgled. Something to do with an incident at Finsbury Park Tube station, and other stuff, but she said she wanted to speak to you first.'

Edie swallowed and sensed the incredible tension inside her body. Suddenly, she felt overwhelmed by everything: by holding together all the different strands, by keeping secrets, by trying to solve the hardest puzzle of her short life. Yet it was more than that, more than feeling beaten down. In that moment, Edie was overcome by something much bigger than her – she was overcome by grief. Or, possibly, the acceptance of grief.

As tears streamed down her cheeks, Edie looked up, beyond her father, to the young boy at the top of the flight of stairs. Her brother had come down a couple of steps from the first-floor landing and was gazing at the photograph on the wall: the one of him and his mum on Hampstead Heath. The difference this time was that Eli didn't seem to care that his sister, and now his dad too, were staring up at him. He was transfixed and reached out with a finger to touch the glass, and the image underneath of his mother smiling on the grass, entangled with her son.

Edie sobbed, choked sorrow soon becoming uncontrollable bawling. Dad wrapped his arms around his daughter and let her head rest on his shoulder. As the wailing slowly settled, in the comfort of Dad's hug, Edie had a moment of mental clarity – the kind of realisation her mum used to say came when your mind was clear and present. It was time to tell the truth.

'It's about Mum,' she blurted out.

Dad eased out of the embrace and looked at Edie confused. 'Mum?'

'Yes. It's all to do with Mum.'

In the lounge, Dad sat on the sofa with Edie next to him. He'd poured a large whisky for himself and a glass of water for Edie. On the armchair in the bay window, Eli settled himself quietly, looking over at his father and sister. Edie took a deep breath, holding tight to the cardboard folder she'd brought down from her bedroom, containing all her investigatory material.

'It started, Dad, at the stone-setting,' Edie began, half-turning to face her father. 'You know my sheepskin coat – the one Mum bought me from the charity shop ...'

'I think so,' Dad replied uncertainly.

'Well,' continued Edie, 'I hadn't worn it since the day Mum died because ... well, because it was the coat I had on when the teacher came to tell me ... the news.'

'Right,' said Dad, wondering where on earth the story was going.

'Well, I hadn't worn the coat for nearly a year, until the stone-setting at the cemetery a few weeks ago. You might not remember, Dad, but I walked back from the grave alone. It was cold and I put my hands in my pockets to keep warm.'

Edie reached inside the folder and pulled out the first clue. 'And I found this envelope.' Out of the envelope Edie took a piece of paper. 'And this note. It's from Mum.'

'From Mum?' her dad said, bewildered. 'Can I have a look?'

'Of course, Dad, that's why I'm showing you!'

Edie handed over the creased piece of paper and Dad

read the note in complete silence. As he made his way through it, the furrows on his forehead deepened noticeably.

'This is unbelievable,' proclaimed Dad. 'It's … it's …. extraordinary. Mum sent you a message from the grave.'

'I know. I was literally sick on the grass when I read it.'

'I saw that,' said Dad tentatively. 'But … I just thought it was the stress of the day.'

'There was something else at the cemetery, Dad,' Edie continued. 'There was a black car, a Bentley, and a man … smartly dressed … with sunglasses. I think the man was watching me.'

From Dad's blank expression, Edie could tell that his mind was elsewhere. 'Sorry, luv. Did you say a car?'

'Yeah, Dad. A flashy one, with a chauffeur. And there was a man … smartly dressed … I think he was watching me.'

'Watching you?'

'Yes. But I'll come back to that later.'

Dad looked agitated and took a slug of his drink. He shook his head, out of confusion and in an attempt to focus his mind. 'Edie, why didn't you tell me about any of this?'

Edie bravely, and comfortingly, took his hand in hers and held it on her lap. 'Dad, you've just got to promise not to be mad at me. Please.' Edie paused then carried on. 'I felt like Mum had given me a task – a challenge – and I needed to see it through.' Edie squeezed her father's hand tightly. 'It's been hard. Really hard.'

Dad wiped away a tear from Edie's cheek and stroked her temple with his thumb. 'It's okay, luv. I'm just … blown away … completely perplexed.' He glanced over at Eli, looking on noiselessly from his seat by the window. 'Does Eli know anything about this?'

'Some of it. Only recently,' Edie interjected, before her brother had a chance to speak. 'I needed his help with something. But nothing's his fault.'

'All right,' accepted Dad, a little more composed. He scrutinised the note more carefully. 'So, what do you think this means: *Only by working through this clue do you get to the next one?*

'I know what it means,' answered Edie positively.

'You know? You've solved this?'

'Sure!' Edie said confidently. 'And you helped me.'

'I helped you? And how exactly did I help you?' Dad asked curiously.

Edie checked out her brother, motionless, watching on with hushed interest.

'It's like a crossword clue, Dad. Mum taught me how to do cryptic crosswords … she taught me but I'd forgotten. I spent days trying to solve her clue until I came home one day from school and you were here … well … over there.' Edie pointed to the seat Eli was in. 'Doing the cryptic crossword. I solved one of them for you, about *Romeo and Juliet.*'

'Oh yeah,' said Dad, his memory jolted. 'I remember.' He looked back down at the note. 'I can't get it – tell me.'

With the piece of paper on Dad's lap, Edie ran her index finger across the clue: 'It's one of those kinds of clues, Dad – only by working *through* this clue do you … You have to connect the different words. If you put "clue" and "do" together, you get Cluedo.'

'Cluedo? The game.' Dad smiled, impressed.

'Yeah. As soon as I worked it out I went to the Cluedo box ... we haven't played since Mum died, y'know ... and inside the black envelope for the murder cards was another clue. The next clue.'

Edie reached into the folder and pulled out a plastic wallet, another piece of paper visible within. She was about to take the second note out but stalled with the wallet on her lap: 'After I solved the first clue, I remembered when we had all last played ... played Clu ...' Edie's voice faltered.

'Remembered what, luv?'

As Edie spoke, she realised that she didn't have to share absolutely everything, including how memories connected with solving the clues were helping with her grief.

'Edie?' There was silence before Dad repeated, 'Edie!'

'Sorry,' Edie gathered herself together. 'Doesn't matter. Just needed a moment.'

Dad pointed to his daughter's lap. 'So, what about the next clue?'

Edie handed the piece of paper to her dad and gave him some time to work his way through the note until he reached the next clue: *What if Charlie got it wrong?* Bewildered, Dad looked at his daughter: 'What does that mean?'

'This one took me a while,' Edie replied. 'Then I remembered that Mum had studied Darwin at university ... for her master's degree. Anyway, I've been doing evolution at school and suddenly it came to me that if Darwin was wrong, then religion was right. If man didn't arise by evolution, then God *created* man ... I mean mankind.'

'So?'

'So, I looked at the Bible in the study – in the Old Testament – and there, tucked inside the Book of Genesis, was the next note.'

'Edie, this is ridiculous … preposterous …' said Dad, exasperated. 'But what Mum did is also quite amazing.'

'I know! But it's all true, Dad. Mum was … Mum is … incredible! But look,' Edie pointed with her index finger: 'This time she asked me to pay special attention to where the note was positioned.'

'In the Bible?'

'No … well, yes … but more specifically in the part of the Bible about creation. So I started doing some internet investigation about creation.'

'Creation?'

'Yeah, the word "creation". I came across all kinds of odd stuff before I stumbled on a pharma … a drug company called Creation. They make Stop It! for diarrhoea.'

'Yes, I know them. Aggressive with their marketing. Their reps are always banging on the surgery doors trying to persuade us to prescribe their drugs. So, what is it about them?'

Edie took a breath. 'Well, it took me a long time, Dad … quite a bit of investigating … but this is what I've found out.'

And, to her astonished and impressed father, Edie relayed all she'd found out about Creation. She told him about the death of the research director, Dr Stephenson; about his links to Vietnam, possibly connected with an outbreak of bird flu; about how she'd visited Dr Stephenson's distraught wife, who was now in hospital, and which was why the public health people had been in touch; and about how Creation was on the verge of a major breakthrough with a new drug called Flu-Away.

'Hold on, hold on, sweetie. Just slow down for a second. Have you got proof of …'

'Dad,' said Edie excitedly, the weight lifting as she let the burden out. 'There's loads more.'

Dad looked over at Eli again: 'And you know about this?'

'A bit,' admitted Eli. 'Edie's been really brave.'

Edie smiled at her brother: 'Thanks Eli, that's kind.'

Dad fidgeted on the sofa and turned back to his daughter: 'Okay, sweetie, we'll come on to the other stuff in a moment, but have you got any proof about Creation?'

'Some proof, Dad, but not quite everything.' Edie dipped into the folder and pulled out all the printouts she'd accumulated and handed them over.

Dad pored slowly over the documents: 'It's interesting … revealing … but it's just internet searching.'

'I think Ethan's also found something,' added Edie.

'Ethan?'

'Sorry, that's Mrs Stephenson's – Dr Stephenson's – son. He's found some important papers of his dad's in the attic but I haven't seen them yet. He drove me home today.'

'So, the Stephenson boy is in on this too?' asked Dad, sounding a little irritated.

'No,' corrected Edie immediately. 'He really isn't. He's just been helpful and kind. Plus …' Edie pulled a file out of the bottom zipped pocket of her school bag, 'I've just been given this from someone scared at Creation, but I haven't read it yet.'

Dad stood up, stretched his back and paced the room.

'Dad, is it possible that Creation could've been doing all of this?' Edie wasn't exactly sure what she was asking but carried on: 'I mean … you're a doctor … is all this … like …. medically possible?'

Dad thought for a bit, stopped by the fireplace and looked at the wedding photos on the shelf to the left – wow, his wife looked beautiful. He turned round to face Edie: 'I guess so. I mean, I'm not an expert, just a GP, so we can ask Dr Montgomery later … but I'm pretty sure it's possible to create a virus – in the lab – to make it more dangerous. You were very young, but do you remember anything about swine flu?'

'Just about,' chimed Edie. 'Maybe from after it ended.'

'Well, I guess you could make a more dangerous version of that virus in the lab, although I think it's illegal.'

'But if you did that, Dad, could you use the new virus to make a medicine to fight it.'

'I think so,' said Dad uncertainly, then got up from his seat abruptly. 'What was that noise?'

'What noise?' asked Edie.

'From out back, maybe the kitchen. Did you hear anything, Eli? You've got better hearing than me.'

'Maybe,' Eli answered. 'I'm not sure.'

'Well, I'm going out to check.'

Edie grabbed her Dad's arm. 'Please be careful, Dad. You haven't heard the rest of what I've got to tell you.'

Her dad appeared puzzled, as if he'd forgotten that there was more. 'It'll be fine, luv, don't worry. You guys stay right here.'

Dad disappeared and the children heard him stepping down the short flight of stairs that led to the kitchen at the back of the house.

'Are you all right, Eli?' Edie asked her brother with concern.

'Fine,' he said, seemingly unaffected, although Edie sensed otherwise.

'Well, thank you for, like, helping me. You've been really great.'

'That's okay,' Eli replied and then, to Edie's surprise, he added: 'I want them to catch the man who killed Mummy. The man in the video.'

'Me too,' agreed Edie.

They waited in silence, hearing kitchen cupboards being opened, before Eli added: 'I miss Mummy.'

'Me too.'

Dad returned to the lounge, prepared for the next instalment with a glass of fizzy mineral water. 'I need to keep my head clear,' he explained, placing the tumbler on the coffee table before sitting back down. 'The flower trough had fallen off the wall on the deck again. Must be the foxes.' Dad focused his attention back on Edie: 'Carry on.'

'Okay,' said Edie, organising her thoughts. 'I'm not quite sure where to go next, but ... okay ... at the stone-setting, Dad, just before I found the note, I saw this big black car, as I said before. And I think I know who it was.'

'How?'

'Well, at the cemetery, he banged his hand on the roof

when he was ready to go, like two or three times, and he had a chauffeur.'

'Okay, so he was rich.'

'No, Dad, it's more than that, much more. When we did the school trip to Creation today, he was there again … same black car, I'm sure … and he banged the roof to let his chauffeur know he was ready to leave. He's the head of Creation, the chief executive, Peter Goswell.'

Although Dad appeared incredulous, Edie knew she was winning him over. 'I need to show you the next thing now.'

'Another clue?'

'Not quite yet.' Edie looked over at her brother: 'Can you go and get the laptop down, Eli? Please.' He jumped up, quicker than she expected. 'Sure.'

A minute later, Eli reappeared with the laptop, set it up on the coffee table and turned it on whilst Edie took the next item from her folder.

'Dad, you need to prepare yourself … but this is what I think happened. It may sound crazy but … well, I think Mum had uncovered something about Creation … that she'd found out about some kind of human rights abuse, maybe of people involved in a drug trial in Vietnam. She was gathering her evidence and Peter Goswell got worried and … and … arranged to have her murdered.'

'Murdered?!'

'Yes, Dad. She says how afraid she was in the first note.

I think she hid the evidence somewhere and the clues lead to it.'

The children could see their father's mind racing. He took another gulp of water. 'She ... Mum ... did mention a case before she died ... about a drug company ... but I thought she'd gone too far with this one.' Dad stared blankly ahead, the weight of the recollection visible in his face, then brought his attention back to the present. 'How do you know she was killed?' he asked.

Edie took out the DVD, inserted the disc carefully into the laptop and pressed 'Play'. The screen was fairly dark but clear enough to tell that it was a Tube platform with passengers waiting for the arrival of a train. Dad hunched forward to get a better view whilst Edie fast-forwarded it to the dreadful minute and second.

'Here it is, Dad,' she explained. 'The moment Mummy was killed.'

In horror, the father of two watched the exact moment his life was torn apart. Tears of disgust, of dismay, spread across his face. As Edie held one hand, Eli moved over from the armchair, sat on the other side of his dad and took hold of the other hand. Then, for the first time, Eli started crying as well, triggering an outpouring from his sister too. Eventually, Dad's sobbing abated enough to ask a question.

'Sweetie, how on earth did you get this?'

No lies. 'I stole it from the control room at Finsbury Park station. Lizzie and Eli helped, but it was all my doing. Don't blame them.'

'I'm not blaming anybody, luv. I just wanted to know.

So that's why the police want to ask you about the station incident ...'

'Now, look at this, Dad,' continued Edie, ignoring her dad's comment, and she showed him the moment, seconds later, when the hood was knocked from the head of the man who'd cleverly made it all look like an accident. 'I think his name is Zero, Dad, and he's the murderer.'

'How on earth do you know that?'

'I'll come back to that in a bit, but see that scar on his face, like a circle ...'

Dad scrutinised the screen: 'Yes, I see it.'

'Well, the same man chased me and Lizzie in Highgate Woods. She hit him on the head with a branch but I saw his face. I saw the same scar.'

'Oh my God, Edie! Were you hurt?'

'No, not at all. But you know what this means, Dad – if I'm right?'

'What?' he wondered, but he was already processing the facts.

'It means it made no difference that you took Mum to the station that day. It wasn't an accident – they were going to kill her anyway.'

Dad reflected for a few seconds on Edie's comment before reacting. 'I wasn't thinking so much about that ...' he posited. 'It's just that I was a bit dismissive of Mum – about the drug company stuff. That's what's upsetting me.'

'Dad,' said Edie seriously. 'Mum had loads of ideas ... lots of cases ... and some of them seemed more important, more real, than others. We even joked about it sometimes,

remember? You always listened to her … supported her …
You just thought some of her theories were better than
others. Nothing was your fault – ever – including the trip to
the station.'

Dad waited, digesting his daughter's mature words.
'But how did he know we would go to Finsbury Park?'

'I don't know for sure,' Edie answered. This had been
troubling her too. 'But I think they've put tracking devices
on our computers – to see what we search – and also maybe
listening devices in the house.'

This information slowly sunk in before Edie broke
the silence: 'One other thing. I also think it was Zero who
burgled the house, looking for the evidence I've gathered.
But he didn't find it.'

Dad was struggling to take it all in. 'What makes you
think he didn't find the evidence?'

'This,' Edie responded immediately, bringing the SIM
card from her locket. 'I stole a mobile phone from Peter
Goswell's office at Creation today. From his secretary's
drawer – his private phone. I had to throw it away later so as
not to be caught with it, but I'd removed the SIM card and
got access to some of his phone and text messages.'

Edie then got on to her Instagram page on the
laptop. With Dad's and Eli's gaze fixed on the screen, Edie
showed them a range of texts between Goswell and Zero –
incriminating exchanges of words.

'And look at this, Dad,' Edie added. 'There's a third
person involved, and he's also on the Creation board. I saw
his photo on the wall. Look at the name … here …' She

pointed and her dad shrieked.

'The pig!' Dad screamed. 'The bloody pig! Wait till I get my hands on him!'

'I know, Dad. You will,' Edie said calmly, holding back from telling him about the kidnapping. 'But we've got to solve the final clue first.'

'Okay,' Dad said, trembling. 'I almost forgot about that.'

Keen to press on, Edie took her father through the next clues – her mum's twin sister and the Lana Del Rey maths puzzle – before bringing out the final clue. The threesome huddled over the strange image with the voice bubble.

Although fully aware of the seriousness of the situation, Edie's dad chuckled: 'It's silly. I mean, I know Mum wasn't that good with the computer, but this ...'

'I know!' Edie laughed. 'It's terrible! I think she tried to use Word Art.'

'But struggled!' her dad interrupted with a grin.

After a moment, Eli added: 'I think it's quite good.' His dad and sister stared in disbelief.

'Just kidding,' Eli corrected with a cheeky smile. 'It's really silly!'

It was the first time he'd managed such a smile since Mum's death. As their grins slowly faded, Edie described the state of play.

'I really don't know what this one means. It's the only clue I haven't been able to solve – and it's the last one.'

'Well,' Dad said, gathering his strength. 'Let's try to solve it together. Three Franklins are better than one.'

Huddled on the sofa, Dad, Edie and Eli peered intensely at the image on the table. Nobody said a word for a while until Dad finally broke the silence.

'Well, let's talk it through. It's a person. Or a person's head, at least.'

'And he's got more hair than you, Dad,' Eli teased.

His father playfully patted the thinning patch on top of his head: 'I'm not so sure about that!'

'How do we know it's a man?' Edie asked.

'True,' said Dad. 'It could be a woman.'

'With very big lips,' Edie added.

'With very big lips,' Dad agreed.

'And the ears look like that man from *Star Trek*,' Eli suggested.

'Spock,' Dad helped, then scrunched up his face: 'But I can't believe this is a *Star Trek* reference.'

'Mum didn't even like *Star Trek*,' said Edie. 'These words, these phrases ...' she continued.

'Yes ...' interjected Dad, wondering where this was going.

'Well, it's like they've been added one by one ... to make this whole speech thing in the bubble.'

'Okay,' Dad followed.

'But they're all negatives,' Edie continued. 'Don't do this, don't do that ...'

'Right. So, what happens,' Dad suggested, 'if we apply each one to the picture?'

'What do you mean?' Edie asked.

'Well, if they've been added one by one, but they're all negatives, what if we apply them to the picture one by one ... in their negative way?'

'Sorry, Dad, I still don't understand,' Edie repeated.

'Well, we could take away the bits from the image that each phrase refers to one by one.'

Now Edie got it. 'Like take away the lips for "Don't smile"?'

'Exactly, we could try that. Let's get a pencil.'

'I've got one,' said Edie immediately, pulling a pencil and eraser from her folder.

'Well, redraw the image in pencil on a new sheet of paper,' Dad advised. 'Now,' he instructed, when Edie had done her best to replicate the strange-looking face, 'rub out the lips.' Edie did as she was told and the image looked even odder. 'Now the nose and ears for "Don't smell" and "Don't hear",' Dad added. 'Rub them out too.' Once again, in silence, Edie rubbed away to reveal a strange, ghost-like picture.

'Mmm,' Dad mumbled, unsure of his plan. 'It doesn't look very promising.'

'But we haven't finished,' chipped in Eli.

'Indeed, we haven't,' Dad acknowledged, putting his hand on his son's knee. 'You're quite right, Eli.' Dad turned to Edie and nodded: 'Carry on, luv.'

With the eraser in hand, Edie waited: 'Okay, but what do I do for "Don't grow"?'

With the threesome staring intently down at the paper, Dad stated the obvious: 'The hair, I guess. Hair grows.'

'And the outline of the head for "Don't think"?' Edie asked.

Nobody had a better idea. 'Give it a go,' Dad said.

Edie did as instructed, pressing down on the piece of paper with her left hand to avoid it from tearing. They all looked down at what remained.

'Mmm,' said Dad, thoughtfully. 'Not very encouraging.'

'It's just a pair of eyes,' commented Edie.

'Maybe Mum's telling us that it's for us to see or that it's in front of our eyes?' wondered Dad.

'But that's not very specific,' Edie countered. 'All the other clues have led directly to something.'

'Maybe it's her glasses or contact lenses?' Dad suggested.

'I've already checked,' Edie responded. 'I've looked through almost all her stuff in the house at some point.'

'Well, we're missing something then,' Dad pondered.

All three scrutinised the piece of paper in silence.

'What does the image mean?' Dad spoke his thoughts aloud. 'What does it mean?'

Silence again, finally broken by a quiet, young voice.

'It's like that thing on a word. An omelette,' suggested Eli.

'An omelette?' repeated Edie, perplexed.

'Yeah, that sign on top of letters.' Eli looked over at his father who'd understand the Arsenal reference: 'Y'know, Dad. Like Özil, the footballer.' Then Eli turned to Edie: 'And Müller, the yoghurts you like.'

'Oh,' said Dad, surprised. 'You mean an *umlaut*! The German grammar symbol.'

'Yes,' responded Eli irritably, as the words sounded very similar. 'An omelette!'

The silence that followed was very different to all the other quiet moments of the evening. It was filled, quickly, with an atmosphere of excitement, almost euphoria, as together each member of the Franklin family came to the same realisation – and shouted one word in unison.

'Günther!'

CHAPTER 15

LAST RITES

Peter Goswell heard the Renault Clio pull away from the house but paid no attention. For a long time, he worked his way through all the family photo albums, towards the end of which he received a call from Margaret. She explained that when she turned on his iPhone a message appeared saying 'No SIM card'. Then Margaret nervously shared with her boss some of the incriminating material that was now on the internet.

Goswell showered. The water felt good on his skin and he washed himself thoroughly. In the bedroom he put on Jane's favourite Kenzo birthday present suit and shiny black leather shoes. Downstairs, he filled Homer's food bowl, the sound of which made the dog come running. Goswell patted his friend warmly on his back before leaning down for a hug. Surprised, Homer turned to look at his owner, then carried on munching.

With the dog distracted, Goswell exited through the back door in the kitchen and made his way to the summer house where, as he'd expected, the girl was gone.

A realisation engulfed Goswell that the game was up. And he'd lost. But then, staring at the family photo on the desk, a very different kind of feeling began to lift his spirits: that he wasn't prepared to lose everything, that he could be a better person.

It took a while but, eventually, they found what they were looking for. Working together the Franklin family first examined the guinea pig, Edie probing his fur as Dad held on to him, the absurd idea in their minds that Mum might've implanted something in the small animal's flesh. No joy, so they moved to Günther's outdoor dwelling, using torches as night had fallen – and that's when their teamwork came to fruition. Eli's deft fingers located a small package underneath the base at the back of the cage, ingeniously stapled and strapped to the wooden slat. Dad pulled it free and, back indoors, Edie unravelled layers of waterproof wrapping to reveal a small plastic box. Inside was a memory stick.

Converged around the desktop computer in the study, the children watched as Dad opened the USB stick to find all the evidence from Edie's mum's investigations. Immersed, Dad worked his way through the files, taking notes as he went along. There was information about a clinical trial of an antiviral drug in Vietnam around eighteen months previously, including the names of the Vietnamese volunteers involved. It was unclear how Edie's mum had obtained the material or how she'd managed to get complex sections translated.

Two files on the stick were solely about the type of virus that was used on the participants, but the classification system of numbers and letters made no sense. Three other files were about money: the costs of running the trial and payments to the participants. From a further file, it was blatant that the trial had been organised and funded by Creation, although there was clearly a concerted effort to conceal the company's affiliation.

'What's that?!' Dad cried suddenly, sitting bolt upright from being hunched over the keyboard. 'That noise – from downstairs,' he continued, agitated. 'Did you hear it?'

Edie shook her head but Eli concurred. 'I heard something too, Dad, louder than last time,' he whispered anxiously. 'I think it came from the kitchen.'

'Stay here,' Dad said forcefully. He turned to his daughter: 'You know how to use the panic button?'

'I do,' replied Edie nervously, but Dad wasn't taking any chances.

'Use two fingers and press firmly upwards on the red button underneath the box,' he gestured in the air with his fingers.

'The box by the front door?' Edie checked, pointing down the stairs towards the small white box attached to the wall.

'Yep. There's also one in our bedroom … in Mum's and my bedroom …' he struggled. 'In my bedroom – well, you know what I mean. By the bedside table near the door, low down. It's rigged directly to the police, so they'll be here within minutes.'

Dad stood up to go downstairs, grabbing a baseball bat that was tucked behind a bookcase, but Edie stopped him.

'I don't want you to go downstairs, Daddy,' she pleaded.

In that moment he saw her as she was: a strong, loving and determined individual but also a fragile thirteen-year-old child who needed her one remaining parent more than anything in the world.

Dad squeezed Edie's hand. 'I'll be fine, sweetie, and I won't do anything silly. I promise.'

Bat held high above his right shoulder, ready to strike, Dad tiptoed delicately down each step. As he reached the bottom of the staircase, a louder sound emanated from the kitchen and Dad looked up at the children crouching on the landing. He gestured for them to go back but they stayed where they were.

Dad turned left at the banister and then took four further steps down, now out of sight of the children. Two paces forward and he was outside the kitchen where he stopped, leant in and turned on the lights.

A dark shadow was lurking outside, behind the still closed double-glazed patio doors. With his right hand, he was trying to force some kind of implement between the doors. The figure stopped what he was doing and looked up, head half-turned to keep his hooded face away from the brightness streaming out of the kitchen. Their eyes locked, just for a second, but long enough for Dad to make out a scar across his cheek.

Unnerved, Dad turned on his heels, leapt up the six stairs, darted across the hallway and activated the panic button.

The alarm blared fearsomely.

In what felt like an eternity – but was actually only eight minutes – police from Hornsey station arrived. Through each of those long minutes, Dad had remained motionless at the bottom of the main hallway stairs, one eye fixed piercingly on the patio doors at the back of the kitchen, the other eye glancing periodically up at the children on the first floor landing. He was guarding his castle and its precious contents with his life.

In the lounge, once the two police officers had carefully checked through the whole house, Dad recounted how he'd found an intruder in the back garden. 'Probably kids, mucking about,' said one of the young policemen, medium height with short light hair. Edie asked about PC Jessica Brearley, who it turned out was on duty at the station. Ten minutes later and the comforting policewoman was at the family's side.

'You've been unlucky, Dr Franklin,' PC Brearley remarked leadingly from her perch on the footstool in the lounge, opposite the family who were bunched together on the sofa. 'Second home entry, or attempted entry, within a few weeks.' The gentle officer could readily have added: *Or is there anything else you want to tell me?*

Still somewhat anxious, Dad was about to say something but Edie kicked off first, feeling implicit trust for the policewoman.

'It's a long story,' Edie said, realising it sounded like a film cliché. 'It started when my mum died a year ago.'

'Okay,' replied PC Brearley, her eyes glancing right and left at the other two. She shifted slightly in her seat and pulled herself upright before adding, 'I'm not in a rush – tell me all about it.'

And so, for the third time, Edie told the whole story: the note, the flashy car, her mum's research, the trail of clues, Creation and Vietnam, the chase in the woods, the man with the scar, the Stephenson family and Public Health England, Peter Goswell's phone and SIM card, and the abduction. For the second time that evening, Edie played the DVD recording of her mother's death at Finsbury Park station. Finally, Edie brought out the memory stick and the evidence that pointed to Creation Pharmaceuticals.

PC Brearley listened to it all attentively and with concern. When the young girl was finished, the policewoman placed a hand on the fledgling investigator's shoulder. 'You're an extraordinary girl, Edie,' she stated with half a smile. 'And quite the detective.'

PC Brearley reached for the radio strapped to her uniform. Before she pressed the button she looked over at Dr Franklin. 'I need to speak to the chief inspector,' she told him.

A sleepless night had been anticipated but, in fact, quite the opposite had transpired. It was late when the police left, and even later by the time Dad, Edie and Eli were tucked up in bed: all together, in the one large, queen-size parents' bed. Surprisingly, they'd all fallen asleep pretty quickly: emotionally and physically exhausted, and comforted by the two police cars stationed outside the house. They awoke at eight o'clock and had only just finished breakfast when the doorbell rang.

'Good morning, Dr Franklin,' said a fresh-faced PC

Brearley. 'This is Chief Inspector Penrose of the Metropolitan Police,' she added, introducing a tallish uniformed man in his fifties, who removed his flat police cap and tucked it under his arm. 'And behind are my fellow officers from Hornsey Station, PC Wilkins and PC Wiltshire.'

'Good morning, Dr Franklin,' said the senior officer, shaking the doctor's hand very firmly before turning to the children. 'And you must be Edie and Eli,' the chief inspector added. He held out his hand to Edie, who accepted it, before addressing her seriously and squarely in the eye: 'What you've done is quite something,' he praised. 'Nancy Drew has a modern day rival.'

Turning to Eli, he continued: 'And you're a sort of young Sherlock,' to which Eli blushed.

'Do come in,' Dad said, welcoming them in, and led the group into the kitchen. PC Wiltshire closed the front door and stayed in the hallway on guard duty.

'Coffee?' Dad asked.

'No, thank you,' replied Penrose curtly. Dad, the children, PC Brearley and PC Wilkins all took seats around the kitchen table, allowing Penrose to begin.

'Quite a business your daughter's uncovered here, Dr Franklin,' he said. 'My team have been up all night looking at the material provided by Edie: your wife's investigations on the memory stick, the notes and clues she left behind, the phone, plus of course that DVD of the ... incident at Finsbury Park station.'

Penrose fiddled self-consciously with his cap. 'Sorry, incident is not the right word, nor accident ...'

He pondered, but for too long.

'Murder,' suggested Edie.

'Yes,' said Penrose. 'It is looking increasingly so. And it must've been dreadful for you – for all of you – watching that recording.' No response, so he carried on.

'It looks like we have a rogue pharmaceutical company manufacturing a new antiviral drug, but doing so illegally, but I'll let the fellow from Public Health England explain that in a moment. I've asked them to come over – they've been working all night too.' Penrose glanced over at Edie. 'But, as I said, we may also have a murder here and, by the looks of the Finsbury recording, an assassin we've been trying to catch for some time.'

'You know him?' asked Eli, to everyone's surprise.

'Yes, young man. We think he's a man known – as Edie noticed from Goswell's phone records – by the name Zero.'

'Because of the scar on his face?' interrupted Edie.

'I believe so. He – if it is him – has been involved in a range of violent crimes over the last two or three years, but it's been hard to pinpoint things, let alone catch him. The video and phone are good evidence.'

'But how did he get that scar?' questioned Eli again, fascinated.

'Well, that's an interesting question. He's ex-special forces, top-notch British military. Served a lot overseas in tough places – Iraq, Afghanistan, Rwanda – but on his last mission he survived an IED ... that's a bit like a landmine ... when the rest of his team were killed. The explosion may have caused the scar, but in the aftermath ... apparently ...

something awful happened that made him go off the rails.'

'What?' asked Edie, perplexed.

'I'm afraid that's classified. Anyway, he was court-martialled, dismissed from the army and came to London. He apparently had problems with post-traumatic stress disorder, depression and antisocial behaviour. He went off the grid and the army lost touch with him, although we – the police – have suspected his involvement in gang violence and other serious crimes. Seems he became a sort of gun for hire. An assassin.'

'A hitman?' said Eli.

'Yes, young man. A hitman.'

Edie posed the obvious next question: 'And you think the chief executive from Creation, Peter Goswell, hired Zero … to kill Mum?'

Eli and Dad sat stock-still waiting for the inevitable answer. 'Yes,' said Penrose, 'that appears to be the case. I'm so sorry. We're picking up Goswell later this morning, but I know you wanted to be with us for one particular arrest.'

The doorbell rang, surprising the distracted PC Wiltshire.

Unlike the police officers, Dr Montgomery did accept a cup of fresh coffee. He introduced himself as a consultant in public health medicine with a focus on the control of infectious diseases, and also deputy director of health protection for London, working for Public Health England. Two more junior staff members were in tow and were cursorily introduced. They all looked tired.

'We've been working on this through much of the night,' started Dr Montgomery, now seated at the table, 'and we still don't have a complete picture of what's happened. But I'll tell you what we do know.'

PC Wilkins stood by the patio doors to the garden, where Zero had tried to break in, watching a small bird pecking at a feeder in the tree fuchsia outside as Dr Montgomery continued.

'I'll start at the beginning – or, at least, what I think is the beginning.' Dr Montgomery seemed to relish having everyone's attention. 'The R&D director – that stands for research and development – of Creation Pharmaceuticals, Dr Thomas Stephenson, appears to have manufactured – created – a new strain of influenza virus.'

'That's flu, isn't it?' Edie checked. 'Influenza is flu?'

'Yes, that's right. But there many different kinds – or strains as we call them – of influenza. Some affect animals, some humans, occasionally both.'

'Like swine flu?' posed Eli.

'Sort of,' replied Dr Montgomery. 'Swine flu may have come from pigs, but it caused an epidemic in humans – a pandemic, in fact, as it spread worldwide. Normally, though, we just have regular strains, or types, of human influenza, which change a bit from year to year – but not that much.'

'That's why we have a new vaccine for influenza each year,' chipped in Dad keenly.

'Correct,' affirmed Dr Montgomery. 'Now, at the moment there are only a small number of drugs that work against viruses like influenza.'

'Antiviral drugs?' asked Edie.

'Yes. But all they generally do is reduce the period of illness, or the symptoms, a little. Maybe by a day or so ... They don't cure the problem, just help you get over it quicker.'

'So, what did Creation do – and why did they kill my mum?' asked Eli, fidgety.

'Well,' replied the public health doctor, glancing at the police. 'I can't comment on your mother's death, but ... it appears that Dr Stephenson at Creation was encouraged to create a new strain of influenza that was more virulent – or stronger, more dangerous to people – than other types.'

'Like bird flu?' questioned Edie.

'Precisely. Bird flu normally affects only birds ... but when humans do occasionally get it, it can be pretty deadly – way worse than regular flu.'

'Could we get bird flu?' asked a concerned Eli.

'No,' answered Dr Montgomery. 'It's really only people who handle birds, like in poultry markets, and mainly in Asia – say in Vietnam.'

'Vietnam?' quizzed Edie.

'Indeed. We think that what Dr Stephenson did was create a new strain of flu in a laboratory in Vietnam – either human influenza or bird flu, we're not sure yet – but one that's particularly dangerous to humans, so Creation could test out their new antiviral drug on people infected with that virus.

As Dr Montgomery paused, Edie continued his line of thinking: 'They knew that governments are terrified of a pandemic of dangerous flu, so are desperate to have effective treatments …'

'Which they stockpile,' the doctor interrupted keenly. 'That means they buy up millions of packets of tablets to treat the population. Drug companies who produced antiviral medicines made a fortune during swine flu.'

'But isn't it illegal to create a dangerous virus?' wondered Edie. Penrose looked on with interest.

'Sort of,' answered Dr Montgomery. 'It's a difficult … and contested … area of medical research called "gain-of-function" studies.' A circle of bemused-looking faces meant Dr Montgomery had to explain further: 'In these types of research studies, the virus is manipulated to *gain* – or increase – their function, hence the name … and usually they also become more dangerous. From the papers that Dr Stephenson's son gave us earlier this morning …'

'Ethan,' interrupted Edie.

'Yes, Ethan,' agreed Dr Montgomery. 'He found papers in the attic at home, which I've just glanced over this morning. And this is where it gets complicated. In the Vietnam lab, Stephenson seems to have created a more transmissible form of influenza virus – that means easier to transmit from birds to humans or easier for one human to transmit to another – but the virus may also have become more virulent, more lethal, at the same time. That's unusual, because normally when the transmissibility of a virus increases, its virulence decreases – or the other way around – but it's not impossible. Anyway, in the trial it appears they called it regular influenza – not enhanced human flu or bird flu – which is illegal and unethical, and they infected a number of Vietnamese participants. Then they tested out their new antiviral drug. It seems that six of the trial subjects died from the infection, and Creation – although they never used their name – quietly paid off the families with large sums of money to keep them quiet and closed down the lab.'

'That's what Mum knew,' said Edie. 'But she didn't have all the evidence.'

'A courageous woman, your mum,' said Penrose seriously. 'You should all be proud of her.'

Nobody said anything for a while, then Dad asked: 'So, how – or why – did Dr Stephenson die?'

'Well,' said Dr Montgomery, taking a sip of his drink. 'We're not entirely sure, but if he hadn't been to Vietnam for a year, he must've brought some of the virus back to the UK. He could've stored it at their labs in Cambridgeshire. We'll have to check. They continued trials of their antiviral drug, which have proved successful, so maybe he wanted to keep a sample of the virus just in case. But it wouldn't have been stored in the most secure kind of lab, so if he had an accident, or handled it poorly, he could've infected himself. Which I guess is what happened.'

'And then he gave it to his wife,' Dad suggested.

'Indeed. She's been very unwell but is improving. The fact that there are only three others affected in Italy, and nobody else in England, suggests that the virus has quite quickly lost its ability to go from person to person.'

'That's lucky,' said Edie.

'Very lucky. Plus, close contacts of those who are ill, like Ethan, may already be partially protected – say if they've had the regular flu vaccine.'

'I've had that,' stated Edie, 'because of my asthma. And I'd been feeling a bit tired but it's got better.'

'Well, there you go,' said Dr Montgomery. 'We'll continue to keep a close eye on you too, Edie.'

After a pause, Dad looked directly at his colleague: 'Thank you so much, Dr Montgomery – the explanation is really helpful. And … comforting in a way.'

Dad turned to Penrose: 'Are we ready for the next step now?'

'We are indeed,' replied the chief inspector firmly.

'And we can still do it as we discussed earlier – together?'

Penrose nodded: 'We certainly can. And after that we'll go and see Peter Goswell.'

Noticing the nameplate on the door made Edie feel momentarily sick, but a squeeze on her shoulder made her feel safe enough to turn the handle and walk in.

'Good morning, young lady,' greeted Dr Martial agitatedly from behind his desk. He was dressed in a smart blue striped shirt, green tie and grey checked jacket. 'Come, come,' he beckoned, indicating the seat opposite him. The way his stethoscope was pretentiously draped around his neck annoyed Edie. She took a seat, tension churning in her stomach.

The senior partner at the surgery eventually looked up from his computer screen, unaware of what lay behind the door or the disquiet that the presence of uniformed officers had caused in the waiting room downstairs.

'So,' he began, 'how can I help you? Asthma? Do you need more inhalers?'

'No, Dr Martial,' Edie replied blankly. 'My asthma's been okay ...'

'What is it then?' he interrupted. 'Problems with boys?' Martial tried to joke feebly.

'No, Dr Martial,' she said. 'It's nothing to do with boys.' Edie felt nauseated: her heart thumped and her face flushed like a beetroot. But she was going to see this through.

'What is it then, dear? Busy surgery – we haven't got all day!'

The young detective took a deep breath: 'You had no right speaking to the school ... to the head teacher ... about me like that ... especially when you had other motives.'

In a blink, the doctor's facial expression transformed from the demeanour of a friendly family GP dishing out prescriptions and advice, to the severe look of a man not to be messed with. 'I don't know exactly what you're suggesting, young lady,' he said aggressively, leaning forwards in his chair. 'But don't you dare lecture me about my professional responsibilities,' he continued, each word emphasised.

'It's just that I wanted to tell—'

'Now,' he interrupted, turning his attention back to the computer screen. 'If you haven't got any medical issue to discuss, I don't wish to keep my other patients waiting.'

Edie paused, gathering her strength and taking her iPhone from her pocket: 'There was one other thing. Do you know someone called Peter Goswell?'

Martial looked over at her, pursed his lips angrily and stood up: 'I don't know what you're up to, Edie, or what you're talking about, but it's time for you to get out of my surgery. And I'll take this up further with your father.'

Edie allowed the moment to hang in the air. A calmness came over her – a deep realisation that his words could do her no harm. 'I'm sure you will speak to Dad,' she retorted. 'But I thought you'd be interested in this first.'

Edie placed her old iPhone on the desk and pressed 'Play' to initiate playback of the recording the police had allowed her to copy from Goswell's stolen phone.

Oh, hello Peter. Martial here. I was hoping to speak to you about that conversation we had in the pub … with your lumbering assassin … I've given it some further thought. About how we can get the girl out of the picture … and my plan is …

'What the hell is this?' Dr Martial's voice was steady but full of fury. 'Give me that. Where did you get it?' Martial began to make for the iPhone, which Edie grabbed, but he stopped as the door burst open and Dad stormed into the room. Martial froze, confounded, as Dad took a few paces across the floor and squared up to him, just a metre between them.

'Careful what you say,' was the best Martial could come up with.

Dad bore down on him, the veins bulging in his temples. 'There's no need for *me* to be careful at all. You,' he stated, prodding a finger directly at Martial's chest, '*you* disgust me!' Dad grabbed the lapels of Martial's jacket and shoved him hard against the desk. Her father's eyes looked enraged, in a way Edie had never seen before – a visceral, innate fury. Through bared teeth, he seethed: 'If you come near my family again, I'll rip out your eyeballs with my own hands and feed—'

'How dare you—' But Martial didn't get a chance to finish the sentence, as Dad drew his right arm back and thumped his work colleague directly on the nose.

The speed of the movement surprised Dad and also Martial, who stood confused and frozen, blood beginning to stream from his nose.

'Ooh,' he said quietly, as Edie stared in disbelief from her seat. This wasn't what had been planned earlier.

'That was for my daughter,' Dad made clear. 'And this is for my wife.' In a beat, and with all the brute force he could muster, Dad punched Martial again, square on the cheekbone just to the left of his nose. This time the impact made Martial stagger backwards onto the desk, then crumple to the floor.

Police officers rushed into the room, and whilst PC Brearley attended to Edie, Wiltshire and Wilkins restrained Dad from further violence. Penrose walked over to Dr Martial, face bloodied and swollen as he picked himself up from the floor.

'Steven J. Martial, I'm arresting you as an accessory to the murder of Alexandra Franklin, for corporate manslaughter and for conspiracy to fraud. You have the right to remain silent …'

CHAPTER 16

THE PARKLAND WALK

It took a lot to persuade Chief Inspector Penrose. He had to get Edie's plan (or 'crackpot plan' as he'd initially called it) agreed with his boss, the superintendent, as well as with the Metropolitan police commander even higher up the chain of command. Nevertheless, Penrose remained anxious, and Dad even more so.

The planned visit to Goswell's home in Cambridgeshire had proved unnecessary. Penrose explained that local police had gone to Goswell's house, as instructed, to bring him into custody. Expecting difficulty, they'd been surprised to find him sitting calmly on a sofa in his summer house, staring aimlessly out the window. Goswell briefly admitted to everything, without any prodding, but was apparently going on and on about some kind of epiphany. He kept repeating how much he loved his wife and children, and would become a better person for them. According to his distraught family, Goswell hadn't moved from the sofa all night and, following his admission of guilt to the police, wouldn't speak further about anything to do with the drug company – babbling instead about 'making amends'.

So, with Goswell out of the equation, they'd all returned to Edie's house after dealing with Dr Martial. Half an hour later, Edie received a text on her iPhone, which the police had retrieved and brought back from Goswell's home. She was in her bedroom when the text arrived, grabbing some badly needed private time whilst the others carried on discussing the case in the lounge. The text was from an unknown number but the message was simple and clear, as was the presumed identity of the sender.

> I know what's happened, that the game is up, but I need to meet you before I disappear. I want to tell you something important – about your mum. We have to meet in person, you have to be alone. NO POLICE. If I suspect anything I won't make contact. I will text you the destination nearer the time.

Edie was tempted not to disclose the text. She needed to know – more than that, she *had* to know – what it was that Zero wanted to say. Yet, she felt that sharing the text with her dad and the police might stop that from happening. Edie therefore took a little time to conjure a plan before divulging the information.

Initially, Penrose dismissed Edie's idea as too dangerous, assessing the text as merely a ruse to lure Edie in and finish her off. Over the remainder of the weekend, Penrose spent hours trying to find an alternative way to catch the killer – the dangerous loose end who was still at large. Penrose contemplated a national manhunt involving the security services, although Zero would be adept at disappearing from plain sight. Keeping Edie in a protected safe house was an option, although this would only work for a limited period. Other possibilities included offering a reward to the public for information. But Edie was going to remain in danger whatever decision was made, and none of the ideas that Penrose and his team dreamt up was foolproof.

Penrose slowly came around to Edie's suggestion; however, he was well aware of the impossible position it put Edie's dad in. After all, what kind of father places his own daughter at such risk – using her as bait – especially after all Edie had already been through? Significant risk, thought PC Brearley, as she listened to all the scenarios.

Eventually, Edie broke the impasse: 'I *have* to do it,' she announced assertively.

'What?' exclaimed Dad, turning away from Penrose. After all the debating, both men were clearly taken aback.

'I said, I *have* to do it,' Edie repeated. 'I *have* to know. But I'll allow the special police team to be tracking me, despite what Zero said in his text.'

'But you don't know what you're saying!' her father warned.

'Yes, I do, Daddy,' Edie replied calmly. 'I need to do this,' she stressed. 'For Mum, but also for me.' Edie leant over the table: 'It'll be okay, Dad. I've been all right so far, haven't I? Trust me.'

Dad looked at the two officers who, though quiet, seemed further impressed by this young girl's extraordinary resilience.

'Dr Franklin,' Penrose finally intervened. 'I give you my word, my personal promise, that I will do everything in my power to ensure your daughter's safety. But we have to catch this killer or he'll just carry on … destroying more people's lives. I think he's lying in his text message and he won't stop, especially as Edie saw him in the woods. It's a strange professionalism … he'll feel compelled to finish the job. And that's his weakness. That's how we'll get him.'

No media. No press. That's how they kept it over the following days. Staff at the surgery were told a fake story about illegal prescribing to explain Dr Martial's arrest, and were advised not to discuss the matter with anybody. Goswell's family were being questioned by the police and were similarly ordered not to discuss anything. In this way, the tight communications strategy kept the whole story – including one girl's heroism – out of the newspapers. That would all come later. For now, apart from the head teacher at Highgate Hill School, only Lizzie and her surprisingly obliging parents were given the full picture.

Monday and Tuesday at school passed unspectacularly. No further texts. On Wednesday, Edie thought she saw a man lurking on the edge of the playing fields during hockey class, but it turned out to be the school groundsman dealing with a foxes' den. By Thursday, Edie was wondering whether anything was actually going to happen. Extra art after school meant Edie finished an hour later than normal, and as she and Lizzie walked through the school gates, the darkness was settling in and it started to rain. The girls had stopped bothering to try and spot their protectors, which they never could, and in Highgate village they dropped into Costa Coffee.

'Did I see you have a good look at Harry Coranger in the dining room today?' Lizzie teased as they sat down with their mochaccinos.

Edie blushed and said nothing, reinforcing Lizzie's hunch: 'You *were* checking out Harry Coranger!' Lizzie affirmed. 'I bet you wish you had more classes with him.'

Rumbled, there was no point in resisting. 'Everyone says he's cute, so I was just checking,' Edie explained. 'I like his hair ... and his smile.'

'Maybe a bit too cool for your taste?!' Lizzie grinned.

'Maybe,' Edie acknowledged playfully. 'Maybe not!'

For twenty minutes, the girls talked about stuff at school, friendship groups, TV, until the rain had temporarily abated and they left Costa and strode down the hill. It was a slightly longer way round to the Parkland Walk but that was the route they'd been told to stick to by Penrose, who in turn was being advised by the police firearms unit, SCO19 – an elite group of officers reserved for the most dangerous criminals and incidents.

At Channing School they took a sharp left down Cholmeley Park, crossed the busy Archway Road, then zigzagged right and left onto Holmesdale Road where, after about a hundred metres, a metal gate led to a steep incline and steps up to the Parkland Walk. At the top, Edie and Lizzie turned right onto the raised, green public walkway. An oasis of tranquillity in the daytime, the path now felt ominous as the light faded. Edie checked her phone: nothing.

Half an hour until full darkness, Edie estimated as they walked briskly along, but vision was manageable for now. In the middle distance a runner was coming their way and, as the figure approached, Edie's heart began to race. Lizzie was similarly transfixed by the rapidly approaching tall male figure, sporting a tracksuit and running beanie. Was he a member of the special police unit? From ten metres away, Edie could see no facial scars and, as he passed, the man smiled kindly and said hello.

'I don't feel good about this today,' sighed a nervous but relieved Lizzie.

'It's gonna be fine,' Edie answered as the rain started again and the light dipped further.

Deep inside, Edie knew she'd changed over the past weeks, and was only just beginning to understand how. After a year of numbing grief, Edie felt more mature, more confident and undoubtedly wiser too, as the detective work had forced her to stretch herself in ways she'd never imagined. Understanding the true nature of her mother's death had obviously been key, but openly revealing her investigations – sharing and unburdening what she'd learned – was allowing the grieving process to finally begin to settle.

Yet Edie still felt fragile at times, like a pane of glass with a crack. She was certain that catching the killer was the right thing to do – was her destiny – but that child-like feeling of invincibility was now counterbalanced by a new vulnerability.

'I get off here, remember,' Lizzie said, pointing to the steps that led down to Stanhope Road.

'I know,' Edie responded. 'Thanks for coming with me again.' She quickly hugged Lizzie, then waited briefly on the Parkland Walk bridge over her best friend's road. Underneath, Edie saw Lizzie exit the steps and walk quickly up the hill to her home at number 57.

Alone, Edie carried on in the knowledge that only a few hundred metres remained before she too would come off the now-deserted walkway onto busy Crouch Hill. As the wind picked up, a flash of lightning lit up the sky, and the loudness of the thunderclap a few seconds later took Edie by surprise. It now seemed very dark.

With her hand tightly wrapped around the iPhone inside her pocket as directed, ready to press 'Call', Edie continued past a heavily nettled area. Looking constantly around her, she walked straight under another footbridge and, with the skateboard ramps in sight, suddenly stopped. She was now only fifty metres from the exit but something didn't feel right.

The rain was now teeming down and Edie was already drenched. She knew this spot well, though, and looked up at the imposing bricked Victorian construction with tall arches to her left. In one of the arches, right at the very top, the weirdest of statues lurked. It was an unsettling figure – a man-gargoyle hybrid – emerging from the wall. Only the top half of his body was visible, as if the trapped demon was trying to pull himself, with difficulty, out of the wall. Bedraggled locks of long hair flowed in all directions.

Edie bristled as a sound, different to the wind in the trees, startled her. She dropped her gaze, spun around and there he was: a real monster. Motionless, dressed all in black, hooded, hands in his jacket pockets. Zero's demeanour, highly alert although appearing less so, reflected years of training and familiarity with such situations. There had been no advance text about their meeting.

Despite the situation, and a possible trace of alcohol in the air, Edie felt somehow calm. It was as if the past weeks had led inexorably to this moment: she was face to face with her mother's killer. After pressing 'Call', Edie took her hands out of her pockets and let them hang by her sides. The rain pelted down on Edie's head and poured over her face. Wiping water away from her eyes, Edie asked the one and only question on her mind.

'So, what did you want to tell me?'

Unmoved, the assassin stayed silent and expressionless, so Edie tried again.

'What did you want to tell me? And why did you kill my mum?'

This time, Zero twitched ever so slightly and shuffled. Zero was confused, very confused. His head just wasn't right: he'd lost interest in virtually everything, worse than before, and hadn't slept in days. Things didn't seem to make sense any more: he couldn't concentrate and the wires in his brain felt crossed. Only his deeply ingrained sense of professionalism and duty had kept him going to this very point in time.

'Don't move,' said Zero uncertainly, having seldom hesitated in his military career. He wondered, what was it about this girl? What was happening to him?

'I'm not moving,' Edie replied softly. 'I just want to

know what you wanted to tell me.'

Her voice sounded kind, helping Zero's addled brain to remember what he'd offered the girl. 'Your mum ...' he began, 'was an extraordinary woman.' Edie noticed a glimmer of life in Zero's dark and troubled eyes as he slowly continued, struggling to find the words. 'Through my life ... in the army, special forces ... and here in London ... I've come across a lot of people ... tough people ... but I've never met anybody as brave as your mum.'

Edie felt herself begin to choke up inside as Zero spoke. She was desperate to hear what he had to say, whilst the chance still remained. 'I can normally scare people easily,' Zero continued, 'and they do what I want. But not your mum. She ignored my bullying ... my intimidation ... and carried on doing her work ... refused to hide or be blown off course. And that's true courage, in my book at least.'

Zero paused, a blank expression on his face: he wasn't drunk, just lost. Edie's silence allowed him the space to grasp onto what else he meant to say. 'I met your mum three times ... and when I threatened her family, there was a fierceness in her eyes that I've never seen before. Utter resolve. And true love.'

By now, Edie was unable to hold back the sobs from her throat. But Zero wasn't quite finished: 'I wanted to say that I'm sorry for what I've done. I'm so terribly sorry.'

Several seconds passed as Edie digested what she'd heard. Her head spinning, Edie managed – just – to gather her senses for the one still unanswered question: 'So why did you kill my mum, then?'

'Just a job,' Zero replied somewhat coldly, as if a different part of him had returned. 'It was just a job.'

As Edie mulled over those harsh words, the world seemed to suddenly light up. An incredibly bright beam shone down from the footbridge above and torchlights from the surrounding trees illuminated the stage where the two actors stood. Instinctively, Zero pulled a gun from his jacket pocket, adjusted his stance – left foot forwards, knee slightly bent, pistol held in his right hand and supported by the other – and took aim at the main source of light. He glanced around, assessing the situation purposefully.

From a loudhailer a voice boomed: 'Drop your weapon! You are completely surrounded!'

Zero maintained his position, switching his aim between the main light, the torchlights and the source of the voice. Edie imagined his mind working through the various options. Dive for cover? Take out the brightest beam first? Shoot the person in charge – the voice?

Yet, in those seconds – and despite how it looked – Zero had clarity like he'd never had before. Deep down he knew they would be after him. He knew Edie would tell them about the text. He knew they would try to ensnare him. He even knew where they would be likely to do so. Right here.

But Zero didn't care. For the first time that he could remember, he felt that he was exactly where he wanted to be. Trapped by the inevitable. About to be brought to justice. He thought about Katie and Dylan, the only people in the world who meant anything to him. And that he'd miss them.

'I said, drop your weapon right now, or we *will* shoot,'

repeated the deadly serious voice.

All of a sudden Zero understood what it was about this young schoolgirl. He had a flashback to Afghanistan and Edie's uncanny resemblance – not the eyes, but a facial likeness – to the beautiful young girl who'd tried to help him after the bomb had destroyed his vehicle and his comrades. The recognition of this connection calmed Zero immeasurably. He was certain about how this would end. Lowering his gun, Zero turned towards Edie.

'You don't have to do this,' pleaded Edie, intuiting what was about to happen. A lone tear trickled from her left eye. 'You don't have to do this.'

But he did. Zero glanced down at his own chest and clocked four agitated bright red dots, moving ever so slightly, like insects that couldn't stay still. It comes to all of us, he thought, at some point in time. And now is my time. Deliberately, Zero raised the pistol and levelled his aim at Edie's forehead. The movement was immediately met with sharp cracks of gunshot. The loudness stunned Edie, who clamped her hands over her ears.

Bullets ripped into Zero's chest. Holes appeared in his jacket and dark fluid began to seep out, but to Edie's astonishment, he remained standing – motionless. Gingerly, Edie took a step forwards, bewitched by this wax-like Madame Tussauds figure, drawn by a need to nudge him, both to check that he was real and to see if he toppled. Then, unexpectedly, Zero's cheekbone muscles jerked and she could sense the life still in his eyes. Edie took another step closer.

'Don't move any further!' screamed a voice through the

loudhailer, but Edie was mesmerised by the face of the killer and reached out her hand.

In an instant, one of the red dots flew from Zero's chest to his forehead and another loud crack filled the night. Edie ducked instinctively, her face hidden in her arms, as Zero's skull exploded – blood splattering, bone splintering. Edie remained frozen as the monster collapsed to the ground beside her.

Hesitantly, Edie lifted her face as the rain continued to lash down. Time stood briefly still as Edie's brain processed what had happened. Then tears sprung from her eyes, mixing with the rainwater, and she started to wail: strange, animal-like sounds of grief and sorrow. The wailing grew louder, becoming a howl, and Edie started to shake uncontrollably. She looked up at the black sky above and screamed with all the force she could muster.

Out of nowhere, someone appeared with a blanket and wrapped it firmly around Edie's shoulders. A comforting, familiar female voice accompanied the attention.

Edie looked down at the lifeless body. An object had half fallen out of the left side-pocket of Zero's jacket. Was it a small gift-wrapped box?

CHAPTER 17

EDIE MARBLE: SUPERSLEUTH

Somehow, the world looked different to Edie. Or felt different. Perhaps both.

It was almost a month since Edie's investigations had culminated with the police execution of a murderous killer on a rainswept Parkland Walk in north London. Since then, nothing about Mum had been forgotten, but Edie's regular daytime recollections were more peaceful. The dreams too had changed: instead of vivid, dark images that caused Edie to wake in a cold sweat, the appearance of her mum now tended to be associated with warmer, loving feelings. But it was still unpredictable.

Over the past weeks, Edie had taken time to properly read *The Inside-Out Revolution* and now had a much better idea of what her mum meant by the Three Principles understanding of how the mind works and why Mum thought it was life-changing. Browsing other articles on the subject had also helped. Edie was more aware that we don't live in a direct experience of the world; instead, we live in a thought-generated experience of the world. In other words, it's not the unpleasant science teacher or the rainy weather that's making us feel bad; it's how we think about the teacher or the rain that leads to our feelings about them. After all, a rain shower isn't always depressing; sometimes it can be beautiful. And, as her dad had suggested a few weeks back, in knowing that her thoughts were the source of her feelings, Edie now realised that she didn't have to take those thoughts too seriously – which was incredibly calming when Edie was feeling sad, or anxious, or just missing Mum terribly. Those feelings pass, she'd remind herself, because thoughts pass: they always do, like clouds in the sky. And this, in essence, represented the principle of thought.

The principle of consciousness felt more elusive to Edie, however. Despite reading and rereading that section of the book, Edie felt that this principle was more about a feeling than something to analyse or work out. Consciousness was described as the aperture through which our thinking is experienced, and also the mirror which allows us to notice that process; in other words, it's what enables us to be aware of our own thinking. The aperture, Edie read, was a space like the pupil in your eye, opening up and allowing light to come in, but also sometimes constricting and narrowing down. Yet, Edie found it easier to relate to the feeling of consciousness, such as those times when you see things clearly and perform at your best. Edie had felt this when she'd solved the second clue in the shower: a moment of clarity of thought, her aperture wide, when the answer just came to her. Conversely, as Edie was learning, there are times when your aperture is closed tight, when your thinking is clouded and unclear – not a time when many clues get solved.

And so to the principle of mind which, as Edie knew, didn't refer to the brain at all. The principle of mind is about something responsible for the world spinning on its axis, for snowdrops in spring, for the cut on your knee healing, for the magic of a rainbow – and for having faith in the way that life unfolds. Not necessarily God or religion, but equally something beyond our human comprehension. As human beings are inherently part of this something, the principle is also behind the extraordinary capabilities that reside in us all: the ability to love, to nurture, to connect with others, to be creative and to be inspired.

Through trusting the principle of mind, Edie felt like she had a gateway to her inner self and a belief that she would always be connected to her mum. Awareness of the principle had created a resilience in Edie that she'd never experienced before – a true resilience that was built on a deep-seated feeling that everything would be all right, no matter what. *No matter what.*

Had Mum masterminded all of this? Had Edie's psychological journey been part of her mum's big plan with the five clues? Edie wasn't sure, but she certainly felt like an understanding of the Three Principles had provided something that would help her immeasurably through the rest of her life. The best lesson ever. A new power.

A superpower, even.

At school, Edie had risen to celebrity status for a while, as news of her crime-solving had filled column inches in the *Ham & High*, *Evening Standard* and even the national press. There had also been a long face-to-face interview with a journalist from *The Guardian* weekend magazine, complete with photos of all the family. Edie had done a number of radio slots, some pre-recorded over the phone and others live; with the latter she'd been amazed at how the radio crew brought all the specialist equipment to the house, including massive headphones, so Edie was speaking live on the radio from the sofa in her lounge.

Edie had also done several TV appearances for the news channels, including one for BBC News where she'd been inside a small booth – like a telephone box – at their studios on Millbank, near the Houses of Parliament. On the back wall of the booth was a picture of the Thames, so on TV it looked like Edie was in a riverside studio sitting next to the presenter, whereas in fact she was by herself some way away. The glamour soon faded, though, and one TV outing on *Good Morning Britain* went from nerve-wracking to upsetting. On the show, after questions about Edie's uncovering of Creation, the presenter had asked Edie persistently about her mum. Edie had clammed up and realised she didn't like speaking about Mum in public, so Dad put a stop to any more such media events.

There was one moment in the aftermath of the events that Edie had particularly enjoyed. At school, she'd been walking with Lizzie through the tunnel under Southwood Lane that linked the main school with the art and English buildings. As the girls emerged from the tunnel, Harry Coranger appeared from the opposite direction with a couple of friends. With his curly long locks and unusual but handsome face, Harry was popular, funny and also captain of the Year 8 school football team. As their paths were about to cross, Harry put an arm across his mates to slow them down and to make way for the girls. And, as he did so, Harry looked directly at Edie.

'Nice work, Franklin,' he said with a smile, as he waved them through.

There were two tasks, important tasks, to complete before the family afternoon outing – on what was an unusually busy Saturday. Edie was up at nine o'clock: she put on her favourite deep-blue skinny jeans and new black Converse trainers, and rummaged around in the cupboard for a long-sleeved T-shirt. Towards the bottom of the pile, Edie was drawn to one she hadn't worn for a while and tugged it out. White background with pink lettering spelling the word 'CONNECT'. It felt right.

'You're up early,' Dad remarked, hunched over the kitchen table and barely looking up from the sports pages.

Edie wrapped her arms around his neck from behind and planted a wet kiss on his right cheek: 'Good morning, Dad,' she chirped, getting the attention she sought as Dad placed his hand on her forearm and twisted around.

'Good morning, sweetie.'

From the food cupboard and fridge Edie grabbed a box of Shreddies and some milk. 'I've got those jobs to do, Dad, if you remember,' she said, taking a spoon from the drawer.

'Of course I remember. You will be back in time, though?'

'When are we leaving, again?'

'No later than two o'clock, so be back by quarter to – one forty-five. Earlier if you want lunch.'

'Dad. You realise I do know that quarter to two is the same as one forty-five?' Edie said playfully. She was about to take the cereal into the playroom, a weekend TV breakfast treat, but instead sat down at the table, which in turn seemed to jog something in her dad's mind.

'Oh,' Dad remarked, looking up from the paper. 'I've been meaning to tell you something. I got an email yesterday from your head teacher, a message to all the parents. Apparently, they're thinking of running a course next term – for your year and another year – about resilience. And the message said it's based on the Three Principles!'

'Wow!' Edie responded, astonished. 'That would be great. I hope they do. Did it say anything else?'

'No,' Dad replied. 'Just that, a couple of sentences.'

After digesting the information for a bit, Edie changed tack. 'Is Eli still asleep?' she asked. 'Or next door on the iPad?'

'He's still asleep.'

'Did you check on … *you know what?*'

'Yes, I did,' Dad replied. 'Went in first thing, the sheets are all dry.'

'So that's what … two weeks now without wetting?' Edie estimated.

'No, it's three weeks today,' Dad responded, looking up from the football news.

'That's good,' Edie stated.

'Yes, it is,' said Dad with a pleased look.

'One other thing, Daddy.'

'What's that?'

'Thanks for buying the bench in Highgate Woods,' said Edie. 'And for letting us use Mummy's maiden name on the plaque.'

'Looks good, doesn't it? "Alexandra Marble: forever in our hearts",' Dad remarked. 'Even though it's a bit of an odd surname!'

'I know,' said Edie with a smile. 'But it is her name. And it's somewhere special that I ... that we ... can go and be with her.'

First stop, The Zone of Print, opposite the Post Office just down from Crouch End clock tower. Edie could do the seven-minute walk with her eyes closed; so she did, opening them only to cross the roads: left down Landrock, left and right chicane into Uplands, zigzag through Weston Park, arriving on Tottenham Lane at the Queen's Pub. Over the road, Edie caught sight of the red shop frontage of Shelter.

Nobody knew of Edie's secret plan, an idea that had come to her out of nowhere as she'd walked home from school a week or two back. With Birdy's song 'Maybe' blaring through her headphones, Edie had realised she was strangely disappointed that it was now all over. She'd developed an appetite for the excitement of detective work. And then came the spark of an idea, the seed that germinates. Why did it have to end?

At the counter in the printing shop, Edie presented her receipt.

'Are they ready?' she asked.

The shop owner, a portly man in his mid-thirties sporting a green The Zone of Print T-shirt, failed to reply and instead took the ticket and retreated to the shelves at the back of the store. A few moments later he returned with a small cardboard box, which he opened on the countertop.

'How did it go?' Edie enquired excitedly.

'Very well, I think,' he replied with a slight grin, retrieving the contents from inside the box. 'See what you think,' he continued, placing a single business card in front of Edie.

Edie examined the card closely. 'It's great,' she said after a while. 'Just how I wanted it.'

'Does the job,' the assistant agreed. He paused for a moment then continued: 'By the way, aren't you the kid from the newspapers? That bird flu thing?'

'Yeah,' said Edie. 'That's me.'

He raised his eyebrows, impressed: 'Setting up a

business then, are we?'

'Maybe,' Edie answered with a smile. 'I'm seeing how it goes.'

'Just one thing,' the man asked.

'What's that?'

'Have you secured that email address?' he wondered, pointing to the back of the card.

'I have,' replied Edie, before adding more quietly, 'I'm also thinking of ediemarblesupersleuth@gmail.com, but it seemed a bit long for the card.'

'That's good too.' He replaced the business card, put the carton in a bag and handed it over. 'Best of luck with it all.'

Back home, the doorbell rang at precisely eleven o'clock. Dad opened the front door and welcomed in PC Brearley, looking smart in her crisp black uniform.

'How are you, Mr Franklin ... I mean Dr Franklin?' she asked.

'Not too bad, thanks,' he replied. 'Things have quietened down, thankfully, and we're able to get on with our lives.'

'It must've been quite a time.'

'It has indeed. But you know what ... I think we're all the stronger for it, as a family.'

'That's good. And how about Edie? Is she okay – I mean health wise?'

'Oh, she's fine. Given the all-clear by the public health doctor a while back. Seems the flu vaccine she has every year, because of her asthma, was protective against the new virus.

They say the outbreak was contained, fizzled out, although it could've been horrific.'

Edie appeared at the top of the stairs, having carefully hidden the business cards away in her locked desk drawer. That would be a discussion for later, but right now there was an important meeting to attend.

'Hi, Edie,' said PC Brearley.

'Hi, Jessica. It's so nice to see you. And thanks again for doing this with me.'

'Not at all,' the officer replied. 'I'm pleased you asked me to, and I know they're keen to see you. A little nervous, perhaps, but grateful that you've reached out to them. Now, have you got what you need?'

In acknowledgement, Edie patted her brown leather shoulder bag.

'Good, let's go then. I know you've got a busy day today.'

Twenty-five minutes later the police car pulled up at a large Victorian terraced house in Tufnell Park, which had been converted into four flats. Curtains twitched in an adjacent building as neighbours wondered what had brought the law to their neighbourhood. Edie and Jessica stepped out of the vehicle, walked up a narrow front path, bordered by an unkempt flower bed, and rang the bell to Flat A. The solid front door to the house was buzzed open with a clunk, allowing the visitors to make their way along the dark corridor towards the ground floor apartment. When they were still a few steps away, the door marked 'A' swung open, revealing a woman in her mid-thirties in a nurse's uniform. A sad but expectant smile appeared at the left corner of her mouth.

'Thank you for coming,' she said awkwardly, ushering them through a short hallway to a small but homely lounge. 'Do sit down,' the tired looking woman suggested, pointing to a red two-seater sofa.

'You must be Edie,' she announced, to which the young girl nodded. 'Can I offer you a drink? Perhaps some juice?'

Edie declined. 'No, thank you, I'm fine.'

'And you, officer?'

'I'm fine too. Thank you.'

The hostess sat herself in an upright armchair, at an angle to the visitors, and placed her own mug of tea on a coaster on the coffee table.

'Please excuse me – I must look dreadful. I did a late shift yesterday at the Royal Free and didn't sleep much. And I'm back on this afternoon.' She pointed at her clothes. 'Hence the uniform. I don't always dress like this,' she shared wryly.

'Do you want me to leave the two of you alone?' PC Brearley asked.

'No, no,' the woman answered. 'I'm just a little anxious. Let me start again.' She patted down her blue and white dress. 'I'm glad you came, Edie. I'm Katie.'

'It's good to meet you,' Edie replied.

'Let me say first off,' Katie rushed, 'I'm so sorry about what happened … about everything …' But she seemed unable to put it into words and reached into her pocket for a tissue.

'It's okay,' intervened Edie. 'It wasn't your fault.'

A silence allowed Katie to gather herself. 'He wasn't a

nasty man, you know. That's why I can't understand how my brother came to do all this.'

Edie was about to respond but Katie carried on, wiping a tear away from her right eye as she spoke. 'We were close ... he was a lovely little boy when we were kids. Quiet, self-contained ... but also strong. We played together a lot and I always knew he'd be there for me when I needed him.'

'So, what happened?' Edie asked carefully.

Katie thought about the question. 'I think it started when I was eleven ... when our parents died in a car crash. They were hit by a lorry on the motorway – the driver was drunk. We had to live with our grandmother, but my brother withdrew into his shell. He was so close to my dad and just couldn't make sense of it all ...'

Katie gave Edie a consoling look: 'You must know all about that.' Edie said nothing so Katie continued. 'He got in with some rough fellas – "the wrong sorts" as my gran would say. Started drinking as a teenager, in and out of trouble of various kinds.' Katie directed the next comment at the officer: 'A story I imagine you've seen many times.'

Listening attentively, Edie probed what she partly knew: 'Didn't he go into the army?'

'Yes, that's right. Straight after school.' Katie replaced the tissue in her pocket. 'It was good for him. A job, grounded, discipline. And he was good at it ... He was tough and committed. Did well. So they accepted him for Special Forces training.'

'Is that when he went to Afghanistan?'

'Afghanistan. Ukraine. Africa. I don't know where ...

he was posted all over. Couldn't speak about it much as it was the SAS and all that. Stayed with us when he came back for a few days between things. We don't have any other family really.'

Katie glanced towards the back of the flat, where the bedrooms were. 'Dylan adored his uncle – loved it when he visited. All the stories ... adventures ... my brother was a hero to him.'

'So why did he leave the army ... I mean the SAS?' probed Edie.

Katie paused to gather her thoughts. 'There was an incident. A big incident. But even before then he'd been getting more and more disillusioned with it all. Told me about the senselessness of the wars.' Katie brushed a strand of hair away from her eyes. 'Iraq, Afghanistan – it wasn't making a difference, he said. And he hated the way some of the soldiers treated the locals ... like they were lesser people.'

'You said an incident. What happened?' asked Edie, although she had an inkling from the conversation with Penrose.

'Oh, I'm not sure exactly. They don't tell you much, but from what I know, his unit were on some kind of mission in Afghanistan and their vehicle hit an IED. All his mates ... his comrades ... they were all killed. Only my brother survived. He felt unbelievably guilty that he'd been spared.'

'That must've been awful,' Edie said, despite it being her mother's killer.

'It was, but there was one other thing about the incident – which I got directly from my brother – that was perhaps even worse, that seemed to tip him over the edge,' continued Katie.

'Oh?' queried Edie.

'Once, when he was drunk, he started going on and on about it ... started crying ... which I'd never seen before.' Clearly unsettled, Katie hesitated, but Edie felt this was important. 'What happened?' she asked quietly.

'Well, as I remember, my brother described the awful carnage in the moments right after the explosion ... body parts everywhere ... vehicle upside down and on fire ... smoke and dust swirling around ... It sounded just horrific ... and somehow, in the midst of it all ... he was still alive.'

Edie and PC Brearley sat motionless, absorbing every word.

'Villagers were running over ... lots of screaming ... with one apparently ahead of the rest. She was a young girl, thirteen or fourteen, very pretty ... he said ... with dark skin and beautiful eyes.'

Katie took a breath, sighed and looked straight at the girl in the room: 'Perhaps a little like you, Edie.'

Edie felt a chill run down her spine as Katie continued.

'This village girl was holding something out to my brother ... but he couldn't see it ... and ... well ... they'd all been drilled about suicide bombers and detonators ... so he pointed his gun and asked her to put down the thing in her hand ... in English, Pashto, both ... I don't know ... but she didn't ... He asked again but she kept on answering back ... so ... he shot her.'

'He shot her?' Edie responded, stunned.

'Yes ... right between the eyes ... I remember he told me that ... how a small red hole appeared in her forehead before she fell to the ground ... and her mother ran over ... screaming ... It sounded just horrendous.'

Seconds passed as they all took in the dreadful scenario before Edie asked one question: 'Do you know what the girl was holding?'

'I do,' Katie replied solemnly. 'I asked him at the time. The girl was trying to give him some plasters – a small packet of Band-Aid plasters.'

PC Brearley knew Zero's case file well by now, so she eventually pitched in: 'And then he came to live in London?'

'Yes, two or three years back. He was discharged from the army. Services no longer needed. I thought he was treated dreadfully by them ... no support.'

'Did he live with you?' Edie asked.

'Oh no, he lived in Somers Town, near King's Cross, in his own flat. But he was a changed man. Angry, frustrated, alone ... depressed, I thought. I managed to get him to see a therapist and his GP, but it didn't seem to help ... Occasionally, though, when he was round here with Dylan, I saw my old brother back: gentle, kind, fun.'

Unable to hold back, Edie asked: 'And did you know what he was doing? Doing for money?'

Katie backtracked. 'I'm sorry, rattling on like that about my brother when we know what he did ... to your mum. He must've got in with those wrong sorts again ... found an outlet for his rage at the world.'

A silence fell. This hadn't gone quite how Edie had anticipated, but she sensed the need to convey how she felt.

'I've wanted to hate him for what he did … to my mum, of course, but also to others, and for terrifying Lizzie and me in the woods. But when I faced him on the Parkland Walk – just before they shot him – I saw something in his eyes. He seemed so … sad … and alone. I think he'd had enough of the world.'

Katie looked drained and unsure how to respond when light steps were heard from behind: 'Hey Dylan,' she said, standing up and putting an arm around her son's shoulders. 'Come and say hello.'

'Hi, Dylan,' greeted Edie from the sofa.

'Hi,' replied the young boy softly and seriously, head down and eyes on his shoes.

Edie stood up, walked around the coffee table and faced the youngster: 'I'm really sorry about your uncle,' she said.

Without lifting his head, Dylan responded quietly: 'Thanks. I'm sorry about your mum.'

As Katie watched tearfully from the chair, Edie grabbed her shoulder bag from the floor, unzipped the main pocket and pulled out a small, gift-wrapped box. The blue paper was torn in a couple of places and darkened at the edges by dried mud. She held it out for the boy.

'What is it?' he enquired. 'Is it for me?'

'Well, it says Dylan on it,' Edie replied, pointing to the inked lettering on the front. 'It was in your uncle's pocket when … when he died. The police said I could give it to you.

Was it your birthday recently?'

'Yes,' said Dylan, tentatively accepting the late present. 'A few weeks ago.' He gently tore the wrapping paper open, careful not to damage whatever was inside. By now, Katie was off her seat and next to her son. A smart black box was revealed. A pen set, thought Dylan, unsure of himself and with no understanding of 'Omega' embossed on the front.

'Go on, Dylan,' urged his mum. 'Let's see what's inside.'

Dylan snapped open the box and took out the Omega Seamaster Chronometer wristwatch – with its black dial and cool-looking hands. He held it up for his mother to see: 'Is this from my uncle?'

'Yes,' replied Katie uncertainly. 'I think it is. Do you like it?'

Dylan just stared at the wristwatch, thrown by the implications: 'It says it's waterproof to two hundred metres.' Katie was about to respond but Dylan added: 'Can I go to my room now, Mum?'

'Yes, of course, darling.'

When Dylan's door had closed, Katie took hold of Edie's hands: 'It's difficult for him.' She then looked away, almost absent-mindedly, before bringing her attention back to where her fingers touched the young girl's palms.

'I'm so sorry, Edie,' she said, tears trickling down her cheeks. 'Losing my brother has been hard and … with your mother … it must've been unbearable for you and your family. I just hope you can now start to get on with your lives.'

Edie squeezed Katie's fingers and smiled graciously: 'I can,' she replied. 'I will. And thank you.'

Edie glanced over at PC Brearley, who indicated that it was time to go. The officer stood up, donned her police hat and walked with Edie out of the apartment. At the front door of the house, Edie checked over her shoulder to where Katie was standing, half in and half out of her flat.

'Just one last thing,' Edie asked.

'What's that?'

'Do you know why he was called Zero?'

Katie folded her arms and contemplated: 'You know what, I was aware it was his nickname but I never knew why.'

'Was it to do with the scar on his face?' wondered Edie. 'It was almost a circle.'

Katie shrugged: 'I think he had the name before the bomb when he got the scar. Guess we'll never know.'

In his bedroom, Dylan held his left wrist out in front of his chest and proudly examined his uncle's gift.

'Edie, you're late, sweetie,' said Dad as he ushered his daughter through the front door, waving at the departing police car. 'Now, come and have a quick sandwich. We've got to leave in ten minutes.'

In the kitchen, Eli was already decked in his Arsenal shirt – 'HENRY' emblazoned on the back in honour of the golden years – plus club scarf and hat. Standing by the French doors to the garden he was practising the chants early: 'We've got Özil, ooh, Mesut Özil ...'

Dad was tidying lunch plates away as Edie downed a smoked turkey bagel. 'You'll tell me how it went later, luv?'

he asked. 'In a bit of a rush now.'

'Of course, Dad. Though it all went fine. Sad. But fine.'

He looked over from wiping around the sink: 'Well, good.' Dad stacked the last plates in the dishwasher and beckoned Eli towards the table. 'Our first family outing for some time, guys. Shall we go have some fun?'

'Yes!' the Franklin children shouted together.

'One other thing,' Dad continued, taking a sip of water and clumsily downplaying the significance of his next comment. 'When we get back, I'll have to go out soon after. About an hour later.'

'Where?' Eli asked, his attention distracted from match thoughts. 'I thought we were watching *Stranger Things* tonight?'

Hesitantly, Dad lowered his tone: 'I've got a date … I mean dinner out … well, yes, a dinner date.'

'Oooooh,' smirked Edie. 'And who's it with?'

Feebly attempting to deflect, Dad carried on: 'I've got ready-meal curries for you both – there's plenty of food. Edie can stick them in the microwave. I won't be back late.'

'Who are you going out with?' Eli asked steadily.

Dad sighed: 'I'm going out with Miss Watson.'

'Miss Watson, my art teacher!' Edie shrieked with a smile. 'Eeergh. That's disgusting!'

'You're going out with Edie's teacher?' queried Eli.

Dad crouched down to be level with his son: 'Yes. Is that all right? It's just dinner.'

'I guess so,' Eli replied, shrugging his shoulders.

'No! It's embarrassing!' Edie yelped, jokingly whacking

her father's back with her fists. 'I can *never* go back to school!'

Snacks. Water. Red and white face paint stripes daubed across their cheeks. Sunglasses. Jackets. Lock the front door. Go!

In the minicab, Edie's father sat in the uncomfortable seat in the middle, flanked by his two children. Despite rejecting the front passenger seat, he still insisted on chatting aimlessly to the driver from Estonia about Saturday traffic during match day and the quickest route from Crouch End to the Emirates Stadium.

But it felt good, Edie thought, watching the world go by in north London, as the two men – two boys, rather – prattled on about which players would start the game. And, though it was only a couple of months since the stone-setting, life felt quite different: warmer, brighter and with a future. Edie slipped her right hand into her father's.

Fifteen minutes later, walking anti-clockwise around the oval-shaped stadium in search of Turnstile C, Edie was struck by the good-natured way in which Leicester City supporters were mixing with the Arsenal fans. No signs of any trouble. Spirited rivalry rather than animosity.

'Anything that could be dangerous in the bag, Sir?' the steward asked as Edie's father presented their tickets.

'Just water and snacks,' Dad replied, grinning at the children as he half opened the bag.

'Through you go.'

They raced up the stadium stairs, Dad breathless at the back, Eli laughing victoriously on reaching the top level.

Two large Cokes, American size, and they took their seats: Block 102 in the North Bank, directly behind the goal. A man behind, drunk already by mid-afternoon, was swearing before the game had even begun.

'I didn't even know *that* word,' Dad jested quietly to the two children.

Despite no interest in football whatsoever, Edie was enjoying every moment: the announcement of the home team; each player's name greeted with a cheer from the crowd; the blasting out of The Clash singing 'London Calling' just before the gladiators entered the arena; and, better than anything football related, the Mexican wave working its way around the ground. Most of all, though, the pleasure of being there as a family. Not the complete family, but a family nonetheless.

Edie was examining the faces of fans near and far, rather than what was happening on the pitch, when two things happened simultaneously. People leapt off their seats all around her as Aubameyang curled a free kick into the top corner of the net, at exactly the same time as the phone in Edie's pocket buzzed. Dad and Eli beckoned Edie to rise and join in with the celebrations, but her phone buzzed again. The vibration was accompanied by the barely audible ringtone she'd assigned for emails received to her new detective account.

'I've just got to go to the loo,' Edie screamed against the din as she stood up.

'Okay, luv!' her dad shouted back.

As she walked up the stairs and out into the main

concourse, a thought flashed across Edie's mind. Here's a real mystery: how can I have an email when I haven't told anybody about my new detective status?

Edie stopped by the burger bar, took the phone out of her pocket, keyed in the passcode and looked at the screen. The simple message took her aback.

Edie Marble. I need your help.

THE END

NOTE FROM THE AUTHOR

Behind this book lies a strange, yet true, story.

Over a decade ago, I had the initial idea of the plot for *The Five Clues*, including the set-up of a mother who dies suddenly, leaving behind a note for her child – which the child then serendipitously comes upon sometime later. Indeed, I wrote the first two or three chapters of this book back then, but the chapters gathered dust whilst I focused on publishing a book for younger children, *The Amazing Adventures of Perch the Cat*. In-between, and completely out of the blue, my own mother tragically died. She lost consciousness overnight and, although she survived a few further days in hospital in a coma, there was no opportunity for a final hug or a proper goodbye.

In the devastating days after her death, my father, two sisters and I searched all over the house for my mother's administrative papers and affairs – but without success. It was weird: my mother was organised, a planner who left little to chance, and it was hard to imagine she wouldn't have taken great care over her bank accounts, investments and the like. So, a few weeks later, we all gathered one Sunday afternoon determined not to leave the family home – where we'd all been brought up and my father now lived alone – until my mother's paperwork was located.

After an hour or so, my younger sister said she was going back to check her own old bedroom – a shoe-box space with every square inch of floor taken up with box upon crate of memorabilia from my mother's past. Memorabilia gathered in an orderly way, mind: if you'd asked my mum where her own mother's antique hairbrush was kept, she'd have found it in that room in an instant. The bedroom had, of course, been fully checked before, probably twice, only this time my sister manoeuvred all the boxes around, a laborious but necessary task so she could access a small wardrobe in the far corner. And inside that wardrobe, to our relief, were several stacked box files, labelled in my mum's distinctive handwriting and clearly containing all we needed.

Downstairs, we placed the boxes on the kitchen table around which we stood in ceremonial style. It had taken us time and tears to get to this place. Dad opened the first black box file and, right there, on the very top of everything to avoid going unnoticed, lay a handwritten note. A note from my mother to her three children. A communication from the grave, or so it felt: 'Dear Karen, Anthony and Jo. If I should ...'

It was a heart-stopping moment, to be repeated minutes later when the opening of the second and third box files revealed the exact same note – handwritten again, not photocopied – just in case we failed to find the first one. As I said, she was careful and left little to chance.

Unlike Edie's mum in this book, my own mother was no activist and you wouldn't have found her investigating human rights violations. Giving time to support a mental health charity, yes. Devotedly attending to her family, for sure. Playing bridge or enjoying a cruise, most probably. Still, the way my mother's afterlife message unfolded to dovetail with the plot of *The Five Clues* was uncanny, at minimum, or meant to be, depending on your disposition. Either way, it still sends a chill down my spine.

ACKNOWLEDGEMENTS

From start to finish, this book has taken over a decade to complete, although, in reality, the bulk was written over the past three years. During this extended period much has happened, including a global pandemic that shares strange similarities with the public health theme of this book. *The Five Clues* has also morphed into the first book of four in the Don't Doubt the Rainbow series. The series title owes thanks to Wayne Michael Coyne, lead singer of The Flaming Lips, for a story he told live on stage about keeping the faith.

There are many to thank for their love, support and advice along this journey. From the literary world, I am indebted to my wonderful editor-in-chief, Jon Appleton, who has consistently gone above and beyond, and whose top-drawer professional skills are matched by his friendship and kindness. It is hard to measure 'belief', or put a value on the hope that belief engenders, but this book would not have seen the light of day without Jon's unswerving belief in the project.

The team at Crown House have been fantastic – Daniel Bowen, Tom Fitton, Amy Heighton, Tabitha Palmer, Louise Penny, Beverley Randell, Emma Tuck, Rosalie Williams. The care they have put into the book's creation and publishing have been a pleasure to experience. I want to express particular gratitude to managing director, David Bowman. David had the vision to see potential in the book, and indeed the whole series, from the outset. In his own thoughtful and intelligent way, David has guided the project with attention, humility, open-mindedness and great expertise. Big thanks too to Dannie Price for her publicist know-how and astute direction; and to Nina Tara for the wonderful and hugely imaginative cover design drawn from blackout poetry.

I am also particularly grateful to Hugh Montgomery – a singular friend, author, enthusiast of life and all-round extraordinary person – who has similarly backed me throughout whilst always being up for a creative discussion. Although, sadly, she now remains with us only in spirit, I owe significant thanks to the crime writer, Ruth Rendell. After enjoying reading my cat book some years back, Ruth befriended me and my illustrator-daughter, Leone, and generously agreed to read drafts of the opening three chapters of *The Five Clues*. I have kept hold of Ruth's subsequent messages telling me I was 'doing all the right things', and her positivity about my writing and literary encouragement was a huge boon. Colleagues at the fabulous charity BookTrust, where I have the privilege of sitting on the board, have been inspiring and tremendously helpful: John Coughlin, Diana Gerald, Peter Roche and Jill Coleman, as well as other executive and non-executive directors.

In the public health world there are people whose support, once again, has been invaluable – probably without their even knowing it: my mentor David Heymann, Sian Griffiths, Duncan Selbie, Paul Johnstone, Gemma Lien and Professor Jonathan Van-Tam, who kindly advised on virological aspects of the story – at times whilst managing a pandemic. Kevin Fenton's friendship and conversational input have been prized, often across a dinner table; and a particular mention to a special friend, confidant and remarkable individual, John Porter, who has been a guiding light and source of strength.

Around seven years ago, I was introduced to the Three Principles understanding of how the mind works, an approach initially used in psychology, therapy and coaching to address mental health challenges and enhance performance, but now also used in school-based educational programmes across the world, supporting children and young adults in their psychological wellbeing and resilience. Within the Three Principles community, I have had the fortune both to get to know, and also to benefit from the wisdom of, Michael Neill, Aaron Turner, Bill and Linda Pettit, Dicken Bettinger and Brian and Terry Rubenstein. As founders of the charity iheart, the Rubensteins are the embodiment of passion and commitment, and their outstanding programme for schools is a beacon of hope.

Of course, nothing really gets done without the love and help of friends and family. Daniel Bernstein, Peter Oppenheimer and Steven Glancy have all played a vital part through their encouragement, keenness and wonderful long-term friendships; and Mike Crawford has been an anchor, treasure and inspiration all rolled into one. My beloved sisters, Karen and Jo, have held and guided me always and whenever, and have provided grounding and ballast through difficult times. And the backing and reassurance of my uncle and friend, Bernard, has been inestimable.

Even closer to home, there are two young people who share huge responsibility – in the best possible way – for this book coming to fruition. With his wit, astute observations, storyline suggestions, proofreading skills and natural charm (and also just being the greatest fun to hang out with), the contribution of my exceptional and cherished son, Ethan, has been precious. It is fair to say that some traits of Edie Marble's personality are modelled on my super-special daughter, Leone: both are empathic, loving, determined, razor sharp and precocious. But Edie is fiction and Leone is real-life proof that the magic of the universe can, from time to time, create something truly remarkable, a person to take your breath away and remind you constantly that the world – quite simply – is a far better place with her in it.

And finally, Elizabeth. Through the past four decades, I have had the life-defining good fortune to experience Elizabeth's love, extraordinary insightfulness, spirit of adventure and immense creativity – as well as her colossal patience through the extended writing of this book. It was also Elizabeth who provided me with the infinite gift of an introduction to the Three Principles understanding of our experience of the world – an introduction that has been transformative to my life and for which I am eternally grateful. I have been blessed and privileged to have such a magical and uniquely special person in my life.

Sadly, neither my mother nor father are alive to celebrate this book. Although unaware of the significance of her very own note, my mother's stamp is, nevertheless, indelibly ingrained on the project. Her unconditional love persists through supporting me every day and in every way. Much more recently, my beautiful father left this world, a departure suffused with the utmost dignity and grace – a lesson to add to the others he so kindly left us with. I miss them both immeasurably, yet know that they live on within me in everlasting spirit.

OUTSIDE CHANCE

WRITTEN BY ANTHONY KESSEL

THE SECOND BOOK IN THE
DON'T DOUBT THE RAINBOW SERIES

Edie's fame as a detective is spreading fast – but is there room in her life for the intrigue and danger of high-level investigations?

Edie is babysitting for a neighbour, Donna, who has crossed paths, serendipitously, with someone who looks exactly like a long-lost friend of hers from overseas. But it seems Donna has been in the same place at the same time as this familiar face on a number of occasions over the past days – as if they were destined to meet. What's really going on?

Meanwhile, Edie has befriended the popular Harry

Coranger from school. Harry is suspicious of his left-wing activist stepfather, who may be part of an ecoterrorist plot. When Harry bizarrely disappears, Edie becomes embroiled in trying to find him.

As Edie works through these seemingly unconnected mysteries she unlocks connections that push her deeper into danger – but also bring her closer to understanding how she can use her mind to embrace and overcome the most difficult challenges that confront her.

Read on for an extract from *Outside Chance*, the second Don't Doubt the Rainbow mystery, coming summer 2022 ...

'Right,' started Max's mum, her tone hushed and uncertain. 'Right ...' she repeated, staring past the girl, her eyes darting upwards.

'What's the matter, Mrs Redmond – I mean, Donna?' Edie asked gently.

Donna smiled at the young girl's precociousness, then began: 'It's a little hard to explain ... and a little, well ... peculiar ... but let me start at the beginning.'

'Okay,' responded Edie, interested.

Donna exhaled audibly. 'When I was at university – Cambridge University – I had a close friend ... a best friend, actually. Her name was Rachel Summers. We met on the first day ... queuing up for freshers' ID.'

'What are freshers?' Edie asked.

'Oh, sorry. Freshers are "freshmen" ... meaning it's your first year at university.'

'Just a sec,' interrupted Edie. 'I'd like to take some notes, if that's okay?'

'Sure,' Donna agreed, allowing Edie to reach into her school bag and pull out her maths notebook, which she opened at the back inside page. Not imagining babysitting duties taking this turn, Edie hadn't brought her Supersleuth stationery with her, so she had to make do. With pen poised, Edie returned her concentration to the storyteller.

'You said you met on the first day,' prompted Edie.

'Yes, we were waiting for our ID passes and started chatting and ... well ... we got on brilliantly from the moment we met. Although we were studying different subjects, we were both at the same college – Queens' College – and at

Cambridge it's the main place to socialise, for friends … sports … and it's where you sleep … in one of their halls of residence.'

'Okay,' said Edie, wondering what this was all about. 'So you became good friends.'

'Much more than that, Edie. We became incredibly close … and were virtually inseparable. Yes, there were boys and parties … and our studies … but Rachel and I were like soulmates. We spent almost all our spare time together.'

'Can I ask a question?' interjected Edie.

'Yes, of course.'

'You said you were studying different subjects. What were they?'

'Right,' said Donna. 'Rachel was studying medicine, initially, then switched to psychology after the first year. I was studying engineering.'

'Engineering?' quizzed Edie.

'Yes,' she responded, accustomed to people's surprise at her subject choice. 'I loved sciences at school, especially physics, so engineering was a natural path.'

After jotting down a few points, Edie probed: 'And what do you do now, if you don't mind me asking? For a job?'

'I don't mind you asking at all, Edie.' Donna smiled before elaborating: 'After my course finished, I stayed in Cambridge and eventually did a PhD, and after that I got a job working for the government – over ten years ago – and I've been there ever since.'

'For government?' questioned Edie uncertainly. 'Like, in politics?'

'No, definitely not politics for me!' Donna clarified

with another grin. 'Security services.'

'Security services?' repeated Edie. 'Do you mean you're, like, a spy? And … did you hear about my mum's case?'

Donna frowned but otherwise remained stony-faced. 'I did indeed hear about your mum's case: she was a very courageous woman. Now, don't you want to know the rest of my story?'

'Absolutely,' assured Edie, her intrigue rising.

'Well, as I said, Rachel and I were best friends until halfway through our final year at Cambridge. Then, all of a sudden, we had a big falling out.' Donna paused, as if troubled by the memory.

'What happened?' Edie asked.

Donna looked past the young girl towards the stairs that led up to their bedroom, where her husband was still getting ready. 'It was because of a boy, as you might imagine.' With her right hand Donna brushed her straightened long brown hair away from her eyes. 'Rachel was absolutely besotted by this boy – who was also at Queens' – and we talked about him endlessly. He was doing a master's degree in international relations. He was handsome, funny, captain of the college football team … Rachel became infatuated, although he never showed any interest in her.'

Edie was drawn in: 'So, what happened?' she pressed.

'I had an affair with him,' Donna stated abruptly. 'No, sorry, not an affair – that's the wrong word. We … had a kiss at the Valentine's Day college party and then started going out. Rachel was hysterical when she found out … mad at me … inconsolable. She completely froze me out … refused to meet ... to talk ... and ... well, that was it. We never spoke to each other again. It was incredibly sad.'

Shocked, Edie looked her neighbour straight in the eye. There had been fallings out with Lizzie from time to time, but she couldn't imagine things ever getting that extreme. Edie checked: 'You never spoke again?'

'No, we never spoke again, and avoided places where we might even see each other. We finished our degrees in the summer and went our different ways. Some years ago, I learned from another Cambridge friend that Rachel had emigrated to Canada a few months after we'd finished at university – and, as far as I'm aware, nobody has heard from her since.'

'And what about this guy ... this man?' asked Edie.

'Oh,' said Donna. 'He's upstairs. It was Scott.'

As if hearing his name, Scott shouted down that they needed to leave in ten minutes, otherwise they would miss the dinner reservation. Donna was ready to leave, though, smartly dressed in tapered jeans and a black jacket – with her handbag sitting on a console table near the front door. She folded her hands on her lap and straightened herself, as if she meant business.

'Let me get to the point, Edie,' Donna continued in an even quieter tone. 'All of that was just the background, which you needed to know, but things began to get a bit ... how can I put it ... weird ... yes, weird ... about two weeks ago.'

Her attention up a notch, Edie noted the time period in her notebook: 'What happened?'

'Okay, so this is quite hard to explain, even for a scientist ... no, especially for a scientist!' Donna corrected. 'About two weeks ago, I was shopping in Covent Garden and took a break to watch the street performers on the square.'

'Oh, yes,' Edie nodded. 'I went there with my mum a couple of times.'

'Right. Well, I was watching a mime artist, along with ... I don't know ... about thirty other people. As he did his Marcel Marceau mime act, I was looking over at the other side of the semicircle of people and ... there she was. Rachel, or at least I thought it was her. Rachel used to have light brown hair, but the woman in the crowd had hair of that colour but with some dark brown ... probably dyed. And she had large dark sunglasses on. Besides that, I was fairly sure it was Rachel.'

'Did she see you?' asked the detective.

'No, she seemed transfixed by the mime performance.'

'So what did you do?'

'Nothing. My stomach sort of heaved ... the surprise of it all ... but I composed myself and walked away. In the opposite direction to where Rachel was.'

'Okay,' said Edie, her eyes tightening a little, unclear what the problem was exactly. 'Sounds like a coincidence. If it *was* Rachel, she may have been on a visit to see relatives. Or maybe she moved back to England?'

'That's what I thought,' Donna responded immediately, her voice muted, obliging Edie to lean in. 'Except that I was out for dinner with an old school friend in Camden Town a few days later in a restaurant called Gilgamesh, which is very large, and when I went to the washroom between courses I saw her again. Over the other side of the room.'

'You saw Rachel in the restaurant?'

'Yes. From a distance, I was pretty sure it was the same woman as in Covent Garden, so I weaved over between the tables, keeping plenty of space between us. Closer up, I got a good look and it *was* Rachel. No question. She was with another woman I didn't recognise.'

'That is strange,' commented Edie. 'Did you talk to her?'

'No! No way. It ended so awfully at university ... and I'm not even sure if she knows that I married Scott.'

'Okay,' said Edie, puzzled. 'So what *did* you do?'

'Nothing,' responded Donna, as if that should have been obvious. 'I kept an eye on her, finished my meal and then came home.'

There was a short silence as Edie processed the information, before asking: 'And what is it that you want me to do?'

'Wait a moment, I haven't finished yet,' replied Donna. 'You're gonna find this hard to believe. A few days later – last Monday – I was on a lunch break from work in Vauxhall and was about to go into the Pret across the street from my office, when I saw Rachel sitting in the window, reading a book.'

'What!?' exclaimed Edie, sitting up straight on the sofa. 'Again? Did she see you this time?'

'No. Definitely not. She was lost in whatever she was reading and didn't look up, so I just walked on.'

Edie made a note of the days and locations, then posed the most obvious question: 'Do you think Rachel is following you?'

'No,' came the instant retort. 'In my work ... in field training ... we're taught to look out for that sort of thing, but Rachel was completely oblivious ... totally unaware that I was around. But there's one more thing ...'

'You haven't seen her again, have you?' Edie wondered, perplexed.

'Yes! Well, I think so ... I mean, I've been getting a bit spooked so I'm not a hundred per cent sure. But yesterday – I try to work from home on Fridays – I went into the Post Office—'

'Sorry, where was this?' Edie interrupted, scribbling in her notebook.

'Here! Around the corner in Crouch End!'

Edie noticed that her neighbour's hands were trembling slightly. Clearly agitated, Donna took a deep breath and then continued.

'I went in to buy some stamps. Just some stamps. It wasn't planned; I happened to be passing the Post Office and remembered we'd run out. I was at the back of a long queue when I saw a woman at the counter who ... from behind ... I mean, I couldn't see exactly ... but from behind looked just like Rachel.'

'And she didn't see you, I'm guessing?' added Edie mischievously, getting used to the run of things. Only this particular sighting seemed odd to Edie, as if Donna wasn't really sure.

'No, but this time I followed her. From quite a distance ... as I didn't want her to see me. Rachel – or the person who looked like Rachel – walked towards the Clock Tower, left up the high street, then left again onto Crouch Hill. I was quite far back, at least a hundred metres, but I'm fairly sure the woman made a right – once over the brow of the hill – and into that funny place, the Alba Hotel.'

'The Alba Hotel?' repeated Edie. 'Just around the corner from here?'

'Yes. That seems to be where she's staying.' Donna paused then finished abruptly: 'And that's it. That's my whole, rather odd, story.'

From the glaze in Donna's eyes Edie could tell the woman was befuddled and unsettled by what had happened, but Edie still didn't know what the point was. 'That's a really strange story, Mrs … I mean, Donna. But what is it you want my help with?'

'I'd like to hire you, Edie,' Donna proposed quickly, glancing at her watch. 'As a sort of private detective. It's just too strange that Rachel and I would be in the same place, at the same time, four times over the last two weeks. I want to know what's going on, whether Rachel *is* actually tracking me down. I want an explanation.'

Edie tried to stay composed. Somebody, and somebody serious at that, wanted Edie to do some proper investigative work – something she could get her teeth into. The prospect was exciting.

'You want to hire me,' Edie summarised, 'to find out why your old friend, Rachel, has appeared – or reappeared – in your life four times in the last two weeks. Is that correct?'

'Yes,' Donna reacted. 'That's essentially it.'

'But why don't you tell the police what's happened? Let them look into it?' Edie suggested.

'I can't. There's been no crime, so there's nothing to report. And it would sound so silly because what I've just told you doesn't make any sense. And I can't do the investigation myself because ... well, first, I haven't got the time and, second, if I got caught doing something like that, it wouldn't go down well at work.'

Loud footsteps indicated an adult descending the stairs. Whispering keenly, Donna concluded the conversation: 'I'll give you £100 now for ... well, expenses ... if you need to buy anything, go anywhere, that sort of thing, and another £100 if you solve my problem.' Donna glanced secretively towards the hallway, where the clearly oblivious husband was putting on his coat, before holding out her hand.

'Will you do it?'

The young girl looked down. A small envelope was being presented furtively to her. The question, though, was hardly worth asking.

Edie reached out and accepted the envelope, then shook her neighbour's hand and answered, 'I will.'

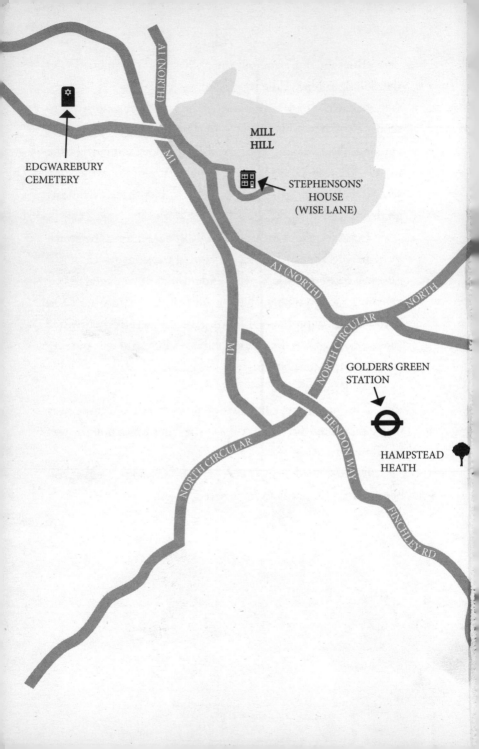